MW00892907

Maggie Awake

Peg Lewis

Maggie Awake Copyright © 2019 by Peg Lewis. All Rights Reserved.

All rights reserved. No part of this book may be reproduced in any form or by any electronic or mechanical means including information storage and retrieval systems, without permission in writing from the author. The only exception is by a reviewer, who may quote short excerpts in a review.

Cover designed by Elizabeth A. Reeves

This book is a work of fiction. Names, characters, places, and incidents either are products of the author's imagination or are used fictitiously. Any resemblance to actual persons, living or dead, events, or locales is entirely coincidental.

Contents

Chapter 1 2
Chapter 2 6
Chapter 3 10
Chapter 4 16
Chapter 5 19
Chapter 6 22
Chapter 7 35
Chapter 8 42
Chapter 9 46
Chapter 10 49
Chapter 11 55
Chapter 12 60
Chapter 13 71
Chapter 14 78
Chapter 15 111
Chapter 16 124
Chapter 17 130
Chapter 18 146
Chapter 19 163
Chapter 20 167
Chapter 21 173
Chapter 22 187
Chapter 23 196
Chapter 24 212
Chapter 25 215
Chapter 26 217
Chapter 27 225
Chapter 28 226
Chapter 29 233
Chapter 30 241

Chapter 31 252
Chapter 32 258
Chapter 33 267
Chapter 34 270
Chapter 35 277
Chapter 36 285
Chapter 37 286
Chapter 38 289
Chapter 39 298
Chapter 40 301
Chapter 41 304
Chapter 42 306
Chapter 43 310
Chapter 44 312
Chapter 45 320
Chapter 46 326
Chapter 47 330
Chapter 48 334
Chapter 49 336
Chapter 50 337
Chapter 51 339
Chapter 52 343
Chapter 53 347
Chapter 54 350
Chapter 55 354
Chapter 56 355
Chapter 57 358
Chapter 58 359
Chapter 59 363
Chapter 60 368
Chapter 61 369
Chapter 62 373

Dedicated to Elizabeth A. Reeves, author, daughter, muse. The woman who allows me to be myself.

Chapter 1

Maggie lay with her eyes still closed, aware that daylight was beginning to penetrate her bedroom curtains. She had just switched over from a dream through the thinnest of membranes that separated her sleepy wakefulness from the dream itself. Her dream had been about mowing the lawn, and now she was thinking about it.

The damp spring had meant tall grass and no chance to mow it. The mower would clog. So Frank had told her. And now the sun was shining and the grass would dry and she needed to mow. It would rain tomorrow and the grass would keep growing and there was no help for it.

Except sheep. She thought maybe sheep had been in her dream. She would get sheep.

And that meant staying in bed, not needing to mow, maybe going back to sleep. She drifted, mostly awake she thought, not wanting to think beyond the comfort of the moment. Moment after moment. Then an instant of clarity revealed the folly of her procrastination. Or, she thought, she could just say that she was dumb thinking she could stay in bed. It hadn't worked before and it wouldn't work now.

The rest of the hallucination evaporated and she realized she needed to mow the lawn. And that she couldn't get sheep. She had neighbors, a neighborhood association, a small yard of her own with wide-open gardens that produced varieties of sheep food like corn and kale. Why would they even eat the grass?

She was drifting again. She didn't want to mow the lawn. She shouldn't have to. Frank would never hire someone to do it. "We can do it ourselves and save money," he had said. "They will charge an arm and a leg and do a terrible job," he had said. "It's good to get outdoors more," he had said.

She was getting mad. She got up and took a shower. She got madder and madder. Frank was still trying to make all their decisions. He had ways of being right even though he was... even though he was dead. She stamped her foot and almost fell in the shower. "He would never let me get sheep," she told herself. "Getting a sheep is a dumb idea, Maggie," he told her brain. She stamped her foot again.

"OK," she screamed. "OK, ok, ok. No sheep!" she screamed. "But I'm going to get a dog."

It was the first time she had heard that idea. It had never come to her in her mind before. A dog? Really?

Frank had said no to a dog from the beginning. (Impractical, expensive, smelly, bossy, flea-ridden....) None of those reasons made any real difference to her. What did was that she was scared of dogs. Big ones, also those small yappy ones. And all the rest.

Even so, she was going to get a dog. She was! She would learn to get along with it. She'd find one she wasn't afraid of. Maybe an old one who needed her?

Because if she didn't, it would be because of Frank. Frank was dead and shouldn't be bossing her around. Frank didn't know everything. He wasn't here to mow the lawn, he wasn't here to point out the folly of getting sheep. He wasn't here telling her they couldn't afford to have someone do it. (Which might be true, she wasn't sure.) AND he wasn't here to tell her she couldn't have a dog.

So, she would get a dog.

She had no idea how to get a dog. Maybe from a pet store. Or the pound.

Still stamping her feet with every step, she marched into the kitchen. She ate her toast and drank her coffee. She opened the garage door and took out the lawnmower. She checked the gas, refilled it from the can.

By the time she got the lawnmower out of the garage, she was smiling. She pulled the cord with great zest. She set off along the edge of the front yard with a bit of a spring in her step.

I am getting a dog!

"I am getting a dog," she shouted, knowing the roar of the lawnmower would cover the sound of her voice. The sun broke through the puffy clouds that covered the eastern sky. The lawnmower slid through the grass. When the grass catcher was full, it came off the back of mower easily, and she had the strength to carry it without effort to Frank's compost pile deep in the backyard.

And once the mower was noisily underway again, she shouted with all her might, "You hear that, Frank? I AM GETTING A DOG!" She heard not a word from her deceased husband.

The lawn was mowed, and a lovely Saturday lay before her. One minute it was an idea, the next she had the phone in her hand. Her dog-loving friend would know what to do.

Chapter 2

"Nancy," Maggie choked it out. "I want a dog!" Maggie said. Her voice was too loud.

The phone was silent.

"I'll be right over," Nancy said.

They found the shelter for aging dogs at the end of a street that dead-ended below a freeway overpass. Then dead factories, broken asphalt, dead nets hanging off of battered hoops.

"And nearly dead dogs," thought Maggie.

Maggie had the shivers by the time they reached the door. The old steel and concrete building was bleak from the street and she pitied the poor residents who were waiting – hopelessly, if the number of cars (none) in the parking area was any indication – for rescue and reprieve. For comfort for their last days.

"Which, you have to admit, is appropriate," Maggie said to herself. "That's what I'm looking for, too."

Nancy was unbearably cheerful. How long had she been telling Maggie about this place? The good work that a handful of volunteers was doing, the pathetic need for homes for aged dogs who had been dumped by their owners when they had had enough of them?

"Frank is dead," Maggie said under her breath.

They filled out an application and paid a fee. Sad noises came from behind a large door with 'Authorized Personnel Only' written on it. And smells, disinfectant and dog. Pee, poop, and worse.

They were led through that door and invited to look around. Endless rows of endless cages lay before them.

"Frank is dead, Frank is dead, Frank is dead!" she said to herself.

"What did you say," asked Nancy."Nothing," said Maggie. "Just that that dog is half dead."

"Well, true," said Nancy.

They were standing before the first cage. The resident didn't move, just lay breathing, possibly asleep.

They moved on. In the next cage sat a droopy bloodhound. When he saw them he flicked his tail. Once. His eyes were bloodshot, his jowls impossibly long. Drool was hanging down all the way from his tongue to the floor in a string. It was collecting on the concrete. The wrinkles on his brow pulled his whole face down. He was going gray all over, with just a bit of color showing, like dried blood.

He sighed, then flopped down on his side. His feet were the size of Maggie's hands.

"He's pathetic," said Maggie in a small voice. " He's so sad!"

The two women stood looking at him. "I'll take him," said Maggie.

"What?" said Nancy. "I didn't think you'd do it."

"Shh," said Maggie. "I could still change my mind."

"I wonder what he's in here for," said Nancy.

"He must be dying of something, right?" asked Maggie.

"That's what they said," said Nancy. "Give comfort and companionship to an old dog during its last days and weeks. Vet bills paid."

"So, what's the risk? It's just days or weeks," said Maggie. "And Frank is dead," she said rather loudly.

Nancy looked at her. "What has Frank got to do with it?"

"Thought pets were stupid."

On the way home the dog lay with his muzzle on his paws, looking toward them. Nancy was driving. Maggie kept looking back at him. He never once closed his eyes. "He must be wondering if this is for real," said Maggie.

"He might be thinking that maybe this is it," said Nancy.

"No, Old Thing," said Maggie. "We're going to make you happy for your last days on Earth." He looked at her. "He's thinking, 'do you mean it?'" said Maggie.

"He's so earnest!" said Nancy. "I think he's saying, 'Love me!'"

"Ernest!" exclaimed Maggie! "You're Ernest! And you're going home. At last."

"I'm not forgetting you said NEVER."

"Then why did you drag me there?"

"Not a bad after-lunch outing...."

"Right."

"And I'm remembering the other NEVERS on your list."

"No!"

"Hmmm...."

Chapter 3

Nancy pulled up in front of Maggie's house. This was it. The house stared at her, its blank windows unblinking. Maggie thought, you have no idea, house, what is about to happen to you.

She opened the back door of the car. Ernest was sitting on the seat, huge, facing her, his giant muzzle at the level of her eyes. She couldn't tell whether he was happy, confused, scared, or what. Hopeful or dismayed? She took hold of the leash, then wondered if he would be ok if he jumped out. She gave him a little tug.

He looked her in the eyes. Slowly he lowered his front legs from the seat toward the ground. Should she try to help him down? She moved in a little closer, thinking she would wrap her arms around his neck. He slid himself down between her and the car and landed on his feet.

Good to know. He could probably make it up the steps and into the house, too.

She and Nancy had stopped on the way home for dog food, the leash, the collar, vitamins, a chewy toy, a bowl. Nancy had done the shopping. Maggie felt she should stay in the car with the dog. The whole time he had sat there quietly, and the whole time she wondered what she would do if he did something else. He smelled of something, maybe disinfectant.

And now she was home and Nancy was needing to leave. She didn't know whether to take him in and leave him while she came back for all these things. Or maybe just leave the door open and let him come and go?

He was standing next to her looking here and there. He didn't seem inclined to run off. She dropped the leash and dug around in her purse for her house key. As she moved toward the door, he continued to stand where he had landed, though he followed her with his eyes. Or maybe his nose. Even as she made a couple of trips back to the car, he simply stood.

Maggie closed the car door. This was it. For the first time, she had a dog. She was on her own with not only a dog but an old dog, a very large very old dog. A big old dog with huge ears that hung to the ground as he sat there not going anywhere.

Unbidden, a thought drifted through her mind: You can always take him back. Tears came to her eyes.

She took the leash, hoping he would follow without complaint. She found herself cooing encouragement, come on you can do it and good boy. He didn't need it.

As she stepped forward, he rose. He stayed at her side all the way to the steps, up the steps, into the house.

She decided to give him a tour. Over here is my bedroom, here's the guest bedroom, this is Daddy's office.

Daddy's office? Where did that come from! Frank's office door was closed, hadn't been opened for what, maybe a year? She didn't like to go in there. It was just as he had left it, three years ago, when he had left her by having a fatal stroke, without warning, without a goodbye, without instructions about what to do with his many papers, with the contents of his file cabinets, with his notebooks full of their financial history.

Daddy's office indeed! Frank, meet Ernest. Ernest, this is ... your father? Heavens! This is my husband Frank. He is dead.

Ernest looked at her. He seemed so accepting. He didn't appear to see ghosts. He didn't seem to wonder about the closed office door.

She told him about the other rooms. Never go in the living room, it is for visitors. We keep it tidy just in case. (When had the last visitor come? Surely someone had sat in those chairs since the funeral.) She looked around at the dusty lamp table, the windows they were always going to cover, when they could decide what they wanted. The pillows on the couch could use some plumping, the bookshelves some serious dusting, if not culling. Frank would never throw out a book.

She went to the kitchen, turned on the light. The grayish day gave way to some real sun. Ernest stood while she microwaved a cup of water for tea. She filled his new dish with water, then tried to figure out where to put it. She could just see herself forgetting it was there as she took her habitual paths through the kitchen and sitting area beyond.

There was really no good place for his water, his food dish, the fat stuffed bed Nancy had indulged in and she had finally agreed to. (How does a dog know to lie down in a certain spot just because we call it a dog bed?)

She stood in the center of the kitchen scanning it with her eyes, trying to find an out of the way place for Ernest. There was none. He would end up in the way.

Yes, she thought. Ernest was definitely in the way. She reached down and hugged him, reminding herself that he would need a bath very soon. He tolerated the hug, resumed his steady standing pose. She realized she was still holding his leash and really didn't need to.

She had thought his bed should be in the kitchen but there was no room. So she lay it in the den next to the place where she always sat. But it took up half the floor space. Finally she put it under the far end of the kitchen table and moved the chair to the garage. No one had sat in that chair for a while and if she needed it, it would not be far away. She filled the dishes with food and water and Ernest ate and drank. She had her tea and made herself a sandwich and sat and ate. She kept an eye on the dog, would rather have gotten back to the novel that sat open at her place at the table but he kept her attention, not that he was doing anything in particular.

Except now. He was looking restless. Ah yes, time to introduce him to the backyard.

Leash? No, it was all fenced. He couldn't go anywhere. She'd go out and sit on the porch steps while he did whatever he had in mind. She hoped he didn't pee on her flowers, the pathetic untrimmed tulips that had gone past maybe weeks ago.

She opened the slider. He followed her out. He sniffed around the deck then hastened after her to the stairs. Rather briskly he trotted down the steps. She eased herself down to sitting. The sun, filtered through clouds, gave her little warmth. She should have put on her jacket. He was exploring the yard, sniffing here and there. Soon he raised his leg, having chosen well: a pile of sticks and brush just inside the back fence. When he was done he meandered back to her, looking up from the bottom of the stairs, eager, it seemed, for her attention.

She said, "Hi, Ernest" but when she made no move to get up and join him, he wandered away, sniffing as he went. She found herself thinking it was not so hard to have a dog. Without him she would have been watching reruns on TV. Now she was sitting in cold bright sunlight watching him. She should have made Frank get her a dog.

Chapter 4

She was startled, then, to hear a voice, a live and human voice. Definitely not Frank's ghost defending himself.

It was Martin, her neighbor. She had never seen him hang over their mutual fence before, but there he was and he was talking to her. What should she do? Should she get up from her step and find her way through the thick grass -- she hadn't mowed way over on that side of the yard -- over to where his face and shoulders were visible through their adjoining cedar?

"Hi," she said and she waved. What was it he had just said to her?

He spoke again. Something about a dog. Yes, he had seen Ernest. Clearly the fence was enough to keep Ernest at his own house, so what was he concerned about? She couldn't quite make out his words.

She got herself up and walked toward him. She hadn't responded to him yet, but he spoke again, in distinct tones as if she were a baby, or deaf. "I see you have a dog!"

She looked around to see where Ernest had gotten to. He was walking their way. “Yes,” she said. “His name is Ernest. He’s an old dog. I rescued him this morning."

Ernest was not looking as though he had needed rescuing, though he still needed that bath.

“Nice,” said Martin. “Was he abandoned?"

“I guess so,” said Maggie. “They found him wandering around somewhere. He’s supposed to die."

Martin looked at her. “You mean he’s sick?"

“I don’t know. When we saw him he was sitting on the concrete floor looking half-dead. I figured I could rescue him because he wouldn’t live long. You know, so if I didn’t like having a dog..."

She trailed off. She looked at Ernest. Her heart skipped a beat. She didn’t want him to die.

Martin said, “I see.” He smiled. “He seems like a good dog. But maybe he needs a bath."

“Yes, no doubt,” said Maggie. She had not come to grips mentally with how she could give him a bath.

“Want some help?” asked Martin.

“What do you mean?” said Maggie. She was feeling wary, a little worried. Did she look like she needed help?

“With the bath!” said Martin. “It might be easier with two people."

“Oh, I don’t know,” said Maggie.

"Well, ok, then, if you decide you need a hand, I don't mind. I've done it before." He turned, disappeared toward his house next door.

Maggie wanted to say 'don't go' but she didn't know how. She would have happily had help with getting Ernest clean and sweet-smelling.

But the moment had passed. Why had she not just said yes?

Ernest stood by her side. She rubbed the big dome of his head. He was warm. She was still standing at the fence, under the giant cedar that shaded a fair amount of her backyard. It was actually on Martin's side of the fence, but its long boughs swept over her yard and blocked the morning sun daily. She went back to the step. Ernest climbed slowly up to the deck and lay down in the afternoon sunshine. She wanted to join him and rest her head on his soft furry side and take a nap. But rather chubby old ladies don't typically lie on decks with their dogs. Do they? She went into the house instead, leaving the door open for Ernest. She got her sweater and cleaned up from her lunch.

Chapter 5

There came a knock at the door. Ernest came in and went to the front door with her. She opened it to find Martin there with a bucket, some brushes, all sorts of things. Ernest was going to have a bath.

By the time they were done hosing him, scrubbing him, combing out some tangled fur, brushing him, they were soaked and Ernest looked amazing. He was a handsome boy, certainly grey at the muzzle and a bit droopy around the eyes, but still a fine example of fit old dog. Maggie went in for some more towels for her and Martin, but Martin said he'd just go home and change. He hosed the suds out of the grass, gathered up all the tools, said bye, and let himself out her side gate. She stood with her hands on her hips, shivering a little, looking after him.

She couldn't be sure if she'd call him bossy or just helpful and practiced in the art of dog-bathing. She'd have to think about it. And meanwhile Ernest glistened in the sun, and also looked ready for a nap.

She went in to change out of her wet clothes, decided to warm up in the shower, thought about taking Ernest for a walk once he woke up.

A walk! When was the last time she'd gone on a walk? One thing at a time.

When she came out of the bathroom, toweling her hair, Ernest was asleep on her bed.

She knew better than to let him stay. He'd get used to it. He'd take over the house. She could end up getting fleas in the night.

It sounded like Frank. It's what he'd always said about having a dog. She stamped her foot. The dog stirred. She quickly got dressed and left the room. She opened the door to Frank's office. Hopeless! Papers everywhere! She closed the door again. She shook her fist at the door. She stomped to the living room. She shook the pillows, threw them back on the couch. She picked up his souvenirs from around the world, his plaques and awards. She put them in his office. She grabbed up his dusty stamp album, not opened these past three years of course, but also, she suspected, not for a good ten years before that. It too went into his office. She slammed his office door. She threw herself on the couch and sobbed, pounding her fists against the cushions, against her chest. She kicked her feet. She screamed out, "No, no, no..."

Ernest came out. He lay his head on her stomach, her round unfit aging poundage, and looked at her. She reached for his head, played with his ears, calmed. "I love you, Ernest," she said.

Chapter 6

Maggie woke from her tantrum-induced nap. Ernest lay on the floor beside the couch. The room was gloomy not with shadows but with an overall grayness due to its location on the northeast side of the house, the shadow of the gigantic cedar not far from the front window, the beige walls, the beige rug, the beige couch, the old books generations in Frank's family and hers. She took it all in with an air of inevitability. She felt gloomy.

Ernest stirred. "Oh you old thing! I suppose you need to go out?" she asked. He rose up and moved toward the kitchen. She pulled herself up slowly. He was waiting by the door. She was stiff. Going out with him would be a pain.

She opened the door. The sun was actually still in the sky, few clouds passing by. The new bright-green leaves were just coming out a block away over to the southwest, but she could still see the shadow of the little island through them. If you could go straight, that little island would be maybe half a mile away, half the distance over land, the other half over water. But you couldn't go straight. There were the houses, the trees, the twisting of local roads, the avoidance of a creek.

The first year they had been in the house, they had moved in in June, just as it was now. She hadn't noticed the island. From all she could tell – though she knew better -- she was on solid ground, on the continent, attached to roads that led to highways that led all over North America.

But she wasn't, they weren't. Their house was on an island of modest size, still big enough to hold a good-sized community of fishermen, ship-builders, merchants at local specialty shops and a few chains, also oil-refinery workers who refined Alaskan oil brought in on huge tankers. And children who played soccer and took piano lessons, of lovers of nature. The town had its own huge wooded reserve full of hiking trails and ponds for kayaking, thoughtfully donated by landowners over the years. The town attracted tourists with whale-watching tours. Headlines in the paper often featured the latest migration of the region's own pod of orcas, J-pod.

But from their house, all she and Frank could see through the tall cedars was other houses. It wasn't until they went on errands that they ran into water. It amazed her -- for months after they moved in, at very least, it continued to amaze her -- that wherever they went, there was water just beyond. Water ahead of us down this street, turn right and in no time, water ahead of us again, she remembered.

But now it was all routine. The highway came into town from the mainland by way of a bridge. It forked, one highway heading to the ferry terminal that would take cars, people, and supplies to other islands, the other taking a turn to the south, to the famous Deception Pass bridge and Whidbey Island beyond, and well before she got that far, to her own house tucked deep in a cul-de-sac above which loomed an impressive ridge covered with cedars.

But from the house, even from the big window in her bedroom, even from the wide outside deck above the garden, the water was not visible, and in summer neither was the tiny neighboring island, though it was only a short distance away. Only the vaguest shadowy mass was still visible even this early in the season, and the very occasional glint that reminded her that the water of the bay was close at hand. A few giant cedars, other just leafed-out trees, and virtually no indication of water. She might as well live anywhere. Or nowhere.

Ernest interrupted the gloomy thoughts creeping up on her again. He had been to the back of the garden and done his errand, and had climbed stiffly back to her side on the deck. He nudged her from her thoughts with his cold black nose.

She was shivering a little, had put her hands in her pockets. The early evening was turning cool again. The warmth of the sun was gone though the sun remained. She was hungry.

She thought she would go in and get something to eat, and what? Go to bed? Watch TV? She turned toward the door, expecting Ernest to follow, but he was hastening down the steps, his whip-like tail wagging. She followed him with her eyes.

"Hello, Ernest," came a voice from the cedar that grew next door but covered so much of her yard.

Ernest seemed to be trying to lift himself up so he could stand against the old wood fence that divided the two properties. She couldn't see what he could because of the huge low-slung cedar branches. But she of course knew it was Martin.

What to do? Call to Ernest, get him back and safely inside?

Or, say hi from a distance.

Ernest wasn't coming back right away. Clearly the two of them were having some sort of conversation. What was she to do? She didn't want to be sociable. She was better brought up than to be rude.

She walked slowly down the steps to the garden, carefully stepped into the same bent-grass path that she had created earlier.

"Hi," said Martin. "Ernest and I are catching up."

Maggie thought, it's been a few hours....

Maggie said, "Hi." And just stood there.

Martin scratched Ernest's head, reaching over the tall fence to do it. Ernest was loving it.

Maggie put her hand on Ernest's back. My dog, she thought.

It came out, in her mind, somewhat like MY dog.

Martin said, "Want some supper? I made soup. Can't eat it all myself."

Maggie turned in a circle, flapped her hands against her side, put her hands on her hips, looked away toward the lowering sun. "What time is it, anyway?"

"About 7:30," said Martin.

That was late for supper. Why hadn't he eaten already? She was hungry for sure. But she couldn't just accept his invitation.

"What would I do with Ernest?" she blurted out.

"I'll bring it over. Then he can stay home and keep getting used to things over there. We wouldn't want to confuse him."

And, she thought to herself, what does it do to him when you're scratching his ears like that? But she didn't say it.

And what about this word 'we', as in 'we wouldn't want to confuse him? There's no WE here! Inwardly she stamped her foot.

Still she dithered. "What kind of soup is it?" She regretted showing her interest immediately. She stamped her inner foot again.

"It's veggie-bean soup. It could use some of your kale."

It was true that Maggie had plenty of kale growing in plain sight, kale that had invited itself into the garden, reseeded from last year's overabundance, which in turn had come up on its own from the year before and the year before that. Kale that she had been ignoring for months.

"Um," she said.

"I'll bring the soup over and heat it up at your place. I'll grab some kale if you think you can spare some?" He didn't wait, but went on. "It will cook in the hot soup in a few minutes."

She looked at him. His voice was pleasant, too pleasant for bossy. But his words made her begin to feel truly mad inside. But then, she was hungry. And she hated to cook for one.

"Ok, then," she said and turned away quickly. She thought that might have seemed rude.

Ernest was at her side so Martin must have left the fence. She wasn't used to being followed, but he was behind her up the steps to the deck and into the kitchen through the slider. She looked out the front window, unlocked the door, didn't know what to do next. She looked around. The table was covered with bills and magazines. She grabbed them up and put them in a cupboard.

"Remind me where I put those, Ernest," she said. The dog was keeping close every step she took.

She set the table with a couple of placemats, found spoons that matched each other, and paper napkins. What would they drink? Most of her glasses were in the un-run dishwasher so she grabbed some old mugs from a hard-to-reach cupboard. She heard the front door close and Martin was putting a huge pot on the stove, his hands protected with potholders.

I must clean the stove, thought Maggie. She didn't look at it. It probably had crumbs and grease spots.

She put bowls on the table.

Martin took a knife out of the rack, then went out, Ernest following.. The sun had reddened and everything glowed pinky-orange. Maggie watched Martin bend over the kale patch, then she turned away before he got back.

He rinsed the kale and tore the leafy parts into the pot of soup. He covered it again and pulled out a chair. Her chair, where she always sat. He was going to sit in her seat. It just showed how presumptuous he was. Then he pulled out the other chair where she'd also set a bowl and spoon and sat there. Her pulled out chair was waiting for her.

Still no words had passed between them, though Martin was having a sweet chat with Ernest. She felt stupid and couldn't think what to do about it. Then a brilliant conversation starter came to her.

"Want crackers?" she said? "Cheese? Butter?"

"Sure!" he said with a big smile. "Do you have any sour cream?"

One moment she was offering him all she could think of that went with soup, and the next she was resenting his suggestion. Sour cream? Who does he think he is, asking for MY sour cream?

He served the soup. He talked about the ingredients, about his love of food, of his love of cooking. Ernest lay on his bed in its spot under the table. She rested her feet on the dog bed too, thankful that she didn't have to dangle: her short legs never reached the floor when she sat on a chair, and she usually ended up eating on the couch, in front of the TV.

"I learned to cook when I was in high school," he was saying. "I worked on a boat for a while and no one else wanted to do it and I didn't want to eat out of cans all summer."

"Where did the food come from?" she asked.

"We all caught fish," he said. "And I had fresh food for days after we were in port. After that it was canned veggies and beans. Real meat was a treat we had only when we were on land."

"I don't like to cook," she blurted out. Then she realized maybe she sounded like she was asking him to cook for her and felt the heat rising in her face.

He looked at her, and his eyes actually twinkled. "Well," said he, "that's perfect!"

He didn't explain and she was tongue-tied.

They ate in silence for a short moment, with Maggie growing agitated as she thought of the clean-up. Would he just leave with his pot of soup? Would he leave his pot of soup? Would she pretend she was bustling as she cleared the table at her typical slow pace? Would he let Ernest lick the bowls?

Frank spoke up from the recesses of her mind, "I told you! A dog will just complicate your life!"

She almost said to him, in her thoughts, "Well, it's not my fault this dog came with a neighbor attached!" That thought almost made her giggle, but she also reflected that it was true: Martin had said maybe five words to her before Ernest came, and she certainly had never spoken to him.

Lost as she was in reflection, once again, on the awful pickle she was in, she was startled when Martin's foot landed on hers, which was still on the dog bed. Ernest was snoring and she was quite certain it was not his foot, his head, any part of him. She gasped a tiny, discreet gasp but what could have given her away was the sudden rapidity of her breathing.

Martin seemed none the wiser. Maybe, just a small chance, he thought his foot was on the dog bed and he didn't realize it was on her foot at all. Given his continuing application of butter to cracker (so MUCH butter, thought Maggie) without even looking her way, she realized that that was actually the case: he didn't know he was pressing his heel into her big toe.

But for one moment, before she knew that was the case, something unexpected had leapt into her insides, a tiny spark you might say, she reflected. Not much of anything really. But for sure a something. She reddened at the thought of it.

And reddened more when she remembered it hadn't happened at all, he had simply extended his long legs -- his very long legs, he must be 6-foot-4 or something -- and had encountered the dog bed and used it as a comfortable place for his feet, as she herself was.

Wait! What hadn't happened at all? NOTHING had happened! Just a mistake on her part to think he had put his foot on hers and then this little ember of warmth.

You can start a whole forest fire with an ember, said Frank. Be careful to put out all your fires. Stamp them out!

She stamped her foot. Unfortunately, she thought an instant later, not in her thoughts at all, but her real foot. The one under his heel.

And then, as she snuck a little peek at him, hoping not to be the least bit obvious, he waggled his eyebrows at her.

These were not ordinary eyebrows, she realized. These were great eruptions of white bristles that when they waggled captured her like a fish seduced by a lure. She stared at him. Her mouth might have been open, fish-like. He was pretending to eat, and all the while his eyebrows – yes they were his eyebrows, she was quite sure – were holding her captive.

As for his heel pressing into her foot, he was now caressing the abused spot with his toes. That little feeling of something flitted past again.

She pushed back from the table. Ernest stood up. She pulled her feet away, regretted it, stood up. Before she could clear her bowl, Martin had gathered an armful of supper things and was carrying them to the sink. Ernest brushed past her and slid to his bowl just as Martin finished scraping the leftovers into it.

He turned on the faucet and gave everything a rinse.

"Detergent?" he said. She pointed.

He was moving quickly, getting everything cleaned up efficiently before she could figure out what to do with herself. Maybe he just wanted to get home. How silly of her to have gotten up from the table when she was enjoying herself, even if she was a bit embarrassed. It was her own fault. If she hadn't gotten entranced by those eyebrows, she and he would still be sitting there. Perhaps she would have summoned the presence of mind to offer him a cup of coffee. Yes, it was her own fault.

Well, no, came a whisper from deep inside her. it was Frank's fault. Forest fires indeed! He had thrown a bucket of ice water on the tiniest of embers and not only would there be no forest fires, but also no warmth, no sun, no light.

In fact the sun had gone down. Martin was not paying attention to her but doing a superb job cleaning the counters, the stove top (quickly, as if it needed very little from him though the truth was quite obviously the opposite).

Ernest was attentive. He went to Martin, who was once again at the sink rinsing out the sponge. Ernest leaned against Martin's leg. Martin dried his hands and scratched Ernest behind the ear. Martin knelt down and felt Ernest's legs, his knees. He stretched his ears out and looked inside. Ernest licked his face. Martin smiled.

Martin turned to Maggie. She looked at the floor. "I'm sorry I kicked you," she said. "It was a mistake. I was mad at Frank."

Martin said, "Oh!" It sounded as though he understood -- that somehow he understood. But he looked confused.

She hadn't a clue what he meant by 'oh'. He said, "Good night, then, and thanks for the kale. It added just the right taste, so fresh and green."

He tucked the potholders into his pockets, picked up the soup pot, and went to the front door. She came to and almost made it there in time to let him out. But not quite. He put the pot down on the tile floor and twisted the nob. Ernest followed along, but Maggie grabbed his collar and called him back. Martin disappeared into the night.

"Thank you," she called after him. She thought her voice was rather feeble, so she called louder, "Thank you."

Chapter 7

She stood mindlessly looking out into the night. So Frank had been right and she had been wrong. She had bought an old dog because she had always wanted one and Frank had said no. Frank had said no because dogs are trouble, and she had gotten one anyway because old dogs end up in pounds because they are about to die and it was a temporary arrangement. And now Ernest did not look like he wanted to die, and she didn't want him to. But that meant trouble. Frank said it would, that it would lead to heartache. Whatever he had meant, he had been right. He was right right now, talking inside her head about the trouble of dogs, and calling out as he did all day long from the grave. She had gotten Ernest, and now she was experiencing heartache.

Because she didn't want Ernest to die, and she didn't want Martin to go away, and she did want Frank and his opinion about dogs and things to go away and that made her horribly depressed. What she wanted was to live, and for that to happen she didn't need Frank. Frank just got in the way. Or she couldn't have Frank, and living now meant avoiding Frank and his opinions, getting rid of them, not letting him interrupt her and her hard-won setting of one foot in front of the other.

But she did need Ernest. He gave her courage. He was loyal to her and he stuck by her and seemed in fact to approve of her.

Here it was, maybe 8:30 at night. She was full of good soup from a total stranger, from a neighbor Ernest dragged home. And she had felt the glow of something missing forever, something fondly remembered from the earliest of days of her time with Frank. Well, she didn't really remember it from back then, but it was familiar even so and she loved it! And now Frank had gotten in the way and she had destroyed it. Or he had.

What could be done? Here she was, defying Frank by getting a dog. And then the spark. Two sparks in one day, Ernest and Martin. Because as awkward as the foot incident, and as meaningless as it had been, in the end, it had still caused a pleasant warmth she hadn't felt until tonight.

Well, Martin was gone. But maybe, she told the black outside and the big cedar tree not fifteen feet in front of her door, maybe -- as unlikely as it seemed and no doubt was -- there would be other sparks. Martin was not the only kid on the block!

A little ripple of joy flashed through her brain, too soon gone but quite nice.

With that she chuckled. Ernest looked at her. She still had hold of his collar, he still wanted to go out, to follow Martin home. He probably wanted to be Martin's dog. But he was her dog and that's the way it was going to be. Until the end of his days. Or hers.

As he pulled against her restraining grip, she thought, well, I want to go too, I want to go to Martin's, I want to be Martin's. And that made her laugh. It wasn't exactly a spark, but it was a happy thought.

"Where's that leash, Ernest?" she said. He perked his ears. He must have known the word from his former life. Well, there was a fine example of the benefits of an old dog: they come with at least a sprinkling of English. "Leash, Ernest," she said, this time to him. He bolted for the kitchen and returned with it.

She clipped it onto his collar. He pulled strongly. "And since it was your idea," she said, "you get to choose where we go!"

His nose had been actively pulling in the air even while they had been standing at the open door. Now she could see he was drawing molecules of Martin deep into his nasal passages and from there into his brain. Not really of course, but something in his nose was deeply connected to his brain, she had no doubt. The moment she put one foot forward, he pulled her without mercy in the direction of Martin's house.

Afraid she would fall, she let go of the leash. Her car in the driveway blocked her view of Martin's property, but a yellow glow, some light fixture for sure, lit up the dark night in that general direction. She inched her way toward that light, imagining that she was hidden in the dark. Ernest's nose knew that she was there, no doubt, but Martin probably didn't. Unless the dog himself, Ernest suddenly arriving, with his leash on, gave her away.

But no, when she got up closer, still in the shadows of her car but with full visibility of Martin's yard, she could see that that yellow light was to help him fix something under his car. He was lying on the ground, his head under the car, a toolbox at one side, Ernest at the other.

Ernest was in fact trying to nose his way under the car. While she watched, Martin's hand came out and scratched the welcoming ears. Maggie kept still.

Though her front yard seemed dark, the sunset still glowed in the west. Her house was silhouetted against the pink and orange sky, the sun itself now out over the ocean somewhere west of Vancouver Island. The air was not too cold, no breeze had come up. She was content to stand there in the shadows watching Ernest try to get under Martin's car. Martin was talking to Ernest, saying she had no idea what, but Ernest was listening intently. His droopy dewlaps hung onto the pavement and he was making a sound she had not heard before, a wuffly snorting. He might have been talking to Martin. Or having an asthma attack.

And then she remembered that she was embarrassed, that she had sort of kicked Martin or rebuffed him, he might think. Her confusion returned, and she felt she had to leave. But not without Ernest. She was stuck again. Did she run up to Ernest as if she were just arriving? Did she sneak up and take him by the leash? Somehow she had to avoid Martin while separating her dog from him.

She decided to tiptoe back to her front door and call Ernest from there. He might come right away. Well, she could hope. Martin might not even hear her from under the car, and Ernest's ears looked like they were designed for long-distance hearing.

She opened the front door rather loudly to simulate her coming out from inside, then called, sweetly and quietly, "Ernest! Oh, Ernest? Are you out there?"

There was the sound of metal-on-metal, some thumping, a quick burst of human language, and then the glow of the light disappeared. No Ernest appeared. Before Frank could whisper anything from the depths of her mind, she told him, "Dogs are a lot of trouble. I know.'

She waited for something to happen. Several minutes had gone by since the light went out.

She was torn by indecision. She walked out into the night, out to the street beyond her car. She was sure Ernest could not have gone past her driveway without her having seen him, nor would he be likely to leave Martin's side. But what if Martin had just gone into his house, leaving Ernest to find his way home? Then he might be out wandering around the neighborhood. He seemed nice enough, Martin did, but what did she really know? That he liked to cook and fix cars. And scratch ears. Well, that counted for something, but where could Ernest be if not lost?

Martin had said he wouldn't take him inside his house, that it would confuse the poor dog who had had just a day to adjust to his new home, her home.

She had reached the street. She looked up and down, trying to see anything at all. Ernest's dark red coat would be perfectly colored for making him invisible in the dark, she thought. Except maybe his eyes? Should she be able to see those?

To the right was the cul-de-sac. Chances are that he was there, or he would have had to pass her house on the corner. If he was there, he was safe. All the houses were quiet. She could barely make out the roadway in what was left of the light of the sunset. The nearest streetlight was a block away in the other direction. She inched along carefully, always on the alert so she wouldn't fall.

She called softly to Ernest, hesitant to disturb her neighbors.

The cul-de-sac was lined with vehicles, first Martin's big motorhome, then a large van for the family with kids that lived next door to him. A boat on a trailer was down the block. She cautiously moved along, her eyes gradually adjusting.

"Ernest!" she hissed. She hoped he'd come bounding up but he didn't. She listened and heard only an owl. She rounded the motorhome, sticking to the side of the road out of habit.

She thought she heard footsteps, not a dog's but a person's. Instinctively, more out of reclusiveness than fear, she moved deeper into the shadows of the motorhome.

Hands grabbed her shoulders from behind.

Chapter 8

Maggie sat on the front steps of Martin's house. Ernest was keeping her warm on one side, Martin on the other. She was shaking not from the cooling night but from a hysteria she couldn't control. Her very insides felt like jelly. Her rational mind, the one that kept saying to her GET IT TOGETHER, was wholly disconnected from the rest of her. All the while it proclaimed that everything was ok, the rest of her ignored it. She shook, she cried, she sobbed, she screamed (but not very loudly -- no need to wake the neighborhood). And all the while, Martin sat there companionably while Ernest frowned, all his many wrinkles descending into his eyes and his panting filling the voids in conversation.

And there was no real conversation. No words passed back and forth. They were like three caricatures of themselves, Ernest the Empath, agitated, whining a bit, drooling a lot, panting, looking here and there, and on a rare occasion getting up and going over for a pat and ear-scratch from Martin. Martin sitting still, calm as could be, tolerant, patient, long-legged. And Maggie herself, shuddering, sobbing, saying things in some disconnected tongue where words were random sound bytes that she didn't comprehend any more than Ernest did. Or Martin.

Sure, she had been startled by the sudden grabbing of her arms, but she didn't think she had been frightened. It was after all her own small and quiet neighborhood. And as she said this to herself as she sobbed, as the thoughts of STOP IT! and YOU'RE FINE, NOTHING HAPPENED emerged from a rational portion of her mind, another part of her was remembering the gentle pressure of his hands on her arms, his pulling her back from the brink of a painful shin bark or fall, her leaning against him for a brief moment. (Also of her regretting having righted herself and standing on her two feet as fast as she could.)

Of the whole awkward and emotional by-play in her mind, what was emerging was just one memory, one startling and traumatic memory, and that was his touch. Not as in HIS touch, but more like his TOUCH. Because, Maggie-girl, her inner Maggie whispered, when was the last time any other human being ever ever ever touched us?

That touch, that human warmth, had been her immediate undoing. Ungluing.

And just that fast, she was done with the whole confusing exhibition. Two new thoughts were coming, side by side: Dry your eyes! And something very new and rudimentary: Touch good!

The last light was gone and still they sat there. But Maggie was growing sleepy, spent, undone -- and now that the trauma of recent events was fading, quite ready to be done with it.

She reflected back on the past hours with total discomfort, from her kitchen to her search for Ernest. And then to her undoing when Martin had grabbed her from behind to keep her from backing into the tongue of his little utility trailer, there in the shadows.

The one part of her, the one that was gaining a hold on her mind now, at last, had realized he had just saved her from an ugly fall. The rest of her had become unglued. All sorts of thoughts had crowded into her mind, this mind of hers that had been pretty much empty for three years, until Ernest. And Martin. First, that Ernest was ok. Second, that Martin was not mad at her or hurt or any of her other wild imaginings. Third, that she was no longer alone.

It was that third wave of thoughts that had unstuck her. She had not known she had felt alone. She had been sleepwalking, that's what it seemed like, since Frank died. And now she was waking up and something inside her was acting like a chick struggling to get out of its egg. Waves of struggle had overtaken her.

Martin must have felt her begin to shake. He had guided her to his front steps and bade her sit.

And now it had been some time, half an hour or more. The night was fully dark. And she was fully embarrassed. Also somewhat enlightened. Because while she might look the same, she was now awakened to ... to what? To all the complications caused by having a dog? Because if the way she felt now was due to having gotten a dog, she was grateful she had yielded to that folly. Because she was alive.

Ernest, that old dying rescue dog, seemed to be her way back to life, to Maggie, maybe. If....

She had stopped shaking, sobbing, acting like a teenager! What, could she not even go for a walk in her neighborhood by herself? Who said? She could feel herself grow angry. On the very day she had decided to be done with Frank, she had acquired Martin.

Well, in a way she had acquired Martin. She was sitting there next to him but his thoughts seemed somewhere else. Like what? Like a babysitter!

Well, she was done with being rescued.

Chapter 9

She jumped up. Or rather, she pushed herself awkwardly off the step in the process of trying to jump up, and that made her madder than she already was. She wanted to jump up decisively, but instead she could hear herself grunting with the effort. Martin was looking straight ahead and she dared him smile, laugh at her, help her.

Ernest eased himself off the step, and she grabbed up his leash. She was going home. She didn't look at Martin. She could get home by herself, it was only next door, yes it was dark but of course she could do it.

But it was seriously dark now, and she knew the truck was out there, the one he had been working on, waiting to be bumped into.

So she walked straight out away from the house, across the lawn, holding tight to the leash. She couldn't see anything but the white of the looming utility trailer that had almost tripped her up. She skirted wide around to the right to avoid it. And she kept an ear on Martin. She was agitated to think that he might come rescue her again, felt more agitated that she might need it, and worst of all that she would have to ask for help.

Because she was done with needing to be cared for. Martin was just like Frank, always assuming she couldn't do things on her own, make her own decisions, even walk around the block by herself.

Which, truth be told, she couldn't.

Ernest stopped short. She felt something sharp pierce her cheek. She raised a hand to find a shrub directly in front of her.

Before she turned around to retrace her steps, she wondered what Martin was doing. With great relief she realized he had not come to rescue her. He had not stayed side-by-side with her. What a relief, but now what was she to do to get home?

She pulled Ernest around. There was no sign of Martin, just a deep shadow where his house was.

She whispered to Ernest, "Take us home. Don't tell anyone I asked you, though."

To herself she said, OK, dog, I need you. I don't need Frank (she said to herself, while listening for Frank to say something about that) and I don't need Martin. But for now, do you think you could just find our way home? Out loud she said, "Home, Ernest."

A light was on, shining out a window at the side of Martin's house. She and Ernest were walking along the road, encountering no difficulty. The window light was no help but from it she could tell that he was inside, unlikely to pounce on her again.

Or to help her.

They got to the door. It was still unlocked. The house seemed empty till they got the lights on. And maybe even then.

The last several steps to the house had been easy. Ernest was at her side. What had Martin said after he had grabbed her? He heels? YES, he heels! He had been right there with her the whole way home.

And that meant she had found her own way home, pretty much. He had given her confidence, was that it?

Chapter 10

That gave her an idea. Why didn't they just keep walking?

"What do you think, Old Boy?" she asked him. He didn't say anything, so she turned, and so did he.

Where had this dog come from, anyway? Why had he been in the pound?

The next thought threw her. What if he had gotten lost, and someone was looking for him? What would happen if they found him? How unusual was a huge blood-red bloodhound in this small town?

Small comfort that the pound was across the bridge, over the boat channel, in another town.

Someone could recognize him! If they were going to go for a walk, good thing it was at night when he might not be all that visible.

Because really, he didn't seem all that sick. Yes, he was a little stiff, a little slow, but then so was she. And she could feel life blossoming in her. Ever since waking up wanting to get sheep. She laughed.

She turned Ernest around and went out the driveway to the street. Then toward the streetlight. Then beyond it. Up the street, or down? Ernest happily trotted along with her.

But then as happy as she was with herself, there was the issue of her bossy neighbor. Was he really just a flesh-and-blood Frank? Were all men like that? She'd have to be careful not to give in to it. She had Ernest! She was ready for new things as long as he was.

They walked for maybe a half hour. She had enjoyed putting one foot in front of the other without thought. But now the wind blew her hair into a snarl. She was getting cold. The blocks were built long and twisting, and sooner or later she would need to head home. Before she or Ernest was ready for sleep.

The wind was blowing stronger but not yet colder. That meant that the clouds had come in and would blanket the earth all night and it would probably rain. She didn't want to get caught, so she picked the way home that seemed the shortest. The shortest way home, but not short. Then the rain started.

She was getting wet. This was no light sprinkle. And home was what? Ten minutes away? She'd be soaked!

Maybe they could cross the brook and cut off almost all the distance. The brook ran through the neighborhood from high up on the heights of the forestlands in a straight line to the sea. Cedars grew along it, and it formed a natural boundary line separating the backyards of houses that were on parallel streets.

And it separated Maggie from her neighborhood a street over.

She could either go down to the crossroad where the brook coursed through a culvert and was no bother, then across to her neighborhood, and up the street on the other side, or she could cut across the actual brook. She'd never done it, never had a reason to do it, but the neighborhood kids cut across regularly. For all she knew they had to take a running leap to stay dry. Or perhaps they easily stepped across on well-placed stones.

She'd take a chance on the brook or else she'd be soaked to the skin.

Too bad Ernest didn't know the way! They'd be home in a couple of minutes.

The rain clouds had darkened the sky, the street lamps cast only the feeblest light, and squint as she would, Maggie couldn't see anything but houses, some with lights on, some completely dark. And cars on driveways, and the shadows of trees behind them. Those cedars would be the ones that lined the brook.

There was absolutely no advantage to dawdling. So without much hesitation -- just a little -- she gave a tug on Ernest's leash and walked down the next driveway toward the backyard. She hoped to be across the brook in a minute, home in two, in a bed in five.

But the backyard sloped toward the brook more than she'd thought, and bushes seemed to bar her progress.

Ernest was standing still, not plowing into the thicket as she was. And then he started pulling her across the yard. She couldn't see a thing, so she held her arms out in front of her to protect her face, and not thinking of anything better, let him pull her. After a good while of plunging into utter darkness, he turned back toward the brook and had them both across and onto a path beyond in a bound. Her shoes were filled with water, her clothing drenched from the splashes he kicked up -- but they'd made it. She was only several hundred feet from home, and she let him pull her there. He strode along with purpose and even went to his own front door!

The rain was warmish, and she stood out in it instead of hurrying inside. Her soaked clothes clung to her and she was tempted to strip them off where she stood. She could see a yellow smudge in the sky overhead, mostly hidden by clouds, old Mr. Moon winking at her. But no, she would go in and take a proper shower.

But what could she do with Ernest? He was soaked too. And maybe he'd get a chill. That bath he'd had was ruined!

She had unclipped the leash, but she reattached it to make sure when they went inside that he did not crawl on the bed in his sodden state. Instead she walked him through the hall and kitchen to the porch, getting towels from the dryer along the way. There was no traffic passing beside her house -- the hour was too late. As she hosed Ernest down, she also let the cool water run over her hair, her face, her shoulders. She took off her shirt and rinsed herself off, working her way down until she was naked. Never had she done such a thing! But of course it was safe, there was no one to see, even if the moon should come out.

She and Ernest were nearly dry when the moon did indeed come out. She scurried for the door, calling to Ernest. She was laughing. She ran into her bedroom and found her nighty, rubbed Ernest one more time with her own towel and went to bed. He crawled in beside her and she gave him a hug full of affection.

When Martin came in the morning, surprising her with oatmeal and the fixings, he let Ernest out while Maggie got dressed. When he came back from the porch he was holding a pile of Maggie's clothing, the jacket, the shirt and pants, the intimate apparel, still dripping. He looked her with a crooked smile and waggled his eyebrows.

Maggie took one look and hurried to take them from him, but he sidestepped her and opened the door to her laundry room, where he dumped them into the open washer. Then he had a long conversation with Ernest until Maggie sat down and helped herself to oatmeal. As her embarrassment wore off, she began to enjoy the domesticity of the moment, and the way this surprising man knew his way around a kitchen. And a laundry room.

Chapter 11

Martin, who had helped himself to butter from the fridge, sat and started to serve himself some oatmeal, but then put down the ladle and took Maggie's hand in his. He turned it over. It was scratched, though she hadn't noticed. It was her feet that were bothering her this morning -- they were red and swollen, maybe from standing in the cold water.

"Hmm," said Martin.

"What?" said Maggie. He still had her hand.

"So, you got yourself tangled up in some brambles last night!"

She tucked her feet under her so he wouldn't see. It was bad enough her hands and arms were scratched. It was as if he had caught her out there at the brook. But how did he know it was last night?

Her sodden shoes were out on the deck. He had left them there, smart since it wasn't raining and maybe they would dry on their own.

He had put her hand down on the table with a gentle pat. "We'll take care of these and your feet after breakfast," he said. And then he'd helped himself to oatmeal, the butter, the banana, some nuts, and was diligently eating it.

Maggie realized she was staring at him, so she tore her attention away and added milk to her bowl, wondering all the while what fixing her scratches and other afflictions would entail. Could be interesting!

"So about last night..." he said.

She ducked her head in embarrassment, a trespasser discovered. Though it wasn't on his property, so why should he care?

"It's because it was starting to rain and I wanted to get home as fast as possible!" she said.

And then he said, "Where did you go? I came looking for you so we could go for a walk, and you were gone. The door was unlocked, by the way."

"I know," she said. "It was going to be a short walk. But walking with Ernest is fun! And then it started to rain."

"Oh," he said.

"So we cut across the brook." The short version seemed more apt to let her keep her dignity.

Martin was thinking things, she didn't know what, and though she had been feeling victorious for getting herself home before the rain soaked her last night, it really had been Ernest who had rescued them. And she'd ended up as soaked as if she'd been caught in a tidal wave because of him.

Martin had everything cleared as she finished her last bite, and then disappeared toward the bedrooms. She rose slowly, painfully, to her feet, thinking she might go find out what he was up to now. Ernest was asleep on his bed under the table so she pushed the chair in carefully, and then Martin was back, with her lotion. From her bathroom! He took her hand and pulled her to the family room couch and sat her at one end, then went to the other.

"How did you know where it was?" she asked. She realized it was pretty obvious, really: You keep lotion in a bathroom drawer or cabinet.

"All you ladies keep your lotion in the bathroom," said Martin.

ALL YOU LADIES! Maggie experienced an instant deflation.

She didn't realize she'd been inflated, but that's what it was: Here was a total stranger who thought he would put lotion on her painful feet (and when was the last time that happened? And how good did that sound?) and it was something he did regularly. And just not with her! This would be a first for her! Except it wouldn't because she'd already pulled her knees up so he couldn't reach her feet. Except he did. One at a time he firmly grasped them, slathered them in lotion, rubbed it in, massaged deeply, worked his way up to her calves with lotion, and after a 15-second struggle on principle, she leaned back on the pillow he'd tossed her and closed her eyes.

Bliss!

Never mind the others. No doubt they were in his deep past, from his younger days. He was old, probably older than she was! These days he would rub feet only in times of need, and probably it would be soothing and comforting but certainly not girl-boy in any sense, not at his age, and not even at her age. Because she was also old. She hadn't been old, and then Frank had died, and just the other day she had awakened and realized she was old, that something had happened in those three years, and Those Days, the ones of touching for the sake of passion, were over.

And then he was encouraging his lotiony fingers beyond her knees.

She opened her eyes, struggled to sit up, pushed her pants legs back down to her lower legs, glared at him, found he was adding more lotion to his hands. A part of her was glad, a part of her was alarmed: what would he apply it to next? She closed her eyes, the better to avoid complicity.

And waited. And nothing. And opened her eyes to see him adding lotion to his own hands. Then he wiped his hands on a towel and started to push himself off the couch.

Oh, she thought.

Fair enough, she thought. And she rolled off the couch and onto her feet, and realized they didn't hurt anymore.

Martin was just then pushing himself up from the couch. Maggie ended up standing somewhat close to him, so she stepped back but Ernest was in the way. She tripped and fell forward against Martin..

"I love you too, Maggie," said Martin.

He took her hand and pulled her along with him to the front hall.

"What do you usually do on Saturday?" he asked.

Maggie looked at him. Her mouth was possibly still open. "Farmer's market," she mumbled.

"Great! Let's go! Grab your bags. Mine are in my truck!

By the time he had said this, he had found the leash and clipped it onto Ernest's collar. Ernest was dancing from one foot to the next. Maggie turned in a circle. "I'll wait for you outside," said Martin.

Chapter 12

It took Maggie minutes to pee, collect her cloth reusable farmers market bags, find her wallet, put on her jacket. Ernest and Martin were sitting side by side in the truck. Maybe she would end up in the middle.

But no, when Martin saw her, he hopped out and ushered Ernest into the little back seat. Maggie was in the process of hauling herself into the rather large pickup when Martin came around behind her. How he managed to toss her in the rest of the way she didn't know. And then he snapped the seatbelt across her. He smelled good.

Maggie held onto the seat belt as Martin backed into the cul-de-sac and accelerated into the intersection. He turned to smile at her while rocketing around a curve and up the hill toward town.

Something was happening to her insides. It must be the speedy way he entered every curve in the road. Before she knew it, they had joined the long line of traffic coming from the ferry.

"What do you need?" he said. He had been forced down to the speed limit by the traffic that was backed up behind the light at D Avenue.

Maggie looked at him. What? What did she need? Good heavens! What DID she need?

"Berries? Eggs? Veggies?" he asked.

OH, thought Maggie. At the market. She hardly knew. Often she planned to go when Saturday rolled around, but lolled about in her PJs for too long and then ended up at the grocery store mid-week when it was crowded and she was grumpy from having no food in the house.

And now he was going on and she was caught not listening again. "...your husband's garden?" It seemed to be a question.

"What?" she asked.

He looked at her and laughed. The traffic was inching along. Ernest was eagerly hanging out the window that Martin had opened for him in the back. Maggie was confused by the direction of the conversation. "Yes," she said.

"OK, so you have some veggies in your husband's garden – what was his name?"

"Frank," said Maggie. And then she turned and looked at him for the first time. He seemed to be driving while looking at her and she wondered how he managed it. "Frank," she said again. "He's dead, you know."

He smiled. "Yes, you told me. And I noticed he wasn't at your house."

"Well, yes," said Maggie. She wanted to keep her answers brief so he'd be able to drive, to look at the road and all the cars ahead of them instead of at her.

"OK, what do you need at the market, and what did Frank leave you in the garden? Because the garden looks like it's full of all sorts of things."

"I suppose so," said Maggie. She realized she wasn't being helpful, but she really didn't know what was in the garden. It was Frank's. He'd had his ways in the garden and her early attempts at helping him had met with resistance. He'd told her, she recollected, that she was not a good gardener. She always did it wrong, and he always fixed her messes and made it right, and she stopped paying attention altogether. But it was true. Many green things were growing there.

Martin had already helped himself to kale.

Martin was waiting, still looking at her. The cars were inching forward, and he hadn't hit any yet.

"I don't know what's there," she offered.

"Well, we can find out later. Let's just go to the market and get some sunshine and say hi to everyone. And maybe take Ernest to the dog park later."

"Ok," said Maggie. She was frowning and he was looking at her with a bit of concern.

"What?" he asked. "We'll have fun!"

"OK," she said.

They got to town and found a parking place not far from the market, not far from downtown or the post office. A general coming and going was taking place. The hour was late for the market, the sun warm. This week's musician was still performing. The crowds were thick around the prepared-food booths and the ever-popular veggie stand of the young dad, Tommy, who farmed an acre and from it earned his livelihood. That was her favorite, too.

But Martin's long legs were taking him deep into the crowds. Ernest was keeping up with him and seemed to pay no attention to other dogs. Maggie had to run a bit but it was easy enough to keep the tall white-headed Martin in view. She tossed a bit of a wave in the direction of some of her friends who had booths. Where was Martin headed so swiftly?

He pulled up, Ernest sat at his feet, and Maggie caught up a bit breathlessly. Martin was fumbling around in one of his market bags, and came up after a bit with a leather object, a holster of sorts that held a knife. They were standing at the edge of the crowd where lawn mowers were lined up against a row of trees. It was the knife-sharpener's booth, and Martin was handing him the knife.

"I figured if I got it to him right away, he might be done with it before we leave," he explained to Ernest. Ernest seemed to think that was a smart idea.

When Martin turned back toward the crowded center of the market, he nearly stepped on Maggie. "There you are!" he said. He gave her a hug of sorts with his arm around her neck, then reached for her hand.

She looked at him through slitted eyes. Yes, most of the crowd was made up of strangers, yacht sailors in at the docks for the day or tourists from the ferries. But she had friends here! What would they think?

And what did she think?

His stride was more reasonable now, and she kept up with him just fine. He had the leash in his right hand, and now he had linked arms with her on his left.

"Do you like cheese?" he asked.

Maggie knew the cheese ladies. They had chatted with her every time she came, over the years. She loved their cheeses, all made at their place from their own cows' milk. Some cheeses had herbs, some were deeply aged and strong, one kind was covered in cocoa. She pulled up to the tasting table and took a toothpick. The mildish one named for a local mountain was her favorite. But she was wary as she nibbled on the sample. What would the two sisters, both older than she was, think of Martin?

Or not exactly of Martin but of Martin holding her hand?

But he had dropped it. Ernest was tugging at the leash, Martin was trying a few samples. "Sit!" he said to Ernest, and Ernest sat.

Maggie smiled at her friends and pretended she didn't know Martin. But the sisters knew him. Despite a couple that had come up since they arrived, the two cheese ladies fell into familiar conversation with Martin, and when he made a selection, they cut it larger than Maggie would have expected from her experience.

Maggie couldn't hear the conversation but he was clearly a good customer – at least a good customer, or maybe he was a friend.

Maggie picked out a little wedge of Mont Blanchard. She held out her money. One of them made change while still talking to Martin. Maggie popped the whole thing in her mouth. She looked around. Ernest was still sitting. The leash was still around Martin's wrist. Martin was still talking jovially with the sisters. Maggie was in the way of the other customers intent on lining up, so she wandered away.

Her friend Sylvia was packing up her booth. The crowd was thinning. She still had onions left, nothing but onions. Maggie hoped that meant she had sold out everything else. She approached her booth. Sylvia had a way of making Maggie sad, and onions seemed just right for the likes of Sylvia. And Maggie herself was feeling a little sad, now that she thought about it. Neighbor and dog were somewhere else and her lovely day at the market was not quite what she had pictured.

Sylvia was happy enough to see her. Maggie helped her put the onions from the table away in a box. There certainly were a lot of onions. They were mostly the white kind, a bit flat, with a fair amount of dirt still sticking to them. Maggie knew Sylvia had a hard time growing enough to support herself, and hers wasn't the most popular booth.

The fact was that Sylvia had a tendency to feel sorry for herself, and right now Maggie was also feeling sorry for herself and she wasn't sure she wanted more of the same.

"Brought too many onions," Sylvia was saying.

"Did you come on your boat, or the ferry?"

"Ferry. I got up too late to take my boat."

Sylvia lived on Guemes Island, just a five-minute ferry ride away.

"Did you bring the car over, then?" asked Maggie.

"No, no, it's too expensive! I sold the car last year," said Sylvia, shaking her head.

"Well, how did you bring all your veggies?" asked Maggie.

Maggie felt something warm and wet on her hand. She hoped it was Ernest, and it was, attached to Martin by the leash. She thought she should introduce Martin to Sylvia, but ...

"Hi, Sylvia!" said Martin jovially.

"What a lovely dog, Martin!" said the suddenly buoyant Sylvia.

"This is Ernest!" said Martin proudly.

Maggie held her breath.

"He belongs to Maggie!" said Martin.

She let out her breath. She looked at him. He was looking at Sylvia.

"Can I help you with that box?" he asked.

Without waiting for the answer, he handed Maggie the leash, stepped behind the table, hoisted the almost-full box to his shoulder, and said, "Which way?"

Sylvia said, "A friend picked me up at the ferry, but she had to leave..."

Maggie thought Sylvia was standing rather close to Martin.

"Well, let's go in my truck then. When is the ferry?"

"Not till 4:00," said Sylvia.

"Well, great! Then we can just go put these in the truck and if you need to do an errand or whatever, we'll have time to squeeze one in after the market closes!"

"I do need a couple of things..."

Maggie stood holding onto the leash. The tablecloth was still on the table, so Maggie folded it. Martin and Sylvia walked together side by side in the direction of the truck, Martin pointing the way. Maggie was a bit slow to follow. She could give Sylvia the tablecloth next week. And if that old guy wanted to come back, she'd still be here. Well, she'd still be here because it was a long walk home and she had come with him. At least she had her dog.

She was a little nervous to take Ernest through the crowds herself, but they were thin now. Technically the market was already closed, but some booths were still open.

Ernest seemed eager to get moving. "You want your daddy, don't you," suggested Maggie. Daddy! Ernest did seem to be pulling in the direction Martin had gone, but she wouldn't let him go that way. Maggie really wanted to get some hazelnuts, which were conveniently in the other direction, if the man was still there.

"You are MY dog," she said.

"Never mind Martin! He can go wherever he wants," she said.

The line at the hazelnut booth was a bit long still. Everyone loved the free samples and wanted to try them all. The sun was warm, the breeze mild, and tourist season full upon them, and even though the market was supposed to be closed, no one seemed in a rush to leave.

The hazelnut man never seemed to remember her. She made her purchase, then decided to taste the peaches at the next booth to see if they were good yet. But the fruit man was closing up his truck. As she looked around, she could see the crowds had thinned even more, the vendors were packing up and many were gone, and she realized that she and Ernest were almost alone in the middle of the plaza.

Now what? It dawned on her that she might have time to go visit Duncan, her lawyer. Well, mostly Frank's lawyer. He used to work on Saturdays, so maybe he was there in his office, just a couple of blocks from the farmers' market.

By now Martin must have gotten to the truck. And taken Sylvia for an errand, wherever that might be. Surely he knew Maggie and Ernest were stranded unless he drove them home! So she would need to wait.

The smart thing would be to wait for him right where he had left her. But now the breeze was picking up, the plaza was rapidly becoming deserted, there was nowhere to sit and no one she knew to wile away the minutes with. And it was too far to walk home. Four miles! She'd never make four miles! Not on top of last night's walk. And not ever. So, she would go to Duncan's office.

She wasn't sure what to do with Ernest when she got there, but.... Well, it was better than waiting. And she'd be gone and back in no time!

Chapter 13

She nibbled at the hazelnuts as she walked along. Ernest didn't want one.

Duncan's office was upstairs in an old building that had once been the town theater in the back, retail shops in the front. Everyone knew it as a fixture of downtown. She and Frank had seen a simple sign in an upstairs window when they'd first come to town: Duncan Graham, Esq. Attorney at Law. They had decided to go check him out, then had been hard-pressed to find the door. It was around to the side of the building, and when they entered they had been confronted with a long stairwell with a landing halfway up. The old theater had had a large screen that ascended well above the second-floor level, and now all the professional offices were built out in that space. Forty steps upward it took to get to Duncan's office, a long climb for her and Ernest.

Today they rested on the landing, hoping that Duncan was in or all those steps would have been in vain. By now he was nearly 80, she supposed. Maybe he was retired and no longer had an office, or perhaps he went home for long daytime naps. Eventually they made it to the top and the sign was there on the door. But no one answered. She'd have to come back, maybe sometime when she didn't have Ernest!

And now she felt foolish and hastened down the stairs and out the door into the sunshine.

She felt as though she must be late, that she must hurry back to the market plaza. Maybe they would be waiting for her. Or might they have gone to the ferry without her? Perhaps Martin would drop Sylvia off at the terminal, then return for her and Ernest.

She hadn't thought of Martin as a thoughtless person, quite the contrary, and the more she pondered her situation the more she realized that Sylvia had probably taken advantage of his good will and made him take her on several errands. She realized it wasn't actually ferry time yet. She had some waiting to do. She could still go to the post office for her mail. That would take only a few minutes. She could go hang out at the knit shop, but he'd never find her there. And the knit shop was not nearly large enough for the likes of Ernest. And meanwhile Ernest was growing restless.

She suspected Ernest knew exactly where Martin was. His bloodhound nose had secret powers of discovery, she was sure.

"Go find him, Ernest! Let's see what you can do!"

Ernest wasn't going anywhere, so Maggie started to walk. At first they wandered back to the market plaza, but then Ernest headed off away from where Martin had gone with Sylvia.

"Good boy!" said Maggie. "You're so smart!"

Ernest was not going in a straight line, but he was going, where she certainly had no idea. They were blocks from the grocery where Sylvia might have wanted to shop, blocks from where they had left the truck and that was in the opposite direction. But she followed. She really had little choice but to follow!

She couldn't remember how far a bloodhound could smell. Whatever his nose was telling him, Ernest was on his way somewhere. He picked up the pace to the point that Maggie had trouble keeping up. They were still on the street that had earlier been lined with cars for the farmers market, though there were few left.

Ernest was tugging on the leash now and taking gigantic steps forward. He was panting. It was warm, and she hadn't thought of water before they left the plaza.

Ernest was picking up speed. Maggie concentrated on putting one foot safely in front of the other.

And then he veered to the left, to the street. She almost tripped on the leash. At the same time she saw a vehicle, and then the friendly voice, "There you are!" It was Martin.

Ernest was all about getting his ears rubbed. Martin had gotten out and walked around to Maggie. "Glad we found you," he said.

'We.' He had said 'we'! Maggie turned, looking around. Sylvia was sitting in the truck.

"Hi," Maggie said. Sylvia was smiling. So they hadn't yet gone to catch the ferry.

Martin opened the passenger door and pulled the seat a bit forward so Ernest could get into the back. Maggie wondered if Sylvia was going to lean forward and make room for her in the back with him. Martin had gotten in on the driver's side. Maggie was still standing at the curb. Sylvia had bags of groceries at her feet.

"Move on over, Sylvia, and make room for Maggie!" said Martin.

Sylvia looked at Maggie and at the groceries, nudging them with her feet. Maggie got the feeling that Sylvia thought she and all her groceries were enough for the front seat and Maggie should get in the back with Ernest.

Martin got out of the truck and walked to where Maggie was standing. He said quietly, "Come on over to this side."

Maggie slid in on his side past the steering wheel and sat in the middle. Sylvia didn't seem eager to make room for her.

Martin said, "Sylvia got too many groceries to take them over on the ferry by herself, along with the box of onions. So I'm going to drive her over."

Sylvia was smiling happily, but looking out the front window, not at Maggie.

"Want to come?" added Martin.

"Sure," said Maggie.

So they drove to the ferry and waited in line. Sylvia had a puckery look on her face that Maggie kept sneaking peeks at. Martin took out his wallet and Sylvia let him. Ernest lay his head on Maggie's shoulder, and Maggie reached around and scratched the ear she could reach. She encountered the hand that Martin had reached around to do the same thing. He gave Maggie's hand a gentle squeeze.

She was flooded with warm feelings for him. The whole scenario washed into her awareness: he was being nice to Sylvia, and he was trusting her to be ok with that. And now that he was so honoring her with high motives, she found herself filled with those high motives and she looked at Sylvia with understanding.

Because they were two old single women, and now she, Maggie, had a special friend in Martin, Martin who had not abandoned her but had trusted her to be a member of his team. Not that Sylvia was all that old but she had a bedraggled, sad look that added years to her -- that was Maggie's guess.

The whole day began to make sense, she herself began to make sense, she and Martin began to make sense, soup, kale, and now driving Sylvia all the way home – it all made sense. She and Martin, and of course Ernest, understood and had an understanding together.

So they drove onto the ferry and Martin paid. Maggie chatted amiably with Sylvia. Sylvia talked about the few customers she'd had. Maggie gave her a hug, really feeling how awful and scary that would be.

And then they drove Sylvia home and helped her unload. They gave Ernest a few minutes to run around and he got scared by some raucous ducks and came back to them for comfort. And then it was time to leave to catch the next ferry, and Sylvia came running to the truck with a dozen eggs fresh from the chickens, none too clean and covered with tiny feathers. She handed them to Martin and then she hugged them both goodbye. And Maggie remembered to give her her tablecloth.

And Maggie noticed Sylvia hugged Martin for longer but she didn't mind, after she thought about it for a moment.

And so they rode home in silence. The sun was high in the sky. He pulled into his driveway. And now what?

She had her packages from the farmers' market, he had the eggs from Sylvia and other packages. He said, "Let's scramble these with some of Sylvia's onions. It won't take a minute. And then I'll work on my old truck."

Chapter 14

The next morning, Maggie's first thought was, let's take a walk. She put it to Ernest and he didn't object. In fact, he seemed to know the word WALK. She tried it on him again, and he ran to get his leash. She wasn't dressed, hadn't done anything to get the day started, but she didn't want to disappoint the old dear, so she pulled on yesterday's clothes, grabbed a few cookies from the kitchen, put on her jacket, and they were out the door in ten minutes.

Ernest had stood there all the while with the leash in his mouth, and now he was dancing from one foot to the other as she clipped it on his collar. Then they were off.

The day was perfect, not that it couldn't change. The sun was just coming over the high ridge to the east. Ernest was well-rested. Maggie was ready, fully aware that it had literally been years since she had taken any walks at all, till night before last. Not that she hadn't intended to.

"And, Ernest, you and I are going to walk every day. We need it!"

Ernest had his nose down and wasn't paying attention. Or he was pretending not to.

They walked around their cul-de-sac. "Are you going to behave, Ernest?" She couldn't imagine otherwise. But there was that fear that he was big and really could take charge if it came into his mind to follow his nose somewhere. She decided to go around the cul-de-sac a second time. Martin's driveway and a gravelly area next to it were filled with vehicles! How many did one man need? He had both a big boat and a small one, both on trailers, a small red truck, his RV. His big truck was missing, no doubt out on some adventure with its owner.

Mostly Ernest kept his head down. Except when they went past Martin's house. The old bloodhound had stopped there and was sniffing deeply.

"No, Ernest, we're not going there, Boy." Ernest must have heard NO from the past. He stopped tugging and stepped along beside her again. He was keeping an easy pace beside her, not that she was all that fast. "You know, Ernest, I am pretty sure I've never walked a dog before. Not that I'm actually walking you. We're just two old friends on a walk, aren't we."

By the time they had gone around the cul-de-sac twice -- and past Martin's house with its blank empty windows twice -- Maggie turned up the street out of their neighborhood. "OK, Ernest, this is it. Keep that nose of yours under control! I am not ready for an adventure."

Ernest kept his smooth pace. Sometimes his head turned to one side or the other, and when they came to a house up the street with a picket-fenced yard and the sharp voices of two or three small dogs, he moved closer to her, went to her other side, pulled to the far side of the street. Then he was moving faster than she was ready for and she felt a bit of panic.

But when they got past the offending yard, he settled back into his stately rhythm, and so did she.

"Let's turn here, Ernest," she said at the next corner. "Good doggie!" she said when he went along. "I'm so glad you're not too old to walk!" she said. And thought, I'm glad I'm not too old to walk. At least this far.

Maggie settled into her thoughts. The quiet streets had little traffic and the companionable Ernest walked sedately at her side. The walk was pleasant, all was well. But where had the young Maggie, hiker, gone? The explorer? As she watched these thoughts, old memories, return to her conscious mind, she marveled that she was old. Old in years, young in thoughts, old in circumstance, a widow, mid-60s, settled, happily going about her routine until the thought that Frank was dead.

So there had been years with Frank, and now they were over. But where had it started, her time with Frank? It seemed so quick now, but it was, what? Forty years! Which maybe had been forty years of no walks, no hikes, no dogs. A garden, yes. A house, this house for half of it or so. A car. A job for a while, his job right up till the day he didn't wake up, dead from a stroke.

It seemed too short. "More happened than that, Ernest." But she couldn't remember what else. No kids, not with Frank. Meals from the garden, trips by herself to the farmers' market. Movies and TV, knitting, crosswords, books, trips to the library for her. Walks with Frank on the dock some evenings, talk of the boat they would get someday, the travels they would do someday. And here we are. "And here we are, Ernest."

"And what's your story, Ernest? Where did you come from? Who loved you? Who lost you? Do they know where you are?" Because, and she didn't want him to hear this, I don't want them to find you -- even if you miss them, even if they miss you.

She picked up her step. She was getting too morose, too dreary. Heavens.

Ernest kept right up with her. They had just about circled the rather large block that made up her neighborhood and now they had to decide whether to go further.

She led him over to the side of the road. From there she could see the ocean. Well, not really the big Pacific Ocean, but a bay off the sound off the ocean, all connected and huge. Japan was over there, way over there. She could see nearby little islands out there, several sailboats, and way off in the distance, beyond the seas that surrounded this island home of theirs, mountains! And even though it was June, snow-capped mountains.

"What can those mountains be?" she asked Ernest.

It turned out Ernest was busy, following his nose back and forth at the edge of the street. From where she stood, not terribly far from her house, the land cascaded downward at a steep angle. A few houses had been built part-way down the hillside. The driveways looked treacherous -- it was so easy to see that a slipped foot could result in a car plunging right through a garage door, right through a garage in fact, so steep were these driveways -- and she was glad her own was flat. Then below the houses another street, with the occasional car, and then more houses and then the bay.

"Look at that, Ernest! Look how close we are to the water! Why have I never walked this way before! We could go down there and maybe there's a beach to walk on!"

Ernest looked at her but only for a moment. Next moment he had bolted past her into the street, and she found herself being whipped around as the leash went taut. She'd heard a car and in this instant her mind was petrified with worry that her sweet old dog was about to be hit and destroyed. As she was still in the process of pivoting, of being yanked around, Ernest came to a halt. And so did the car.

Or rather the truck. Because it was Martin in his pick-up, facing in the homeward direction. And Ernest was beside himself with joy, apparently, because he was making some sound deep in his throat and thrusting himself toward the car window. And now Martin had the window rolled down and his hand out and Ernest was letting his ears be scratched. And Maggie thought that dogs were really smart that way, having silky ears that practically reached up for a scratch.

And now Martin was saying something and it was lost in the throaty noises Ernest was making.

So Maggie stepped closer, as close as she could get with Ernest in the way, only to hear Martin say, "...don't you think?"

Maggie stood with her hands on her hips staring at him. Martin looked bright and eager and maybe a bit full of mischief. And now he was hopping out of the truck, leaving it right there in the middle of the oncoming traffic lane. And now he was taking Maggie by the hand and twirling her back toward the sea and pointing somewhere. And now he was making it easier for her to see what he was pointing at by getting behind her and putting his head on her shoulder and extending her arm with his.

"See that island, Maggie?" he was saying. "It's one of my favorites. It's got a little beach. Let's go there in my boat!"

He had turned her back so she was facing him, not all that far away. "Want to?" he asked.

Maggie didn't say anything. Yes to him, not sure to the boat idea. She'd never been in anything smaller than a ferry. "What about Ernest?" she asked.

"He'll love it! Let's go! Come on in the truck! We can hitch the boat trailer up and be on our way in ten minutes!

Maggie thought that ten minutes wasn't going to give her time to think. And then she thought maybe that was a good thing. She knew already that Ernest was all-in. So she walked around the truck. Martin was there before she was and was ready to give her a boost. Ernest was already in the back of the truck.

Maggie was silent the two minutes it took to drive home.

"Well?" said Martin. "Is that a yes?"

She looked at him. At his eager face. She caught a glimpse of the beloved red dog prancing around in the back. Clearly these two guys were going. The day was sunny, cool and breezy. Thoughts like, 'I could stay home and knit' started to drift into her brain as they had for years.

But NO, she would not stay home and knit. NO NO NO! Today she would go out in a boat. With her guys. With her very real guys who were fun to be with, who did things she had never done as if they did them every day! No more staying home for me, she thought.

But in a boat? Maybe to an island? With a dog, her dog? And Martin?

"Sure," she said, rather quietly. She looked straight ahead, avoiding...what? Avoiding smiling, avoiding letting him know that a happy bubble was building inside and was about to burst out into the world? But she could see he was looking at her and smiling a big smile.

She buried her face in her hands and smiled her own smile. And then thought, it's only a boat ride. With Ernest. And Martin. To a beach. With a picnic. 'It's about time,' said Frank. Or her mother. Or maybe that was her inner Maggie, awake inside her.

They were underway with the larger boat from Martin's yard, also the dog, picnic lunch, fishing things of all sorts, life jackets and sunscreen. "And get a jacket in case it gets cold. I've got extra rain gear." She looked at the sunny sky, then at him like he was crazy. He just laughed.

It was nice to get out. They drove to the boat ramp at the park. Ernest was drooling with excitement. She had to hold him and the boat while Martin drove the car and trailer to the parking lot. No one was around. The morning walkers of the loop trail through the woods, all three miles of it, had finished for the day. Kids were in school, working folks were at work, and they had the park to themselves. The sun was lovely, the sky almost cloudless, the breeze gentle.

Martin was back. He threw all the gear into the boat, then helped Maggie up the boat ladder from where she was standing on the sandy bottom, water up to her knees, just beyond the boat ramp. The water was intensely cold. Ernest bounced up and down, biting at the water, running back to shore, splashing them till they were wet through. Then Martin scooped him up onto the side of the boat. Ernest launched himself forward and landed hard against the other side. He stood looking down into the water as they backed out of the shadowy shallows and made for open waters.

Maggie held on tight to the tiny railing that wrapped around the boat. Ernest came over and lay his soaking head on her lap. She pushed him away. "Lie down, Ernest! You're wet." Ernest looked at her and flopped on his side in the sun. He filled the space at her feet.

Martin said, "Hold this" and handed her the steering wheel. They were speeding along and she was so low down she couldn't see where they were headed. "Wait!" she said.

He said, "We're fine. I just need to do a few things below."

She nervously peered around the width of the boat but still had no idea where they were headed. She could tell their own island was receding quickly. Holding tight, she stood up behind the wheel. Open water spread out before them.

In the distance was a ferry. Of course she knew the ferry went back and forth from their island to other islands and even to Canada. She had seen them for years, had even been on one with Frank a couple of times. Now she was heading straight for one. "Martin!" she said, rather louder than she had thought to do. "Martin, there's a ferry straight ahead of us."

'Ok," he said.

She continued to keep her eye on it. It seemed to be approaching their island, but not very fast. She relaxed a little.

Martin returned from down below. “Can you keep steering while I get the fishing gear ready?” he asked.

She nodded. She was still concentrating.

“Look at the seal,” said Martin. He pointed.

She didn’t see it at first. “What happens if we hit it?” she asked. “Will it get out of the way?”

He nodded. Otherwise he was concentrating on the fishing pole.

She settled into a dreamy state induced by the warm sun and the gentle rocking of the boat. Other than small waves that had reached them from the ferry, the minutes passed in calm, even serene predictability. It was very nice, she decided.

“All set,” said Martin. He had slid the pole into a holder and was coming back to take the wheel.

She started to step aside, but he stepped behind her and took the wheel from there. She was wrapped up in his arms, the two of them steering together. He was swaying with the rhythm of the swells. He guided the wheel around to the left. “Let’s go over here,” he said. “This is my favorite fishing spot.”

She couldn’t tell one spot from the other. She was content to let him steer. Still holding the wheel in one hand, and that meant still keeping her between his body and the wheel, he reached down and turned off the engine. They bobbed in near-silence on the small waves.

Still he held her. There was not much steering to do. They had rounded a tiny island and no other boats were nearby to worry about. The wind seemed to be blocked by the island. The sun was warm, the air a bit cool but pleasant. He said, "Do you need your jacket?"

"No," she said.

In her life jacket she felt huge, awkward, unbalanced in the narrow space except that Martin was holding her. Ernest lay still, giving her little room for her feet. She and Martin had only a few square feet to share by the wheel. But they didn't need to guide the boat now, with the engine off. He turned her toward him, continuing to hold her. Her arms were pressed to her sides, and since she was a good foot, maybe more, shorter than he, she had her head pressed against his chest. He was hugging her, but she wasn't hugging him back. She couldn't with her arms pinned, and she couldn't figure out if she wanted to. A hug was an escalation already, a reciprocated hug even more of one.

But then, she didn't want to not hug him. What would that tell him?

And what did she mean, anyway? What did she want?

She wanted just what was happening right now, a nice hug from a nice friend.

But then what?

She sunk her head into his chest, or actually his life jacket. His hand rose up and pressed her head to him. Her one arm was free now. Still feeling ambiguous, she reached around, gave him a squeeze, and patted his back in what she thought was a friendly maybe non-committal way.

He raised her chin and kissed her, full on the mouth.

She was shocked. Not displeased. Quite thrilled, really. And embarrassed.

She was standing rather close to find out what was going on on his face. She wanted to see his eyes, his crinkles, his mouth. But if she put her face up, she'd be begging for another kiss, it would seem.

And is that what she wanted? It was complicated.

For one thing, he lived next door! How complicated could it become!

Martin held her out at arm's length, which meant leaning her against the wheel, and looked at her.

"What?" he asked.

She didn't know what to say. A good chunk of her wanted to just kiss him a few more times to get a clearer idea of what she thought.

"Let's fish," he said.

"I'll watch this time," Maggie said, and sat down behind the wheel.

So Martin busied himself with fishing gear and Maggie watched. She was still feeling the kiss on her mouth, and enjoying it, and she was also enjoying watching that guy who had kissed her. The day was perfect. The boat was lulling her into a peaceful empty-minded timeless place of pure enjoyment.

Martin was catching a fish now and again and throwing it back. Ernest showed interest in the first one, but then he too seemed to sink into a soporific state of peace. Maggie's heart was getting a real workout as she looked from one friend to the other.

But now Martin seemed to be hurrying to put away his fishing gear. "Hold these," he said as he thrust the tackle box then the bucket at her. He was taking apart his fishing pole.

Maggie looked around. The wind had come up, though she hadn't realized it. And there was now a bank of clouds off to the west. The sun still shone warm and lovely, but the breeze was more chilling than before. And really, she thought, it was more than a breeze. And the boat was rocking in an unsettling way.

Martin had turned on the engine. He took her hand and pulled her to the wheel, set a course, and asked her to stay on it.

"Just aim for that tall tree," he said.

She thought she knew the one he meant. It was way over on an island, the pointy tree, probably a cedar, that stuck up above the rest.

He came back to her. He needed to get close enough to be heard. "I think this will calm down this afternoon. Let's go over to the island and take shelter there. If it isn't calmer, we'll have to go home.

Maggie looked at him. She was a bit concerned about how jostling the waves were, how the boat was rocking so much that she felt in danger of falling. She grabbed the wheel, but that knocked them off-course: even she could see that the boat was now no longer pointing at the tall cedar.

Martin took the wheel in one hand and wrapped his free arm around her, steadying her. He didn't seem to be tossed around. His feet were apart, his stance steady. Instead of grabbing the wheel again, she held onto his arm that encircled her and leaned back against him.

She could see the island getting closer, but it took far longer than she'd thought it would and the wind was stronger. The whole boat was slapping the waves. She clutched his arm more tightly. She was trying to figure out if she could survive if she let go enough to get under the canopy and down the little flight of stairs to the bunks below.

But Martin had closed the opening to the boat's insides. And good thing! Salt spray was wetting everything, and when the boat slammed against a wave and a good-sized splash reached them, Ernest stood up and whined.

"Lie down, Ernest," Martin said.

Somehow Martin was standing firmly in one place undisturbed by the tumult of waves. And now he was rotating her around and guiding her arms around his waist and taking the wheel with two hands. She held on as tightly as she could around the bulky life jackets.

She didn't notice right away that the waves had abated, that the boat was barely bouncing at all. So she held on tight as though her life were still in danger until Martin pried her arms from his torso, gave her a kiss, and sat her down behind the steering wheel. Facing forward she could see the waves were nothing but little ripples on a smooth sea.

"We're in the lee of the island," he said with a smile.

In a few moments they were close enough that she could see a tiny harbor ahead, just big enough to shelter a few boats, she thought. And to get to that harbor, a narrow inlet.. As they entered through that narrow neck, she could see a house hidden in the woods halfway up the hill, A single lone house. The sun was directly overhead, midday. One other boat lingered there, possibly owned by the residents of the house. There certainly was no other way to this small island than by boat. Or possibly by helicopter.

As soon as they entered the tiny harbor, the wind ceased entirely. She was wet enough to be chilly. They had not yet eaten their lunch, and she was ready for it. Maybe they could get dry in the sun.

Martin continued driving the boat until he came to a sandy beach, tiny and unoccupied and sunny. He busied himself up at the bow. She could see him toss the anchor. Then he surprised her by stepping off the side of the boat. He landed in water halfway up his thighs. Maggie wondered what was wrong with the ladder and in consternation wondered how high the water might come up on her. Ernest, watching it all and trying to help, leapt off after him.

Maggie was still sitting behind the wheel wondering what to do. But Martin called her and guided her down the ladder. At the last minute he pulled the stern of the boat toward shore, so that when she stepped off she was only up to her knees in water. Cold water. But not as cold as she'd thought it might be.

They slogged through the water for the remaining twenty feet or so until they were out on the beach. The water here was pleasant on her legs. Warmed by the sun, she thought. She lingered in it, walking back and forth up to her ankles, squishing sand between her toes. Ernest bounded in and out of the water, then ran to the back of the beach and into the bushes. She was having fun watching him enjoy his freedom.

Martin had gone back to the boat for the picnic lunch and a blanket. The sun felt wonderful on her face. Now she wished she had worn shorts. She thought, I might have to buy some.

They explored while they chewed on their sandwiches, finding the bushes that lined the beach mostly ended in a wall of rock, not man-made but more like a pile-up from some landslide deep in the past. At least that's what Martin thought. Signs of recent tides included a bit of seaweed, an occasional broken shell. Once Martin had pointed it out, Maggie could see an eagle nest high in the tallest cedar far up on the hill, maybe the cedar she had steered by. It seemed to be empty, or else maybe it had eggs or babies. But no parents were about, none that she could see, and it was too late in the season for babies. There were no seals sunning themselves, no gulls flying overhead. If there was someone in the house, there was no sign of it except possibly the little boat. They were alone, the three of them.

Maggie found it uncomfortable on the blanket so she kept walking around exploring. Martin was sitting cross-legged on the blanket slowly peeling and eating a mango, using a knife to skin it, slice off the flesh, put it in his mouth. He looked at home and at peace. His weather-beaten face, lined but well-balanced, pleased her. His eyebrows were outrageously bushy. His ears were large. His eyes were blue and intelligent and piercing. He used them in disconcerting ways, she thought. They looked and looked as if searching for something hidden away, some truth maybe. Like what he'd said about the rock wall, which to her were just ... rocks.

She had taken off her lifejacket when she got out of the boat. It was a bit tight for her. No surprise. She had been glad for the freedom. And so had Martin. And now they were drying off in the sun, and Maggie wasn't chilled anymore.

And so here they were. As adventures went, it was all very new and she liked it. Earlier Martin had barely begun to fish before the waves had come up. But then he didn't seem surprised or disappointed. Maybe that's the way it was with fishing. She'd be willing to go again and learn more about it if this is what fishing was all about.

Overall she felt not exactly at peace. She was happy to be here, but she also was thinking about lips on lips and a certain buzz that made her want to find a need to wrap her arms around him again. Now he was exploring with her, and as they wandered about, poking around at the high-tide line for shells and whatnot, she found she kept drifting closer to him. It wasn't exactly a decision, and when she noticed she was doing it she grew a bit embarrassed and strode away in what she hoped looked like a purposeful direction. But where did she want to go but back into his arms, and once again she found herself standing quite near him while he probed in the seaweed for treasures.

And he was onto her, apparently.

"Maggie, look at this," he said. What he had in his hand seemed unremarkable to her but she looked closely and more closely. She realized her body was on high alert to be that close to him.

Ernest wanted to be part of it. He ran over, smiling and panting and galumphing and tossing up sand. He licked Martin's hand and whatever had been there disappeared. And he knocked Maggie over in the process. She landed with an oooph and Martin put his hands on his hips and laughed at her and she was this way and that way about it until she saw his smile.

And then her hand went out toward him of its own accord as if she wanted a boost back onto her feet, and he saw it and pulled her up and then kept pulling and then she ended up in a giant hug that could have gone on, she thought and sincerely hoped, except that the galumphing dog wanted in and ran between their legs and Maggie needed to steady herself and Martin stepped back and gave Ernest a huge ear-scratching.

Maggie was actually feeling that she had had enough sun. She found herself looking around for shade, even just a little, and Martin caught her at it and asked what she was looking for, and in the end suggested they could maybe have a swim and then get out of the sun in the cabin of the boat if there was enough breeze so they wouldn't roast down there.

Maggie thought the idea of cooling off in the water sounded great but she didn't have a bathing suit with her, just the jeans and shirt she was wearing. Which she pointed out to Martin.

"There's always skinny-dipping!" he offered, with a twinkle.

It dawned on her that perhaps he was baiting her, seeing what she would do. She looked at him. What kind of guy was this? She was a well-brought up lady! And then to herself she thought, OH, he knows that! He's kidding! So she smiled at him and said she was fine.

So he unbuttoned his shirt and took it off. Kicked off his sneakers. Started to unbutton his shorts. And Maggie went running up the beach into the bushes with Ernest running after her. She had no idea what Martin was doing, didn't dare look, though she might take just a little peek, thought how embarrassing it would be if he caught her peeking, finally peeked anyway, and couldn't see him anywhere. But there was a pile of clothing on the beach.

She scanned the water and still didn't see him. She squinted. Nothing. Then the boat swung around in the breeze and there he was, his head showing above the water, just beyond the boat. She waved. He waved back and started to stand and she turned her back on him as fast as she could. But out of the corner of her eye she had seen all she needed to see, which was that he was wearing his shorts -- his undie shorts she was pretty sure.

"Come on in, Maggie!" he called.

Ernest heard him and ran to him, swam to him. He knocked Martin over in the water, and in that commotion Maggie ran back to their pile of things on the beach, picked up a towel, and put it over her head. Now what?

Suddenly Ernest was all over her. The sand was flying. She fell back. Ernest stood over her to lick her face, and dripped on her and scuffed up sand all over her.

And then she heard Martin's voice very nearby and she didn't dare look in his direction. The man knew no shame, that was clear. And then he said, "Come on, Maggie. I'm trying to help you up. Move over, Ernest."

And then he reached down and pulled her to her feet and got behind her and walked her into the water fully dressed and kept pushing against her back till she could submerge herself and wash the sand off.

And while she was doing it he went back to the beach and removed his undershorts, exposing his trim backside to her and the staring windows of the house on the hill and pulled on his outer shorts and buttoned up his shirt. She had always thought that if you've seen one guy-butt you had seen them all, but not so. She stood up in water up to her waist, then strode to shore. Her jeans were heavy with water and the ponderous weight of her upbringing.

But now the boat was turning quickly on its anchor. Little ripples of waves sprang up everywhere. The sun had darkened due to a dense cloud that had appeared when she wasn't paying attention. Martin gathered everything up, washed his hands and the knife at the edge of the water, and called to Ernest. He seemed to be hurrying. Maggie wondered what she could do to help, but he was already loading her up with the picnic supplies and blanket. She waded over to the edge of the boat so she could toss them in. He grabbed the stern as it swung around and held it for her. She dumped everything in, then held the stern while he chased down Ernest to toss him in.

When Ernest landed in the boat, Maggie lost hold of the stern and landed on her knees in the water. The stern swung back and knocked her over. It caught her on the shoulder and knocked her the rest of the way so that for a moment she was underwater. Looking up as she sank, the water above her brownish and full of scraps of who knew what, her surprise turned to a brief moment of fear before she bumped the bottom and got her legs under her and pushed upward as if she was in real peril. Then Ernest came to her rescue, knocking her once again underwater. When she came up, Martin was standing a short distance away extending his hand.

She pulled up against his solid stance. Now she was cold. They hurried to finish loading the boat, getting all of them aboard.

He went forward as if to raise the anchor but then stopped. Maggie was shivering violently and was huddled down as low as she could get to avoid the wind. Martin came back and with his face close to her ear, shouted "Get down below!". He was pointing to the little cabin.

With the boat tossing as it was, she kept low and moved her hands from wheel to whatever she could grab. She wondered what he had in mind for Ernest. Her glasses were spattered with drops of driven rain -- or maybe it was seawater -- and if she'd had a spare hand she would have taken them off. Finally she saw the door he had opened ahead of her and stood so she could step into the opening. Martin was right behind her with Ernest in tow.

The space was tiny. Martin closed and hooked the door behind him. He kept Ernest from joining Maggie on one of the beds, the only place she could find to get out of the way. She was aware that she was dripping, as were they all. Martin held Ernest's collar while he reached into an upper cupboard. Inside was a stack of towels.

He tossed a towel to Maggie, then wriggled out of his jacket and set it on the floor near the door. Maggie did the same. Her jeans were dripping so she stripped them off. Martin was using a towel on Ernest, whose back was soaked to the skin. Ernest was shivering as much as Maggie was. She toweled her hair and wiped her glasses. She tossed her jeans into the pile at the door. She added her soaked jacket to the pile and crawled under the blanket on the bed. She curled into a ball and continued to shiver.

The boat was tossing about. Martin looked out one of the tiny windows and shook his head. He stripped his sweater off and added it to the pile. He lay some dry towels on the floor between the two narrow beds and pointed them out to Ernest: "Sleep, Boy!"

Maggie said, "Aren't we going home?"

Martin said, "I'm taking a chance that this squall will let up quickly. I'm hoping we're safer here in this little harbor than out in the bay. Of course the safest place would be home, if we could get there."

Maggie nodded. The boat was churning so violently that she had to hold onto the edge of the bunk, but certainly it could be worse, she could see that. She wished she could see out, to be sure they were still anchored. What would happen if somehow the boat tore loose?

"What would happen if the boat tears loose?" she asked Martin.

He looked at her. He knelt down over Ernest so he could take her hands in his. "It probably won't, Mags," he said. "And if it did it would probably beach itself on our little beach."

"Probably?" said Maggie.

"No guarantees on the sea," said Martin. "I won't lie to you, we could end up on the rocks at the base of the cliff, or knock into that other boat and maybe even spring a leak. Or we could drift out to sea through that little inlet. But I think we'll just stay here at anchor till this storm passes."

The bunk she was on was long and narrow with little shelves where the walls of the boat were, not like boxes but odd shapes to fit the shape of the boat. Martin started to get into the other bed, but then came over to Maggie. “Put your legs out straight, Maggie, so I can get in there and get you warm.”

Maggie didn’t have to think twice. She made herself as thin as possible and backed up against the shelves. Martin slid under the covers and pulled them to his chin. When Maggie brushed against his bare arm, she was startled by how cold it was. Without thinking she pulled him closer to her. He was shivering. His back was cold. His hair was wet. His feet were very cold. She wiggled her trapped arm under his head and shuddered from the feel of his cold hair. Her free arm she used to cover as much of his back as she could reach. But she still had her damp shirt on. She rearranged herself so she could unbutton it, sat up long enough to take it off, and tossed it onto the pile. Her bra could stay. She lay down again and covered him as much as she could.

Ernest was snoring.

Martin and Maggie shivered for a bit longer, but the arrangement suited them. Their body heat conserved, the tiny space cozy, they began to warm up. The storm raged. During a lull, when they could hear each other, Martin pointed out to her that they could feel that the anchor was holding: the boat would go so far in one direction, then stop and swing back. They were ok. And if the storm abated at all, they'd make a run for home.

Before long another torrent of wind and rain blew through. They could hear it in the whining of wind and the jostling of waves, ever more intense now.

Maggie was feeling drowsy, but before she could fall asleep, Martin said, "Tell me about your husband! Tell me about Frank."

Maggie stopped breathing, just for a moment. Because when he said to tell her about her husband, just for a little moment she had thought he meant Simon. Simon! Why Simon?

But he didn't know about Simon. She didn't think of Simon at all. When was the last time?

He felt her breath catch, and said she didn't have talk about Frank if she didn't want to.

And she said, "No...."

She meant, no, it's not Frank! It's Simon!

He had closed his eyes. He mumbled, "that's ok" and his breathing was beginning to slow.

And right at this moment she thought, yes, Simon! And out loud she said, "You mean Simon!"

They had twisted around until they were on their backs. Maggie was talking about Simon. Simon her first husband. Simon who had disappeared. Simon whose brother was Frank and who had let Frank marry her. "Well, it's complicated," she said.

But Martin said, "The sun is shining!" and they got up. The clothes were of course still soaked and they were nearly naked, the two of them. Martin rummaged in a narrow vertical closet at the foot of the bed and came out with an old tee shirt, soft and too big at the shoulders, which he tossed to Maggie. "Think of it as a dress," he said.

She held it up. She could barely make out the old faded heart, the faded letters that spelled I LOVE YOU.

When she put it on it covered her nearly to the knees and that would do. Meanwhile he had found a pullover sweater for himself. He still had on his outer shorts, which were only damp at this point. They were dressed.

Martin opened the hatchway door and stuck his head out.

"Where are we?" asked Maggie.

"On the beach," said Martin. The anchor is still attached but we're on the beach anyway."

They both got down to work salvaging their lunch bucket from several feet of water. Martin showed Maggie how to clean up the debris and wipe off the cedar needles that had stuck to the boat due to the violence of the wind. But more than anything Martin kept looking around.

"What are you looking for," asked Maggie.

"Another storm cell," said Martin. "And I think that's one out there to the west, and not all that far away. Let's go!"

They let Ernest sleep, they let the pile of soaking wet clothes remain on the floor. Martin turned on the engine and installed Maggie behind the wheel while he clambered to the bow and lifted the anchor. He hopped off the boat -- how cold that must have felt, thought Maggie -- and pushed against its hull until it was free from where it had come to rest in the sand, then pulled himself onto the ladder, ascended, and pulled the ladder into the boat. Maggie was steering with care. She knew they would need to thread themselves through the inlet into the bay.

She could see the bay stretch out ahead of them. There was more chop to the waves than on their way here. She braced herself for them. Martin kept an eye to the west and let her steer. And she was glad: she was getting a feel for it, enjoying it, feeling an unaccustomed bit of exultation, feeling brave and competent. And trusted.

After they were safely in the bay he pointed the direction they would need to take to navigate around the headland and not run aground.

The sun was fairly low in the sky. Martin pointed to it. "We want to get back before dark. I think we can do it. Do you want me to drive?"

Maggie said, "No, I can do it. You'll need to point the way, though."

He smiled. She was standing behind the wheel. She could just see enough ahead of her to make her confident that there was nothing to hit. The engine rumbled reassuringly beneath her feet. Martin took one more look around, then came to stand behind her. He wrapped her in his arms -- his warmth was welcome -- but he kept his hands off the steering wheel.

And then they were almost home. He guided them in toward the boat ramp, then at the last minute took the wheel, turned off the engine, handed her the painter, told her to hop out, and jumped into the water -- all 6 inches of it -- so he could go get the trailer.

Maggie shivered all the way back to the house. Martin had said he'd made soup and he'd bring it over to warm them up. Maggie nodded, then went back to looking straight ahead. She wasn't seeing anything, not the rosy light of dusk or the bright planet Jupiter overhead. Not the deer family at the side of the road or the scurrying rabbits or roses and ripening apples in the seaside gardens.

Instead she was seeing a darkened lab, a university lab, a head bowed over a stack of paper lighted by a desk lamp, Simon. And stepping back from the scene , in her memory, another head, her own. This memory was newly awake in her and she ventured a step fully into it.

But then someone was saying something, here we are Maggie and get out Ernest and be right back, and with some effort she pulled herself back to the modern day, her clothes wet and uncomfortable. She got out of the truck. Ernest was already at the front door. She let them both in and left it open for Martin, who would be back with soup. Martin, who had kissed her.

And Simon. She and Simon had kissed. Not at first. And not yet, not at the time of that memory. But soon after. She remembered when.

She went into her bedroom, stripped off the wet clothing, got in the shower, heard the front door close, decided not to linger. Ten minutes later they were eating Martin's homemade tomato and kale soup, the two bowls heated in the microwave so they wouldn't have to wait for the full pot to eat. And Maggie was still shivering. She got up and put on a sweater. She got up again to put on another pair of socks.

Ernest was asleep on his bed under the table. He was also shivering. She felt him to see whether he was dry. Mostly, she thought. Maybe just a little damp. She got up and got him a blanket. Then she wiggled her own feet under it and kept them warm against his furry side.

"Eat, Maggie!" said Martin. "It will warm you up!"

But still she shivered. The sun had set, the night was clear and starlit. The moon was a sliver, chasing the last signs of the sun, sharing the last rosy tones. Martin went to the closet and found her winter coat. She thought that was a bit much for a mid-summer night, but then she was the one who couldn't stop shivering. Then he went somewhere and found a blanket and pillows. He opened the slider and took her hand and pulled her out. Ernest didn't stir, so he closed the slider.

He made a nest for Maggie on the porch, and one for himself right next to her. He pulled her down onto the decking and covered her, and covered himself. He put his arm around her and pulled her close, pulled the big bulk of her and her layers of socks and clothes and sweater and winter coat close, and made sure every part of her was covered with the blanket. He kissed her lips and her cheek, and he pointed up at the sky and named some constellations, and pointed out Mars and Jupiter.

And then he said, "Who's Simon?" And he kissed her again.

But she was sleepy. Warm now, and sleepy. One more kiss and she might fall asleep. So she waited a bit before answering him. And then it was all Simon.

Chapter 15

Maybe he had walked her to her bed. She was sure she could remember him climbing in on the other side of the bed, with Ernest between them, both of them keeping the old dog warm. And now she could feel herself waking up. The man next to her was stirring. Warm rosy feelings had filled her for hours and now she rolled over, her arms ready for an embrace. But Ernest wasn't having any of it. He stood on the bed, stretched, stepped off, left the room.

It was an hour before Martin arrived. He handed her a buttered bagel. No hot oatmeal today! And he didn't sit down, not at first. But she did. She wanted to ask him about last night, tell him about Simon and their early cozy days together, have another bagel. She sat there looking at her empty plate, contemplated getting up for a piece of toast.

And now Martin was sitting down. His bagel was gone too. And she realized he'd been speaking for a while. What about, she wondered. So she shifted her attention. It took some effort. What she heard was the improbable word 'trip'.

"Trip?" she parroted.

"Sure!" He said, with great enthusiasm. "Don't you love road trips?"

"I've never been on one, I don't think," she said.

"Well, then! About time!" His eyes were twinkling wildly.

All sorts of images flitted through her mind, a lot of them -- she was embarrassed to admit this even to herself -- involving beds. Tents and sleeping bags. Motorhomes and vast king beds. Hotel rooms with their two queen beds, one entirely unused.... STOP IT! She screamed at herself. But no. Maybe there'd be a secluded beach.....

Out loud she said exactly what she had been thinking and exactly what she knew she could never say to him, "What about sex?"

He paused exactly where he sat, a cracker part-way to his mouth. She saw that he was quaking a little and his lips were curling up. He was about to laugh despite himself. She crawled under the table and grabbed Ernest around the neck and curled up there with him on his dog bed.

Martin peered under the edge of the table. He smiled. He said, "It's lovely. What do you want to know?"

"OH BROTHER!" she screamed. "I know I know I know I know I know. But I, I mean we, well..."

"Well, if you don't like it we don't have to do it," he said.

She pounded her fists on the dog bed and Ernest got up and left the room. He licked Martin's hand as he went by.

"Come on out, Maggie," said Martin. "I won't bother you. I won't kiss you even."

"YOU DO BOTHER ME!" she screamed. Ernest came back and looked at her lying on his bed, and whined.

"Well, should I leave?"

"NO!"

"OK, then, hands off? I tell you, I am not sure that is possible. I may find I'm taking Ernest on a lot of walks."

She started to cry. "I CAN'T STAND IT!" she yelled. Then she blubbered and her nose began to run.

He reached under the table till he could get a hold of her hand. He pulled. Maggie slid along with the dog bed under her until she was next to Martin's feet. Ernest had retreated somewhere. She grabbed Martin around the legs and hugged and wouldn't let go. He eased her chair over so he could sit on it, then pulled her up in front of him. He embraced her, arms and legs both and kissed her tears, then her mouth.

"You are confusing me," he said.

"And you are confusing me."

"Why? I'm simple enough. If it had happened that you liked sex, well then, we could just hop in bed and have some. Or are you not that kind of girl?"

"I've never been that kind of girl." She sniffed. It sounded like she was being a little contemptuous.

"So does that mean you do like sex, or you don't?" he asked.

She looked at him. This was a rather unseemly conversation. She'd rather just fall into his arms and pretend it never had entered her head to think about it, just like in the old days. But that was hard because she had thought about almost nothing else for a week now, ever since Simon. Or had that been two weeks? Or had it been just a day? She nodded ever so slightly.

"You do?" he asked.

She nodded again, just a tiny delicate proper sort of nod. The raging fire in her snorted in contempt.

"And are you the 'gotta be married first' sort of girl?"

She nodded yet again.

"So love is not enough?" he asked.

This was getting confusing. She had said nothing about love, had in fact not really thought about it. And he was thinking about it or the word wouldn't have come out so easily. Right? Well, when had love come along ever? Had she been in love with Simon? Frank? It was only Ernest she was sure of. She loved Ernest.

But what about Martin?

As she thought about it, a soft smile began to form on her lips. She thought, I think I love him!

"What was the question?" she asked.

He held her again. She was still standing in front of the chair, which meant he could kiss her neck and throat and chin but if they were going to kiss on the lips, she would need to stop pretending she was an innocent bystander and bend over and reach her face toward his lips. Avoid his nose. Get close enough.

Her legs were getting wobbly, no doubt from too much standing. She loved being pressed up against him. It made her ever more aware of his long torso. She had thoughts of what it would take to unbutton that shirt, but she banished them. She should pull away and sit down and have a reasonable conversation with him. And he with her. But it was hard with his hands, his very large hands, pressed firmly against her back keeping her pressed up against him.

Finally she gasped, "Martin!"

He relaxed his grip. She moved away a bit. "What?" he said.

"What do you mean by road trip."

"Well, it's where you go on a trip not just to town but something that takes a few days. Like in a motorhome.

Or a truck. With a tent. Or maybe you get a motel for the nights. Or stay with friends." He was smiling and his eyes were dancing.

She pulled away. She turned in circles. Her mind was spinning. He wanted to go on a road trip with her. And Ernest. Was that right?

"How old are you, Martin, for heaven's sake?"

"Seventy," he said. "Well, 76."

"Seventy-six! I mean, you want to go on a road trip with me? To motels?"

"If necessary."

She looked at him. "Can you...." But she knew the answer already. "Never mind," she said.

Of course they would never go on a road trip, but it was fun to think about.

The next day Maggie awoke with Ernest next to her. He was getting restless. She stretched.

"Hi, Old Thing," she said.

He nuzzled her vigorously, leaving a bit of dampness on her face. That was it -- she would have to get up.

"But I don't want to get up, Ernest!" she said.

He stepped down off the bed and trotted out the door of her room. Time for her to get the slider open. She grabbed her robe in case any old-guy neighbors happened to be hanging over her fence. What about her hair? She didn't have time to deal with that.

"Hold on, Ernest!" she called out.

He woofed. She hurried to the slider and let him out. He ran down the steps. "Must have been a close call!" she thought.

But no, instead of hurrying to the back fence to do his business, he ran under the cedar boughs to the fence that divided her yard from Martin's. She decided to sit on the steps for a while. The sun was warm, the breeze gentle, and she was still half asleep. From here she could see what would develop.

Because really a day with Martin -- even a few hours -- would be really nice. Aside from that absurd road-trip idea. So far he had shown a real flare for hometown adventures, and maybe he'd come up with something for today. It was after all a beautiful day.

She was daydreaming. She had laundry to do, but it could wait. She should get breakfast, take her shower. But the yard smelled like roses -- Frank's beautiful roses -- and garlic. It was amazing the roses kept blooming year after year with her complete inattention. Well, at least she could pick raspberries.

She went inside for the picking basket. And some clothes. Ernest was still at the fence. Would she miss Martin if she took a quick shower? She dithered, put a spoon and bowl on the table, opened the slider in case Ernest wanted to come in, went to her room, made it a really quick shower, got dressed, could hear Ernest at her closed bedroom door. And Martin's voice some distance away. She hurried out of her room.

She heard him again. "Unlock the front door, Maggie! Hurry!"

She did. He was there with the now familiar large pot of steaming oatmeal held with potholders. She got out of his way, and he put it on the stove. He lifted down the bowls from the cupboard.

Ernest was dancing around Martin.

He got the pot of coffee from the porch. Ernest stayed on his heels the whole time, his tail snapping side to side. Maggie stepped back. She couldn't think of anything to do but stay out of the way. She had long since learned he didn't want to drink her coffee, the microwaved cup of water with granules stirred in.

Once they were seated, and Ernest had settled down on his bed under the table, and Maggie had mumbled thanks for the breakfast to Martin and God, a silence threatened to overtake them. Martin was diligently adding butter to his oatmeal, and nuts and bananas and cream -- all of which he had brought and set on the front porch along with the coffee. He typically made at two trips from his house. Maggie made her oatmeal his way. She never ate oatmeal normally, only when he made it. She had noticed he didn't add sugar and he hadn't brought his maple syrup. She had never had oatmeal without sugar, not until today. It was still sitting in the cupboard, too too far away.

She took a tiny taste of the oatmeal. It was good. He was already eating with gusto, and was done when she'd barely begun.

"It's a beach day," he said. He wiped his mouth. Aside from the boat trip they hadn't been to the beach, and beaches were everywhere. Including ones you could drive to and home again and not have to spend the night.

Maggie looked at him. She hadn't been to the beach in a while. Maybe it had been a year. There was the stony beach at the park, the steep one on the other side of the island, the tiny one that was mostly a smooth rock at the edge of the fresh water at Little Cranberry Lake, and then other ones farther away.

"Which one?" she asked. She realized she could have sounded more enthusiastic. "Nice day for it," she added, hoping to appear positive. She really did want to do something with him, but beaches had seemed something of the past. She and Frank had sometimes walked on one of the long beaches on Whidbey Island....

Martin had really blue eyes and they were staring off into space. Maggie looked at him, then looked down at her oatmeal and kept eating. It was really good! And she didn't want to get caught staring.

"Let's go to the state park," he said. "It will take half an hour to get there."

He was looking at her intently and his mouth was twitching. Had she missed something? She was feeling uneasy, had begun twisting her hands around, thought she might get one more bite out of the remnants in her bowl, took up her spoon again....

He was saying something, and this time she had definitely missed a few words. What she heard was, "....in the rig."

"What?" she asked.

"I wondered if you were listening," he said.

"I think so," she said, with no certainty. "But could you say it again? Please? After the part about the state park?"

"Oh, that. I just said we could take the rig. I've stayed there a lot. It's nice. Good people."

"Stay?"

"Yeah, you know, take the RV, park it in the campground, go for some hikes, play cards in the evening."

She gawked at him. She knew her mouth was hanging open. A tiny misbehaving piece of her brain was letting joy trickle in, but her better brought up parts were in shock.

"Um..."

"Yes, exactly!" he said. He leapt up and cleared the table, rinsed out the dishes, loaded the dishwasher, and said, "So, can you be ready in 15 minutes?"

"Ready? You mean to go to the beach? I guess so. I'll just get my hat and sunscreen."

"Well, about the...the how did you put it? Ummm?"

"Um," said Maggie before she thought of what she was saying.

"Exactly!" he agreed.

She was pretty sure he was misunderstanding her on purpose. The little tickle of joy found that concept rather appealing, but the rest of her was squirming with impending embarrassment. After all, um seemed to mean 'spend the night in the RV' if she understood any part of this conversation.

"Um," she said again.

"OK! Glad you agree!" He was bounding for the door. He called over his shoulder, "Pack your toothbrush!"

Ernest tried to follow him but Maggie caught his collar. In that quick moment, Martin made his escape. She stood looking after him with her hands on her hips.

Little twitches made the corners of her mouth turn up. Wispy thoughts wandered through her head. They seemed to say, "Aha, Girlie! Looks like an assignation!" or some such, whatever her mother would have said at a time like this.

And what exactly was a time like this? She was 65. Had been married. Twice. The guy who had moved in next door was a playful kid who made her feel young. Of course she wouldn't actually crawl into bed with him, but they could enjoy the whole day together. And the whole night? Maggie's mind clamped shut.

And now came the dilemma. How should she pack for such a ... day. Such a DAY. Hat and sunscreen. Then her intentions would be obvious. She would not go prepared to spend the night with him, even on the couch, even on the floor. Because if she did take something to sleep in, a toothbrush, a curling iron, it would suggest she was ready to spend the night. And whether she was ready for that or whether she wasn't, she didn't want to look like she was. Because she was. But she shouldn't be. She took her mom's words more seriously now that she was 65 instead of a third that age. She didn't sleep with guys she wasn't married to.

Not that anyone had asked. It was all theory. She had been married forever, and then she had been a widow asleep and out of circulation for three years. So not much chance to be asked. But it was something she knew about herself: She didn't do that sort of thing.

So she got her hat and sunscreen and put them in a little drawstring bag. Went back for her sunglasses. Saw her toothbrush on the sink and slid it in.

Chapter 16

They left a little more than half an hour later. She hadn't ridden in this kind of RV but it was very comfortable and spacious. First they would need to get food, Martin had said, so they headed to town. They parked in the Safeway parking lot near the back edge to stay out of the way of traffic. They left Ernest in the rig on his bed under the table -- it had been Martin's idea to bring it along -- and descended into the parking lot. Martin was obviously in a buoyant mood, walking almost faster than she could keep up. She was relaxed in the warm sunlight and gradually settling into the mood for an adventure, and now the handsome guy had grabbed her hand and was pulling her along. He didn't let go when she caught up to him.

The parking lot was bustling with morning shoppers. Pedestrians deftly scooted shopping carts around entering and exiting cars. And then Maggie squinted at a familiar figure. Halfway across the parking lot, standing facing them, staring at them it seemed, was Nancy. Nancy who had helped her rescue that old bloodhound she now loved so fiercely. As they got closer, Maggie could see Nancy had her mouth open but nothing was coming out.

"Hi," she said. She was staring at Martin. "And who's this?

Maggie felt caught in an illicit act. "Martin," she said but it came out like a whisper. "Martin," she said almost fiercely. Her mind was in turmoil. She was standing in the Safeway parking lot with two friends, and she felt naked, caught in the act. Granted they didn't know each other all that well. Granted she had been thinking of what her mother had taught her. Granted it looked as though she had traded in the old rescue bloodhound for an old rescue human. Though in truth he looked pretty good, pretty healthy, pretty all together, especially in that blue oxford button-down that made his eyes blue blue blue and that chino zippered jacket and plaid shorts that came only halfway down his long thighs that were covered in copious amounts of white fur. And his hat, his bashed fisherman's hat with the tie tucked up over the rim that covered his shiny pure-white full head of hair....

But yes, Nancy. OK, "Nancy, this is Martin. He lives next door." She decided to stop there. If she went on she would tell all. All there was to tell and all she had been thinking about, no doubt.

Nancy was staring at Martin, maybe at a button on his shirt, maybe at the hairy well-tanned V of his collar. Her mouth was still open. He was smiling pleasantly at her with not much interest, Maggie thought. Then she felt him pull her closer and stepped toward him as he circled her waist with his arm.

Nancy looked at Maggie, back at Martin. "Hi," she said.

They all seemed to shuffle around a little. A car wanted to get past. Martin was exerting a slight pressure on her. She guessed he wanted to get into the store and get the food. Nancy's eyes seemed full of questions. Maggie's mind was sending out jabs of laughter that she was afraid would become manifest. All she could think to say was, "Let's get together next week!"

Nancy said, "Yes, how's Tuesday? How's Ernest? I must see him. He's ok, isn't he?"

They parted. Maggie looked over her shoulder to wave one more time to Nancy, and saw her staring at the rig. A deep howl was coming from it. "Busted," thought Maggie.

Maggie could see it play out in her mind before it had fairly begun. Nancy started walking, then running, in the direction of the rig. It's true that Ernest did sound as though he was in dire straits, but Maggie was now used to his song. Nancy was going to go rescue him. She would realize that this was their vehicle, hers and Martin's, that they were on their way somewhere. Did people do errands in huge RVs? No. They just went places to spend the night.

Maggie could let it play out that way. Or she could run over to the RV and ease the situation along and explain the bare minimum -- bad choice of words -- to Nancy. Because the next scene to play out in Maggie's mind was Nancy calling for help for the poor dog within. Nancy didn't know it was Ernest. She didn't know it was Martin's rig. She just knew some beast was suffering inside. Maybe it was hot in there! Maybe it was being abused! Maggie knew Nancy's imaginative mind. Maggie needed to stop all this before it began.

Meanwhile Martin had a shopping cart and some fruit and if he heard Ernest at all, he didn't seem worried. Maggie needed to communicate with him fast or a whole crowd would be gathered around Nancy as she made a dramatic rescue. Maybe she had called the fire department! So she just said, "Ernest!" Martin turned and looked and clearly heard and fished the keys out of his pocket and handed them to her.

Maggie took off at a fast-paced waddle, wishing she could go faster. She was sashaying, that word of her mother's that fit so perfectly the motion she was in. She paid no attention to rights of way but fixed her eyes on the rig, her ears on Ernest, and her every effort on getting there before Nancy.

But Nancy had a head-start. She was already trying the door and Maggie was only halfway across the parking lot. Ernest paused for a moment while Nancy's hand was still on the door handle, but resumed again when she gave up.

Maggie had gone only another twenty feet when Nancy reached a nearby phone booth. "Stop!" shouted Maggie. But she was breathless and knew her voice would not carry. She bustled on, waving vigorously at Nancy. But Nancy had her head down while she punched in the phone number. Maggie could imagine she heard the tones: 9-1-1.

Nancy lifted the phone to her ear and looked off into space. Not toward Maggie, who was gesturing in vain, but toward the rig. Ernest was earnestly practicing his scales.

The dispatcher answered the call just as Maggie arrived. Maggie could hear, "What is your emergency?" Nancy was opening her mouth to speak when Maggie, still breathless said, as loud as she could, "It's Ernest!"

Nancy looked at Maggie and Maggie could see the truth dawning. The whole truth. It was Ernest howling in there. That meant that was Maggie's vehicle. And

Martin's vehicle. Nancy said, "Never mind, my mistake" and hung up.

The word 'overnight' seemed to hang in the air unspoken as Maggie unlocked the door and caught the slobbery and overjoyed Ernest before he could leap into the parking lot. Nancy was looking at Maggie but not saying anything. She reached out idly to stroke Ernest's head. Martin arrived with the groceries just as the police cruiser came by to check on the call.

"Everything ok here?" the officer asked.

"Just our dog, Officer," said Martin. "He gets lonely when we're shopping."

The use of 'we' was not lost on Nancy, Maggie could see that much in her face. She looked from Martin to Maggie and from Maggie to Martin, and then to Ernest. She said, "No such thing as one potato chip," turned on her heel, and left. Martin laughed. Maggie blushed. Ernest licked them both.

"I'll call you," Maggie mumbled.

Chapter 17

By the time they were underway, Martin was in a jolly mood, and Maggie, after thinking through the whole encounter with Nancy a second time, was beginning to see the humor in it. And she was also feeling a bit proud, maybe a bit smug. Look at that guy, Nancy had seemed to say. How did that happen? To you?

And Maggie's inner person had said, "Why not me?" and now she was riding along in the passenger seat thinking, "Indeed, why not me? Indeed, MOTHER! Why not me? and why not this? and why not any of it?" It was an amazingly courageous and unfamiliar mindset.

She had been over the Deception Pass bridge by car several times, and she had tried to check out the swirling water below, but she had never seen it up close, and this is what Martin was describing as they drove along. They would walk the beach, have lunch, and then might take a hike over to the bridge, seeing it from below. And checking out the wildly swirling water up close. From up here on the bridge she could see the water surging and churning, something she had entirely missed when she was alone, when she was the driver.

In a moment they were turning into a side road and just ahead was the entry station with a sign announcing Deception Pass State Park.

Martin was signing in for two nights in the campground! She tried to become very small and looked out the passenger window so her face could not be seen by the man in the booth. Her earlier elation was fading, squelched by embarrassment. She wanted to have time to talk all this over with Martin. Two nights! She had never intended one night! He would have to take her home. Later, after they'd had time to walk on the beach.

The whole time Martin was making the RV fit into the little driveway of the campsite they were assigned, Maggie stayed hunkered down. She and Frank had come to this park, she realized, but she hadn't known it had an overnight campground. But maybe someone she knew did. Maybe when she stepped out a friend from the knit shop or the farmers' market or the library would be standing right there and would instantly know what Maggie and Martin were up to. She hid her face in her hands.

Meanwhile Ernest had begun prancing and probably needed to go out. She pretended she didn't see him looking so anxious, and now he was beginning to whine a little.

Finally Martin said, "Maggie, come here and park this thing so I can take Ernest out!"

Maggie realized three things all in an instant: She couldn't park the RV, he didn't really want her to park the RV but to take Ernest out, and she was going to have to go face all her nosy friends herself.

She got the leash, opened the door, and there right in front of her was ... a picnic table. No people. No one she knew, and no one else.

She was being tugged by the impatient possibly urgent Ernest, and since she had nothing to fear, she followed him to the nearest bush. When he was done with his business, he seemed to want to keep walking. Maggie was ok with that.

In a few minutes they had covered the whole of the RV park. It was small, and it was empty. She was relieved.

When they got back to the RV, Martin was just descending the steps with his backpack. The pleasantly cool breeze was blowing in from the ocean, and now they were walking together down the path and it was all very much like home. The beach was only ten minutes away.

When they got beyond the main parking lot, they kept going on the beach itself. Maggie couldn't keep up. The sand was soft, making it hard to walk. Her legs were growing tired and they had barely begun. Maybe this wasn't a good idea. The Martin part might have been, but not the keeping-up-with-Martin part.

Martin had brought lunch in his backpack. He had pointed out some picnic tables on the grassy slope above the beach maybe half a mile away. Ernest was padding along contentedly between them except when his nose distracted him. Seaweed was fascinating to him for a while, and there was plenty of it. Maggie was glad when he had to go back and revisit a fascinating piece of kelp because it gave her an excuse to stop.

Martin seemed to be just as fascinated by the oddities that had been washed up on the beach. Ernest had just stopped at a strange globule of clear jelly and was sniffing it deeply. Martin poked the jelly with his finger. Ernest made a deep growling noise and kept sniffing. Martin knelt down in the damp sand and leaned over as if to smell the blob. Maggie was curious too and wanted to be with her special guys, but she was reluctant to leave her hard-won advance and stood her ground, looking back at the two dear heads but not joining them. She had known each of them for such a short time, and her life was so much richer for them both. She gazed over the sea, watched the waves, feeble ones, inch closer. Tide must be coming in. The sea always put her in a trance.

"Jellyfish," Martin said, surprisingly close. Ernest had loped up the beach a short distance. Martin took Maggie's hand in his. She wondered if it was the one that had poked the jellyfish.

Somehow the stop had rejuvenated her and now she was walking easily, keeping up easily. Martin was talking about sea creatures he had known, whales and halibut and an octopus he had seen pull off a remarkable escape from the Shannon Point Marine Center a couple of miles from Maggie's house.

"We were standing at the edge of a boat ramp that went into the building where they kept all sorts of sea creatures," he said. "We had just been inside talking about a tiny octopus they had in an aquarium. Or had had. He had escaped over and over but this time he was gone for good. No one had seen him for days. They looked everywhere! The doors were kept closed. Where could he have gone?"

Maggie was trudging along, keeping an eye on the picnic table, which at last was growing nearer. She turned to look at him. His face was lit up like a kid, delighted as he was to be talking about the little octopus.

"So," Martin went on, "we left the lab and went outside to see some tide pools. And then we saw a small movement."

Here he stopped. Maggie looked at him. He looked at her and his eyes were twinkling.

"What?" she asked.

"Well, what do you think? The little octopus was just then emerging from a drainage pipe that went from the lab to the outside, maybe forty feet."

"Did he get away?" asked Maggie.

"Would you like the story better if I told you he got away?" asked Martin.

"Sure! He deserved it!" she said with a rather strong voice.

Martin laughed. Ernest came back to see what he was missing. Martin put his arm around her shoulder. "Yup," said Martin. My friend the professor said, "Ok then, go. I'm not watching!" and the little octopus slithered into a stream of water and took a ride back to sea."

"Oh!" said Maggie. "How big?"

"About the size of my hand."

Whether he'd meant it to or not, Martin's story about the little octopus had distracted Maggie and to her surprise she found herself at the picnic table. Martin was taking off his backpack. Ernest was chasing a scent in the greenery at the edge of the beach.

Maggie looked around. The cool breeze off the ocean was a bit chilly, and she wrapped her jacket tightly around her. But it was also refreshing. The gloom and irritation that had overwhelmed her since Martin had committed them for two nights together in the RV began to leave her alone. Irritation maybe because she hadn't seemed to have a choice.

But now she could look at him. Now she wasn't feeling quite as victimized by his one-sided decision to sleep with her. Or at least very near her. Now she saw that he was sneaking peeks at her while he was trying to lay out the lunch things in that gusty breeze. Now she understood that he was in fact a bit nervous with her. Maybe he was nervous about a night in the RV too. Or maybe he was concerned more that she might be upset with him.

And she didn't want him nervous about her. But she was still unhappy at the thought of their spending the night together.

And why, Maggie-girl, would he want to, you know, have sex with you? YOU! You of all people. At your age!

True enough, thought Maggie. Why? (And was that Frank saying, yeah, why?)

"SHUT UP, FRANK," Maggie blurted out.

She looked at Martin to see if he'd heard. And how much had she said out loud? But Martin was coolly tucking napkins under cups of water and not looking at her at all.

And surely it was her imagination that he was sneaking peeks at her from under those bushy white eyebrows. And that his mouth was twitching a little.

Maggie's heart was beating a little faster, she could feel it, and she wondered what to do about that. This was a very very nice man she was with. Rather tall. Certainly very friendly. And so far his only real fault was that he ... Well, he wanted to spend the night with her.

(And hadn't her mother warned her about such men? When? 50 years ago?)

So she continued to scan the sea and looked down the length of the beach and watched Ernest for a while, and then Martin handed her a tuna sandwich. And without thinking, she smiled up at him. He was very close, and as soon as she looked up all those extra inches above her head to his face, he kissed her on the lips.

"Welcome to Deception Pass, Maggie," he said. And he waggled his eyebrows.

She was undone. Quickly she took a bite of sandwich and turned away. She knew she was blushing. Because that one kiss suggested all the rest of it that she had been thinking about and she didn't dare look at him or he would know it. But now she could see that a night in the RV would be, could be ... what?

Delicious, supplied the inner Maggie.

"Delicious sandwich," said Maggie to Martin, and then nearly choked.

They sat across the picnic table from each other. Martin reached for her hand and she let him hold it and felt some lightning bolts stab her here and there. She kissed Ernest on the nose -- he was on alert in case a crumb of sandwich should fall, and in fact several of Maggie's had already fallen -- but she still held onto Martin's hand.

The kiss was still lingering on her lips and if it would stay there forever she would be fulfilled, she thought, but then the idea that maybe another kiss would be OK came to her. Not that she could do anything about it, but she did keep a good hold on his hand.

But think, Maggie-girl, of how many kisses might happen overnight!

She blushed and looked out to sea and he smiled. "What?" he asked.

She was smiling, she couldn't help smiling, so she covered her face, which required taking her hand away. She didn't want him to see her telltale face and guess all.

But he had gotten up from the table and she had to see where he was going. He went out on the beach. Ernest went, too. They walked back and forth, Ernest sniffing at things, Martin poking at objects at the high-tide mark. She couldn't resist either of them. She got up and joined them.

Martin was leaning over something in the sand. He picked it up and showed it to her: a fragment of shell with a corkscrew shape inside.

"Amazing, isn't it?" Martin said.

Maggie nodded. It was all she could do to keep from hugging him. She loved his passion for, well, for everything! And maybe that was why he liked her: maybe even though she was a little broken like the shell, she was interesting on the inside. Anyway, it was nice of him to see the good in things, the beauty in the broken shell, and that made him irresistibly huggable.

Except he was looking for more shells. Where did that fit in her romantic view of his shell collecting?

Martin pocketed the first shell and picked up another. Maggie wandered off. Ernest, who had been following scents all along, was now flopped out under the picnic table.

Martin went back to the table and put away the residue of the lunch. Maggie went with him, then sat down on the sand next to Ernest and gave him some ear-scratches. He made a contented growl and lay his head in her lap. Martin put on his backpack and sat down behind Maggie.

"Here, lean back," he said. "It's hard sitting for long in the sand."

So she leaned back against him. The wind was picking up, though, and sand was blowing all over them. Martin got up and pulled her up too. "Come over here, Maggie," he said.

Still holding her hand, he walked her down the beach another longish distance. When her legs grew tired, he pulled her gently along, giving her the extra oomph to allow her to keep up. Even Ernest was plodding now, not frisking his way down the beach. Only Martin seemed to have energy to spare.

Just up ahead of them was an enormous array of huge logs. Some were on the beach, others on the green growth at the sand's edge. All were stripped of their bark. Some were piled up on each other. All were the size of very tall trees, but they no longer had their branches or any signs, actually, that they'd once been alive.

"They look like they're waiting to be built into a log cabin," said Maggie.

Martin smiled. “They’re called beach logs,” he said. “I wish I knew where they were from, where they grew. Or how long ago they were living trees.”

Maggie thought about that. No trees this truly big grew here anymore, not any that she had seen. Maybe they had been chopped down for lumber in some previous generation and then had flowed down some river to the ocean. Or maybe they had come from far away. .

And that led Maggie to the thought, “What about you, Martin? Where did you come from? And where have you traveled?” But she didn’t ask out loud.

And then the inner-Maggie added, “And you, Maggie-girl? Where have you been? And with whom? Maybe he’d like to hear about that! About those various husbands. And about, you know...”

But maybe they’d never have these conversations, and maybe that was good.

The rain had started, the wind was blowing, they had walked a good while, and they would be soaked if they went back to the RV. Martin had pushed Maggie along, and now Martin was pointing to the piled-up beach logs, where an entrance of sorts was big enough for them to crawl in and get out of the elements.

Maggie looked in, and wonderful to see, the sand deep in the center of the pile was dry. Maggie crawled in and called Ernest to her. Martin took off his backpack and tossed it in. The wind still whistled through the logs but they were out of most of it. The space was barely large enough for the addition of Martin, but he wiggled in on his belly and lay curled up in a semicircle with Ernest in the middle and they all fit.

Martin fished a small towel out of his backpack and handed it to Maggie to dry her hair. Then he used it to rub Ernest down. The old dog was shivering.

Rain clouds had dimmed the sun. Rain was coming in the openings between the logs, and then dribbling on them in random places. Wind that found a way in was keeping them chilled. And the only option they were in charge of was to dash back to the RV, half an hour away. Maybe it would keep raining, maybe it would stop. This was summer in Washington, and nothing more could be said about it.

And this is when Martin started talking.

"I've waited my whole life for you, Maggie," he said with a smile. "You're such a surprise."

Maggie stared at him. Clearly he hadn't waited for her at all. All sorts of women knew him, and he acted familiar with them. And that she had found out after just an hour or two at the farmers' market. It was such a silly thing for him to say, it made her laugh. And though she might not have chosen to laugh right out loud, she did.

He looked hurt for a moment, then sighed.

Maggie was searching her brain for some clue about why he might have been looking for her. She could think of a dozen ways in which she was uninteresting. For example, she had just spent the past three years knitting and watching TV and going to bed early.

He looked as though he wanted to say something more and was thinking hard about it. She figured he was done, though.

But he wasn't done. "You're honest. What you see is what you get."

Maggie didn't find this particularly reassuring. What you saw, what she saw in the mirror, was round and gray and wrinkly, definitely unfit, uncolored.

"Hm!" she retorted.

He laughed. "Exactly!" he said. He fished for her hand across the big red dog and brought it to his lips.

"Look!" he said. He had raised her hand upward. He was smiling and it dawned on her that he was pointing out the shining sun. It wasn't raining anymore.

That was good. It was certainly uncomfortable there lying on the sand, and as she looked up at the criss-crossing logs and saw how massive they were and wondered how stable they were, how long they had held each other up and whether they would stay put while they lay there, she was yet sorry that this cozy moment was over. She was with her guys and she liked it!

But he seemed in no hurry to get up. "Maggie!" he said. "I want to know all about you! You are such a mystery!"

Maggie scrunched up her face. She was at a loss. "I'm just me," she said.

He laughed. "Exactly! And you are a delight and you make me happy."

Maggie had nothing to say. She sat up as much as she could, avoiding bumping into the logs in case they might become unsettled and fall on them and kill them. Ernest stirred. Martin let go of her hand and wiggled his way backward out of their cave. Ernest fit well in the little doorway, but Maggie had to crawl out and felt awkward.

"And," said Martin, "you don't have to spend the night with me in the RV. We can go home. It's only a half-hour drive."

This was a very confusing man! He knew all sorts of women, and maybe they had all spent the night with him in the RV and maybe she was just another one of them and maybe he had told them all that they made him happy. Maybe he had a great capacity for happiness!

And she couldn't deny knowing what he meant, because he made her happy.

But what a concept! She hadn't expected happiness. She hadn't thought about happiness at all, not forever.

And then had come Ernest, and right then, that first day, that big old dog had made her happy! Just because he was Ernest. And she hadn't quite realized it until now. And then had come Martin. And yes! He made her happy!

So if she made him happy, she knew what he meant. But of course she was still surprised. Because she was just Maggie.

And now he was saying, "So, night here or night at home -- that's the question!"

She looked at him and felt overwhelmed by a wave of...something. Something good and appealing and deep and tingly and warm and very much like what she felt about Ernest but more more more more more.

"Home," she said.

Chapter 18

They walked back to the RV hand in hand. It was shorter, it seemed, than the walk on the way out. She were almost back before she even thought to be embarrassed at holding hands.

And then they were back, and Martin patted her hand and gave her a boost into the RV, and Ernest too, and said, "That's my Maggie." He drove them back across the Deception Pass bridge and home.

All the way Maggie wondered what it would be like when they got home. Awkward? Sweet? Abrupt or loving? Would it be over? Or maybe they were too tired for it to be anything but a parting with thoughts for another adventure another day. Maggie's legs were tired from walking in the sand, and she did all she could to enjoy the scenery, the rugged pass, the setting sun, without nodding off.

And then Martin was talking. "Maggie, look, let's come back tomorrow. This is such a great park. And we can spend the whole day together here just as if we had never left."

She looked at him, out the window, out the windshield. She reached for his hand on the steering wheel, thinking only to pat it reassuringly. She couldn't think of anything she'd rather do than spend the day with him, just as if. As if. Yes, as if they were spending the night together back there instead of going home and coming back. He even still had a campsite he had paid for!

"Yes," she said. "Yes."

He turned and smiled broadly at her. They were home soon after, and went their ways, and the plan was set for a morning departure -- only not too early.

The day dawned with a shower that turned to rain. They hoped while they ate their oatmeal that the rain would stop, and a couple of times it seemed to. Martin said, "Let's take a chance" and she hurried to grab her jacket and out they went.

Once they were settled in the RV and seatbelts fastened, Martin said, "I have to take a letter to the post office. Might as well do it now."

Maggie looked at the rain. It was not too heavy. She always tried to avoid errands in the rain but of course this time she could stay in the RV while Martin dashed through the drops and got his special stamp or whatever. It would be only a tiny detour, and maybe by the time they were underway again, the sun would be shining.

The errand was indeed quick. But then Martin was saying, ‘let’s stop by the farmers’ market -- it’s Saturday you know’.

The problem was in finding parking spots. Despite the rain, downtown parking was filled up, and their RV was welcome only on certain streets. After two passes, two times around the block that took them past the docks and railway depot where the market was, and the dog park, they found a spot. They needed their umbrellas for sure. And what about Ernest?

“I’ll stay here and watch him,” Martin said. “And you can grab some veggies and cheese.” He pulled some dollars from his pocket, and she scurried off. Ernest was clearly disappointed that she closed the door in his face.

The market was in truth nearly deserted. The vendors had all brought large umbrellas or were wearing slickers and hats. Maggie made a hasty circuit of the necessary stands, noticed that Sylvia wasn’t there, went back for some hazelnuts, and then walked as briskly as she could in the direction of the RV across from the dog park. It was a good solid 5 minute walk and she’d be soaked to the knees from splashing.

Then she saw Tommy’s stand, and at it a basket of fresh peas, her favorite! She hesitated to stop, but she was salivating thinking of the stir fry she could make, and besides, there was no line.

She was about to step under the awning of the stand when someone beat her to it. She plowed into the man, who was clearly getting soaked: he had on only a light jacket and no hat. She backed up and apologized in mumbly tones. It wasn't someone she knew, maybe someone from out of town. And what a bad day to visit! Here they were having one of the last spring storms -- though it was definitely summer on the calendar -- so maybe it had caught him by surprise.

He was standing in front of her at Tommy's stand, which left her partly out in the rain. She thought she'd step to one side to get closer and out of the storm, but just as she moved to do that, he also stepped to the side.

And then he turned around. He glared at her with great intensity, then reached for her arm. She stepped away and he looked -- what? Hurt?

"I'm sorry," she said, though she didn't know what she had done, and stepped to the stand. As he walked rather quickly away, she looked after him. Even though he was perhaps vaguely familiar, he sure didn't have his farmer's market manners on! And he hadn't even bought anything, she didn't think.

Once she had the peas, she hastened down the street to the RV, which she could see just behind the dog park.

And much to her surprise, Ernest was galumphing about in the park playing with -- or maybe avoiding -- another dog.

Her glasses were constantly being bombarded by raindrops and she could see better without them -- though none too well. But she was certain Martin was in the dog park enclosure, too. He'd be getting soaked. Nice of him to let Ernest play while she was busy at the farmers' market!

There was virtually no one else at the dog park, just someone all bundled up in rain gear and a hat. As Maggie got closer, she could see that this woman -- she was at least small enough to be a woman -- was talking to Martin.

So maybe it was this woman's dog Ernest was avoiding.

As she got closer to the dog park, Maggie could see a tiny dog. It was yapping at Ernest, who was sometimes chasing it and sometimes fleeing from it and trying to get behind Martin.

By now Martin had seen her and waved, and she shifted the shopping bags so she could wave back. In a few more moments she had reached the outer gate of the dog park, and as she arrived she saw the woman -- a slender blond long-haired youngish woman -- step closer to Martin. Possessively, Maggie thought.

The next moment the woman had her hand on Martin's arm and was straightening out his cuff as someone might do to protect a child from the rain. She had fancy fingernails.

Ernest ran toward her when Maggie called to him. "I want to get these put away inside, Martin," Maggie said. She thought she sounded normal, but Martin looked up at her with a peculiar expression on his face.

"Maggie, please come here first and meet Dede," he said. "We're old friends," he said. "Sometimes we go to the dog park together," he said.

But Maggie was thinking, you don't have a dog.

And then she said to herself, I have a dog. But YOU don't have a dog.

And then she said to herself, but you seem to have a woman. Who is this woman and what is she doing with her hand on your arm and what are you doing not looking surprised or even noticing?

So she said, "Hi," and she turned on her heel and went to the trailer. Came back for the keys. Called to Ernest. Kicked the tire of the RV as she went by. Old friends. What did that mean?

She didn't say anything as they wound through the back streets of the town and waited at the traffic light at the highway. The road was almost empty of cars: the locals were most likely at home, the tourists were probably aware of the weather report and had stayed in Seattle for the day. Martin showed his receipt at the gate and drove directly to the same campsite he had been assigned the day before.

Maybe it was where they were, down by the sea, but the rain was raining much harder. They would be soaked if they stepped out the door.

They had brought a couple of packs of cards. Maggie had her knitting and a magazine in her big purse. Martin had a whole shelf of books he traveled with, neatly secured with a bungee cord. Ernest had his big red bed. The cupboards were stocked with staples, and the fridge with the Safeway groceries from yesterday. Let it rain!

But where to start. Maggie wandered around the rig looking at things, seeing things that were perhaps a bit personal. Clearly Martin stayed here often. It had razors, a bottle of aspirin, sunscreen, all in permanent-looking places. Probably if she opened the drawers she would find deodorant or underwear or ... Whatever it was that single guys needed. But she left it all alone, except for what her eyes could see.

When she completed her tour, she sat on the couch. Ernest looked up but seemed happy to stay put on his bed. Martin was lying on the floor with his head under the dashboard, tool in hand. She thought she might knit but didn't have the ambition for it. The magazine seemed like all the others she had read. So she watched Martin.

Not that she could see what he was doing. Instead she admired his long legs and wondered idly about his history, his story. He had been born -- where? He had been employed -- where? He had been married, no doubt. Well, probably. Maybe he even had had kids, still had kids. Still had an ex. Had lived -- where? In town, in a house he had owned? Or somewhere far away?

And who was that woman, the one with the fingernails?

The rain was loud on the RV roof. She wondered that it wasn't cold in the rig -- these rains no doubt had floated down from Alaska. She was amazed at how cozy the rig was, a regular little home.

Without warning she was overwhelmed by a deep sadness. She didn't know why. Tears were filling her eyes, and her breath kept catching, leaving her gasping. What was it?

She didn't want Martin to hear her. There was no way to explain to him if she herself didn't understand. And Martin kept working under the dashboard. But Ernest did hear her and got up and came to her and licked her. He was agitated, whimpered, danced about, all the while looking at her with his wrinkles drooping, his face so sad that she hugged him around the neck to comfort him. And that helped her.

But not entirely. Another wave of sadness hit her. Why?

Here she was with her two boys, where she wanted to be, happy as she hadn't been in years. So why so sad? Or why the tears?

Wisps of the past, of something like loss, chilled her heart, but she couldn't place them.

She closed her eyes and felt herself growing calmer. Ernest settled at her feet. She felt Martin sit down next to her. He had taken her hand, and was now pressing her head to his shoulder. She nestled closer to him. He wrapped his arms around her.

Some time went by like that. Whatever it was, the storm was passing. Outside as well as in, perhaps: the rain on the roof seemed diminished.

But then a blast of wind hit them broadside and the whole rig, heavy as it was, shook and lurched. Martin got up to check the door. They were still safe. Whatever had been agitating her was gone, past.

She stood up, peeked through the blinds. Rain was slamming against the windows so heavily that it ran off in sheets, and through them she could easily see the swaying of cedar branches and the tearing away of bark and sprigs of needles. She knew cedars, and this happened only in the worst storms.

"Martin!" she said. "It's a big storm!"

He turned on the radio. It was indeed a big storm, due to a low pressure area far off the coast, strong enough to draw heavy winds and rain not down the coast from Alaska but up from the south. Late in the season for it, said Martin.

"No walk on the beach today, Mags," he said. "Do you want to go home?"

She hadn't thought about that. Of course he could just start up the engine and they'd pull out and in 30 minutes they'd be home. And go their separate ways, most likely. There were things to do at home, chores to attend to.

"No," she said. "Let's stay. It's ok."

He looked at her, stood up, pulled her up, took her by the shoulders, searched her eyes. She didn't understand.

"Mags, look," he said. "This is a huge storm. It might not be over for a couple of days. If we don't go now, we may not be able to go till it's over. There'll be flooding, trees down, no electricity."

Maggie understood, of course. They could go now, or they would be spending the night. Maybe a few nights. And she was good with that. She felt content with it. She felt happy about it.

"Good," she said aloud. She smiled at him, a confident smile with no wavering.

He looked at her with a hint of a smile. He searched her face. She knew he was looking for doubt, and she knew he saw none, because she had none. Come what may, here they would stay. Together.

It was maybe a half hour later that a thrill went through her and left her thinking about kisses. Lots of kisses.

The storm grew stronger. They sat across from each other at the table and dealt out the cards. Maggie thought the air in the RV was growing colder, had already put on her jacket over her sweater. Martin had put a sweatshirt over his sweater.

"I can turn on the heat," he said. "But if we use our propane for warming the rig, we may run out of it for cooking. In case we can't go home for a couple of days."

Maggie looked at him. She was cold. But there were blankets. They could wrap up in them.

So they bundled themselves in blankets, pulled on some heavy socks that Martin had stashed away, and sat on the couch side by side to keep each other warm. Martin rearranged the blankets so they were in one big cocoon, and when he took her hands in his, her shivering stopped.

Outside the rain beat against the RV and the wind rocked them first one way, then the other. Then a sharp crack startled them both, the lights went out, and Ernest, who had been sleeping, looked up and growled. Martin unwrapped himself, covered Maggie again with the blankets, and separated the blinds to look out the window behind the couch. Nothing there, it seemed. And then he checked the window across from them.

"A big branch came down, Maggie," he said. "Looks like it just missed us."

Maggie huddled down deeper into the pile of blankets. She was shivering again.

"I'm going to make you some tea," he said. "Good thing the stove still works."

They sat warming their hands on the cups of tea. The RV shook in sudden jerks. Maggie had heard some of their neighbors pull out, and wondered if they should have headed for home, too. They could be in their solid house -- their solid houses, in reality. Two houses, or one RV? She had made the right choice!

Martin had taken the two cups to the sink, and was now standing over her with his hands on his hips. He seemed to be studying her face. Enough for her to say, "What?"

Instead of answering her, he turned and opened a narrow closet. Inside she could see boots, a paddle, a pump....He was groping around in the back of the closet, his body mostly blocking her view. When he turned back to her, he appeared to be holding a raincoat. Two raincoats. And two hats. These were the kind of rain gear that fishermen wore, rubbery, orange, huge!

He held one out to her. “Try this,” he said.

She stood up. Ernest raised his head, but only for a moment. She reached for the raincoat. But it was actually a raincoat and rain pants, whatever they were actually called. She held them away from her and looked curiously at Martin, who was holding another set. He smiled at her.

“Let’s take a walk!”

“In this?” She had meant in this rain, but he interpreted her question to mean the rain gear.

“Sure!” he said. “Unless you’d like to take a nap. I could go either way, a walk now and nap later, or a nap now and a nap later!”

She spent the next two minutes not looking at the bed but exploring the pockets of the rain jacket with great diligence. She pulled out a packet of gum. A file card with pencil writing on it. A tea bag.

She looked at him. He was watching her. “Well, which would you prefer?” he asked.

She would not look at the bed, not now. So she turned and lifted the blind to the great outdoors. The campground seemed completely empty. Had they ridden out the storm alone? Was the storm over? Was it raining? She couldn't tell through the drops on the window. But she could hear the wind, ferocious wind. And she could see tree parts being blown about.

Still not looking at the bed, being very careful not to look at the bed, turning awkwardly from the window so she couldn't see the bed, she said, "Walk."

"Good girl!" he said with great enthusiasm.

And what if she had said 'nap"? Would he have shrugged in resignation? Or would his enthusiasm be even greater? She'd never know.....

He was pulling on the waterproof pants over his regular ones, and she did the same. Then the jacket. Then the hat. It all fit just fine. She had expected to have to roll up the pant legs quite a bit but she barely needed to make a small cuff.

And while she was doing that, she began to see. Not anything she wanted to see, but she was seeing that this waterproof gear was in the closet for some other woman, the gum was hers, the file card, all of it.

The fact that some woman had been his before her -- not that she was his, she reminded herself -- and not that he was hers, said Frank, the suddenly interested dead ex-husband -- was unsettling. Had that woman been thin? Fit? Young? Had she chosen a nap? Before or after the walk?

Maggie felt an attack of claustrophobia come on. Was that it? She had to get out of here! And she had to get out of these waterproof clothes. And she realized that in reality she might do either but not both: it was seriously wet outside.

She started to take off the rain pants. To do that she had to sit on the couch. And Ernest was covering the couch. She roughly pushed his legs out of the way to make a space for herself. She had never treated him roughly before but she was doing it now. She was even hissing at him to get out of the way.

Martin had noticed. He grabbed her hands and raised her up to her feet. The rubberized pants were down around her ankles and even if she had wanted to go somewhere -- and there was only the kitchen and the sleeping area -- she would not make much headway as she was. But her thoughts of fleeing and realizing she couldn't were now being interrupted by that scoundrel of the many women, who was pulling her to him to .... To kiss her, actually. Which he was doing, and which she was doing back, come to think of it. But she really wasn't thinking all that much.

"So, nap then?" he asked. He was twinkling. He put his foot between her feet on the bunched up rain pants so she could pull her feet out. And she almost did it. But then she remembered the other woman -- women, no doubt -- and she reached down to pull them up again. It was tricky bending over because his arms were around her, and she gave up.

"I can't take a nap with you," she whispered.

"Why not?" he whispered back.

Ernest looked at the two of them, and stretched his way off the couch, then turned to the door.

"Not now, Ernest," said Martin.

Maggie didn't know which way to turn. She was trapped. Yes, she was in his arms, and no, she hadn't tried to remove herself, and yes he was kissing her again, and yes she was kissing him back, and yes she was forgetting about packs of gum and whatever and yes she wanted to take a nap with him and see what that was like, and no she didn't need her rain gear for that.

And then her thinking took a break. Even Frank seemed lulled or distracted. Her lips were tingling in an exotic sort of way she had never felt before, and while she was thinking her arms had found their way up around Martin's neck, and he was making little humming sounds while his lips found her neck and the little pockets there that his kisses fit into, and she thought, hmmm, what about that nap?

Martin was saying something. She thought he was sort of mumbling, but it wasn't just humming. Maybe he'd say it again and this time she would listen. And then there it was, something about walking in the storm?

He was of course joking. But then he was inserting her arms into the sleeves of the jacket and zipping it up and putting the hat on her head. And he had put his own things on, and even had Ernest's leash in his hands, and where had she been all the time he'd been doing that?

He gave her a gentle shove toward the door. Opened it by leaning over her shoulder. Held her hand while she went down the steps. The wind hit her with a blast from the right, another slammed her from the left. Cedar debris was flying around in front of her.

He said, "There are no trees on the beach. We'll be safe there." And he took her hand and pulled her along. And she thought, "What?". Her entire blood supply seemed to have left her brain and was deposited elsewhere in her body, such as in her lips. They felt swollen and tender and lovely. And then they were at the beach.

Chapter 19

They had the whole beach to themselves. Not counting gulls, and some bird on the beach not far from them, something rather large. Maybe it had been injured in the storm. Maggie thought it looked like a bald eagle, but it was dark all over. "Baby bald eagle," Martin said.

The baby bird let them approach. He didn't move at all, but stood nearly in the tide looking at them. Ernest approached curiously but cautiously. Martin called him back. Without saying a word to each other, they veered away from the young bird before continuing on down the beach.

It was really too raw and blustery for a long walk, though Maggie was loving the wind blowing her hair in disarray. She had taken off the hood of the jacket when she realized it wasn't truly cold out, just windy. They had already turned around to head back to the RV.

Maggie was a bit leg-weary but Martin was fairly bounding up the beach, walking on ahead, then circling back for the old dog and his equally worn-out mistress. He seemed as cheerful as any time she had known him.

The sun was setting through clouds on the horizon. Twilight had taken over and would last for hours more. The RV, just now appearing as they rounded a curve in the footpath from the beach road, caught the last flickers of sunlight and nearly blinded Maggie with a reflected beam off its window.

So they were nearly back. And that meant Maggie would need to regather her thoughts. All along the beach she had been in a pleasantly unconscious state with no cares, just an ongoing enjoyment moment after moment, mixed with a sense that the path back was remarkably long and her legs were remarkably sore.

But now she was abruptly attentive and troubled and excited and perplexed. What did Martin have in mind? What, for that matter, was going on in her own mind?

Surely he could not have meant sex, not right there in the state park, not right there in the RV parked ten feet from the place where another RV might park if the weather cleared up. Even if that's what Nancy thought.

The remembrance of Nancy's expression gave her the giggles, and once she was laughing the whole situation seemed absurd.

Which in reality it was.

She was 65! She'd been a widow for three years! She'd been in a rather celibate sort of marriage! SURELY Martin wasn't thinking about sex!

Her boys, Martin and Ernest, were back at the RV and Martin was unlocking the door. She stopped. She had fallen minutes behind the two of them, and now she stood with her hands on her hips, staring at the RV and the old man helping lift the old red dog up the stairs. If she'd been over there he would be lifting her too. Surely sex was absurd.

But what to do? How to find out before she appeared to be going right along with whatever plan he had? What had he said back in her kitchen? She couldn't remember exactly.

So she continued to stand. Martin and Ernest were inside. And now the awning was unrolling into place over the picnic table. Probably Martin would not do that if he was planning on leaving for home. Probably he would not have brought the RV unless he planned on sleeping in it. And she had even agreed to whatever plans and thoughts he was having.

In fact, the old dog was probably right now disloyally curled up on his bed under the table inside the RV.

What could she do? Where had her confident resolve gone?

The door of the trailer opened. Martin filled it with his height. "Come on!" he said.

She looked at him. He was holding the screen door for her, but he was distracted by something inside. Maybe she could hide somewhere....

She put one foot in front of the other. She walked up to the steps to the RV. Martin reached out his hand and helped her in.

Chapter 20

Maggie set about laying the table with spoons and bowls. Martin was ready to dish up the soup he'd made at home and reheated. Reheating had taken a while on the little stove. Maggie was learning where things were, though so far she had to ask about everything. It was homey, but it wasn't her home.

It was a beautiful little space, though, she thought. Just enough room for this and that, the tiniest imaginable bathroom, closets, stove, fridge, table. Small windows with little plaid curtains. Tiny drawers. Clever storage spaces here and there, just like on a boat. And a geranium in a flowerpot sitting on the counter where Martin was laying out his soup ladle, where the potholders lay that he was now picking up to use to carry the big soup pot.

"Slide in, Maggie," he said.

The table was surrounded by a bench, so she slid part-way round. There was plenty of room for Martin to slide in on the other end of the bench.

But after he put the soup pot down, Martin slid in the tiny space next to Maggie and moved the bowls and spoons over so one set was in front of each of them. He smiled, put his left arm around her, kissed her on the mouth.

"Martin!" she said.

"Yes?"

"I need to go home!"

"Why? Have you left something on the stove? Are you worried about Ernest? Do you need to mow the lawn?"

"No, no, no!" she said.

"What then?"

What indeed! Here they were, in a strange little home away from home, playing house! With kissing!

"Well!"

"Eat your soup, Maggie! Then we can do what we always do, me and my friends, when we're camping!"

Friends! Did he mean a bunch of friends hanging out? Or was that more like one at a time? What sort of man was this? He was more fun, she thought, than anyone else in her whole life. He was always up to some adventure. He always knew how to do things, how regular folks did things. While she, she had to admit, was a rather out-of-it sort of person whose greatest expertise ran to TV and the farmers market.

But now he was saying something else and she had missed half of it again. She had better turn into a better listener or who knows what might happen? She might have time to think if only she knew what was going on enough to think about it!

"...cards," he ended.

"What about cards?" asked Maggie.

"Scrabble or cards," he said. "Those are our traditional games. Sometimes we play late into the night."

Maggie felt some sort of relief at that. They were there, quite possibly, to play games. And then they'd fall asleep, each in their respective spaces, and in the morning they'd go home.

She was almost sad at that moment that tomorrow they would go home. She looked wildly at him to see if she could read his mind. He grinned at her. Or maybe it was a leer.

Martin taught her how to play some card games she'd never heard of. She relaxed into the role of happily losing every round, because after all she was the new one at this and what could you expect? As long as he was happy playing cards, all was safe and in fact quite innocent and normal and not even unusual. Except they were doing it at a state park, not at home.

She could even hear the surf, and a bit of wind, and after some more time, rain.

The rain on the roof reminded her of the little space they were in. How intimate it was! Martin was eagerly winning every hand and poking fun at her and she was having a good time. And Ernest was snoring a bit as he slept on and on.

And in fact it was getting late. The last thing Maggie wanted to do was to yawn and remind Martin of the hour and the need, sooner or later, for sleep! Ah, yes – sleep! But the yawns were getting hard to suppress.

Finally she yawned a big yawn and Martin looked at her and said, "Poor Maggie! I've kept you up too late! Look at the time!"

"That's ok," she said, yawning again. Once she began, she couldn't stop.

The rain had turned into a torrent, and the wind had picked up. The RV swayed. Maggie looked around.

"Are we safe?" she asked? "Does it ever leak? Or tip over?"

Martin stood up, and so did Ernest. He let Ernest out to do his business.

"He's going to get soaked!" said Maggie.

"I suspect he'll stay under the awning once he sees how wet it is," said Martin, still holding the door open. Ernest was back in in a moment, shivering a bit. He lapped some water from his bowl, then went back to his bed under the table. Martin covered him.

Martin was wiping off the counters and putting away some spices. "Come here, Maggie," he said.

She looked at him. She was still over by the table, several feet away. When she didn't move, he wiped his hands on a towel, then stepped over to her. He reached his arms around her. She was shivering, maybe from the cold or maybe from the windy weather or maybe from being there with Martin, she didn't know which.

He nuzzled her ear. He said, very quietly, "Don't worry."

But she was worried. She didn't want to make a fool of herself, didn't want to make Martin sad, didn't want to make Frank mad, didn't want to leave Martin's arms, didn't know what she wanted or what he had in mind. She shivered some more.

He found her lips and kissed her, softly. He kept his mouth on hers and nibbled at her lower lip. He kissed her again. Then he held her head against him, which as always was at the level of his chest. She thought she might lose her balance and wrapped her arms around his back to steady herself. The wind whistled, the RV rocked with the buffeting it was taking, the rain came more heavily, and she found herself clinging to him for protection.

She fully expected him to guide her to the bed at some point, and she was tired enough to go willingly with him and snuggle under piles of covers, if he had such a thing in the RV. She didn't even want to go home, she just wanted to go to sleep.

And guide her to the bed he did. It was not far away, just behind a curtain down near the bathroom. Behind the curtain was a queen-sized bed made up just as if it were in a house. He pulled the curtain aside and set her down and pulled her shoes off. "Pee?" he said. "Teeth?" She nodded.

He let her up to use the bathroom and when she returned the bed was turned down. But only on one side.

He unbuttoned her jeans. "Comfier that way," he said. She was so sleepy she didn't care. Then he lay her down, pulled her feet up onto the bed, covered her, kissed her on the lips and eyes, pulled the covers up to her chin, and said, "Good night, precious Maggie, see you in the morning." And with that she fell asleep and slept very well indeed.

Chapter 21

Maggie awoke the next morning because Ernest was suddenly giving her kisses she couldn't fit into her dreams. She was feeling a great deal of love for Martin in that dream, and now that she was awake, and could see where she was, and could tell it was sunny outside and maybe even a bit late for getting up, she was still feeling that love.

She took care of her bathroom business, then stretched a big stretch and hoped to see Martin sitting at the table. Or making breakfast. He couldn't be far. Or maybe he was already out walking. Maybe he had had it with her slow ways and was striding about on the beach with his big strides that she could never match. But then why was Ernest here? Surely he would love to run on the beach and frolic in the morning air!

Maggie considered. Should she go out? How did she lock the door? Where would she go? She wasn't used to out-of-town, or even many out-of-doors adventures.

Meanwhile Ernest had moved to the door and was staring at it in his polite I-am-an-old-dog-and-know-how-to-be-patient way. He wanted to go out -- didn't seem to need to go out -- and that was enough for Maggie. She put on her sneakers and her jacket, clipped on Ernest's leash, and braced herself against the doorframe in case he went bounding out and pulled her down the steps.

Martin was sitting at the campsite picnic table with a woman, a totally gorgeous, stylish, young, thin woman with -- and Maggie didn't see this at first but Ernest alerted her to it -- a very small dog-in-arms, the woman's arms.

Dede, she said to herself

Martin got up. He looked tousled, as if he had just gotten out of bed. "Maggie!" he said with great warmth. "Maggie, you've met Dede. My wife."

Maggie surely had tripped over a rock or something, because she fell where she stood, cushioned only by Ernest from a serious bruise.

Martin was close enough to offer his hand. He pulled her to her feet, leaving Ernest to bound frantically toward this woman Dede only to sprint away and circle back. Maggie didn't know if it was about the woman or the tiny dog she held, the miniature something-or-other that was now yapping in staccato high-pitched deafening barks.

But above the din, Maggie could still hear 'my wife' and she took her hand from Martin's grasp, turned back to the RV, pulled Ernest in after her, locked the door, sat in the driver's seat, fiddled around with the adjustments until she could reach both gas pedal and brake, and, when she saw the keys were still in the ignition, started the engine. With a tiny part of her mind she did realize that the awning was still out and the wheels were chocked. And now, as she considered whether she cared whether the awning got stripped off the RV by some low-hanging branch, and found herself looking out the window at the two or three of them if you counted the small dog, she noticed that the awning was sagging. And it was sagging because of all the rain that had accumulated last night. And that same slice of her brain realized that whether she accelerated forward against the chocks, or jammed the brakes on, that awning was going to dump itself onto the picnic table and everything within 8 feet of it, and while she was trying to decide whether forward or backward or stopping was the best choice, her foot put on the brake rather abruptly.

Ernest skidded across the kitchen floor. The awning trembled and rippled. The pool in the awning leapt upwards. Then down.

Maggie turned off the engine, ran as fast as she had in her whole adult life to the bedroom, tried to fit in the narrow closet, tried to get under the bed but there were drawers down there, and then sat down on the far side of the bed and pulled all the covers over her and the ever-faithful Ernest.

It was that same Ernest who popped his head up from the hiding place a moment later when Martin opened the door and walked right to her hiding place and stood over her with his hands on his hips and water draining from his fishing hat.

All was quiet, Maggie was glad not to hear the small yappy dog, Martin wasn't saying anything. She really couldn't see him because of the large pile of blankets and the dog standing on her licking her face, probably because it was so salty. She wished she knew who was doing what but she couldn't tell.

But what she did know was that Martin was married. That was his wife, that little dog was their dog, this was probably their RV, that was certainly their bed. Their bed. The bed she had slept in in reality and the bed she had slept in in plenty of fantasies.

She wanted to pound him. And now he was lying on the bed above her, where the covers had so recently covered her while she had slept, dreaming lovely dreams, keeping her cozy and warm. And now he, the subject of those dreams, was pulling the covers away from her face and meanwhile pushing Ernest out of the way.

"Go lie down, Ernest," Martin said rather more firmly than usual.

And Ernest, who was no dummy, went and laid down.

And that left Maggie staring up into Martin's face. She wanted to pound him. She wanted to kiss him, and that made her cry because all their kissing days were over. She was realizing she was trapped by how much she loved his kisses, also by how narrow the space was between the bed and the wall of the RV. In fact she couldn't get up. There was nothing to grab ahold of, and she was gradually spreading out and settling into the little space next to the drawers under the bed.

And so she had to accept Martin's hand and arm that were now extended to pull her out.

He had removed the pile of blankets and pillows she had pulled over herself as she hid from him, and now he was prying her off the floor. She wouldn't look at him, but she couldn't avoid accepting his help. Gradually she became unstuck and found herself half on the bed and half on her knees on the floor.

And that awful adulterous neighbor was kissing her cheek and smoothing her hair.

He also had his hand firmly on her back so that she couldn't move, couldn't get up from the bed or off of her knees.

"Now before you beat me up, my dear," he said, "I want you to listen to me for one minute."

And what right did he have to say 'my dear', she thought, and let's just see if I listen to him!

And she would have said something smart and put him in his place, but actually, she realized, he WAS in his place. And it was HER place too, that woman's. And she started to cry all over again. And then she realized he was talking and she had missed the beginning. In fact, all she heard was,

"....divorced."

And then he was done, and he let her get up and now what did she do? Because he was looking sweet and maybe sad, and definitely expectant.

She covered her face. He sat right there on the foot of THEIR bed, his and his wife's, and she sat on the side of it, and time went by. She still had her face covered, so she didn't know what he was doing. Ernest had let out little squeaks from time to time but each time Martin had said, quite gently, actually: 'Stay."

And so Ernest did not come to the rescue. In fact, they all stayed, right where they were.

Martin might have thought Maggie was thinking over what he'd said, but Maggie had no opinion on that at all, because she didn't know what he'd said. Just 'divorced'. As in 'I could always get divorced.' Or 'for years I've been divorced'. Or 'I don't believe anyone should get divorced'. Or 'if you and I got married we'd only end up divorced'. Or 'We got married the other day because I was tired of being divorced'. Meaning him and that woman of course.

And then Maggie had a few of her own, such as, 'I think you should get divorced.' And 'Why didn't you tell me you weren't divorced?' Or "Most people who get married today end up divorced.' Or, worst of all, she thought of him having said, "I didn't think you'd care if I didn't bother to get divorced."

But then, what did being divorced have to do with it? He wasn't divorced. He had a wife and her name was BeeBee or Fifi or PeePee.

Her head was swimming with all the possibilities, or rather all the new impossibilities, the ones that had been there all along.

And where was that confounded woman anyway?

Maggie couldn't reach Martin. Maybe he was making sure of that. So she flopped down across the bed and kicked. She hit the window with her foot but she didn't think that was a good idea, so she shifted around until she was kicking the wall.

She fully expected Martin to grab her ankles and subdue her. But he didn't.

She didn't hear him go, but when she looked up he was gone. Maybe for good, she didn't know.

Maggie continued to lie across the bed, but she stopped kicking once she realized he wasn't there. And then when ten minutes or so had gone by, and she was feeling seriously bored, and probably hungry, she got up. She washed her face and put on fresh clothes -- she had never really started the day earlier, had just gone looking for Martin and found him sure enough, not playing frisbee as she had imagined, but sitting companionably with That Woman.

So she began again. She would take Ernest for a walk and then she would come back, and then...who knew. She doubted she could actually drive home, not in a vehicle of this size.

But at least she could put up the awning. Remove the chocks from the wheels. Have a snack....

At least this time there would be no Plus Three at the picnic table looking like she belonged, looking like she owned Martin. Who did she think she was? And actually, who was she?

So Maggie clipped on Ernest's leash. He was more than ready to go out. She leaned over him once again to open the door, pushed the screen out so he could go down the steps, stepped out herself, and ...

She sat down on the steps. She put her elbows on her knees. She pulled the eager Ernest to a halt and told him 'no' rather sharply.

He growled. She didn't blame him.

"Hi," said Martin.

"Hi," said Dede. "Did you have a good rest?" Dede smiled a toothy fake smile. She and Martin were holding hands. Her flaming-red nails glistened in the sunlight.

Maggie was embarrassed. She felt like an intruder. She didn't know whether to go hide in the trailer, or hasten to take Ernest for a walk.

So she got up, but before she could take a step in either direction, Martin was at her side. He took the leash. Ernest ran over and licked his hand. Maggie looked at her feet. Martin raised her chin and kissed her on the mouth. She thought, he's probably doing that to say good-bye.

Then Martin took her hand and led her to the table. He sat her on the bench opposite Dede, and sat next to her.

Dede was making a great show of talking to her tiny dog. Ernest was being content to lie at Martin's feet. Maggie was looking at her lap but trying to sneak peeks at Martin, and an occasional one at Dede. Martin had Maggie's hand in both of his and was kissing it. And in between kisses, he said, "Maggie, this is my wife Dede."

Dede smiled at the air and at one of the RV tires. It was a bit of a forced smile, Maggie thought. For her part she had no smile at all. Now she knew that she had not heard wrong before. He had not said 'ex-wife' or anything like it. Dede was his wife.

So then what was he doing nibbling at her fingertips?

She sat in confusion. She wouldn't look up. And then her dawning sorrow turned to anger.

She yanked her hand away from Martin. Or tried to, but he was too fast. She gave him the worst dirty look she could think to make. Finally, when he seemed undisturbed by all she was casting his way, she stuck her tongue out at him.

This caused him to kiss her on the lips.

Dede made a great show of looking for birds' nests in a nearby cedar.

Martin slid closer to Maggie. She wasn't sure if he was hugging her or trying to make her behave. Rather loudly and firmly he said, "Maggie!"

He grasped both her hands, and said, "Dede and I used to be divorced. And then we got married again. And now we're just as good as divorced again, but we decided not to bother with the paperwork."

Maggie thought that she didn't really know what 'just as good as divorced again' meant. Should she just not worry about the details, or should she accept that this previously loveable, handy, fun, sexy neighbor was, you know. Married. That he had a wife, a gorgeous wife.

He was kissing her again, but she wasn't kissing him back. And wouldn't, she resolved, until she got this figured out.

And, speaking of figuring it out, what did it mean for them to be as good as divorced again if she was here at the RV when he was here with her, Maggie, and early in the morning at that? For all she knew, Dede had spent the night in the RV! Because Martin had been gone already when she had awakened.

But no, Ernest would have alerted her.

It was dawning on Maggie that whatever their situation, Martin was acting as though he was divorced from Dede, and almost like he was married to her, Maggie! She HAD spent the night in the RV! Maybe Dede didn't know that. Or maybe if she did, maybe she thought they had, you know, slept together!

And what was Dede doing here? Why had she come? When would she leave?

Martin, reading the direction of her thoughts, said, "Dede, tell Maggie how you got here and why!"

Dede gave him a bit of a dirty look, or so Maggie thought, or maybe she was giving Maggie a dirty look, but now Maggie was growing curious, so she looked at Dede and waited for the explanation. And while she looked and waited, she couldn't help but notice that Dede was looking damp and bedraggled. How could that have ever happened?

"I went over to Marty's last night and the RV was gone, so I figured he was at some park. This is our favorite, so I tried here first."

Maggie blurted out, "You were here last night?"

But what she was thinking was, 'Marty?'

"Yes, I tapped on the door. It was before midnight sometime, just when the lights went out."

"But Ernest would have made a ruckus. Because of your dog."

"I left my dog in the car. And I brought Ernest some leftover mac-and-cheese."

"So...." Maggie looked at Martin through squinty eyes. He looked back at her with a frank sort of look like, yup, we're here to get the truth out on the table. But Maggie wasn't sure what the truth was. Because he didn't look sheepish. He looked more like, let's get this over with.

So he took up the monologue.

"Dede scratched at the door. I was not entirely surprised. I wrapped up in a blanket and went out to tell her to go home."

"So I went home," said Dede. "I thought maybe we could spend the night together, but no..."

Maggie cringed. Some kind of behavior for 'just like being divorced!"

"I thought he was alone," Dede continued.

"I guess!" thought Maggie.

"You were married, Maggie, weren't you?"

Maggie looked at Dede. How much had Martin told his WIFE about her? Or was it just a good guess? She looked at Martin, but he was looking at Dede with surprise.

Maggie had to decide right this instant whether Martin loved her or whether he was the scoundrel he might be. And from now on whether she'd be with Martin and his baggage -- Dede, yappy dog, blue eyes, long legs, helpful ways, Sylvia, possibly all the women at the knit shop, possibly all the women at the farmers' market, possibly all the women period -- or whether she'd abandon him because of this woman sitting here.

And then she realized this woman wanted her to abandon him, and a surge of rebellion took over and Maggie looked her in the eye and said, "Yes! I was married! To Frank! For forty years!" And then she added, "And we never got divorced even once!"

And Dede said, turning to Martin, "I wonder if that's the guy from the bar, the one I hung around with for a while when we were divorced."

"I don't know," said Martin. "You hung around with a lot of guys. Remember?"

Maggie had grown a little bored with their reminiscences, except she was keeping track that so far no one had said anything about 'that woman you were hanging around with at the bar' about Martin. That's what she cared about.

But Dede was continuing, "because his name was Frank! I wonder if it's the same one!"

Maggie had just returned from daydreaming to the conversation. "You can't mean Frank, my husband Frank!"

And then all the forest sounds, all the surf sounds, and certainly all the people sounds, stopped. Complete silence engulfed Maggie. And Martin too it seemed.

He turned to her in slow motion, and she looked him in the eyes. And a new possible Truth passed between them. Martin turned back to Dede, also in slow motion. She was saying, "That's it! Frank!

And at that moment Maggie said to the silence and the Universe and anyone else who was listening, "Really? Frank? Frank, as in my husband Frank, was hanging out at the bar? With Dede, with Martin's wife?!" And Frank seemed to have nothing at all to say for himself.

Chapter 22

Maggie walked away. First she took the leash from Martin's hand, ever so calmly. Then she and the ever-faithful Ernest walked across the campground roadway and kept going in a straight line, oblivious of what was underfoot or in the way. She crossed the next campsite, barely altering her beeline for the picnic table next to their camping neighbors' fire pit. Then she walked into a grove of cedars. And she kept walking.

And while she walked she was having a conversation with herself about Frank. Because he might have been on the cool side as husbands go, not with-it cool but, well, a little cold in the emotion department. And he might not have been chatty or one to have the fellas over or one to go bowling with the boys. No indeed, not Frank.

Because Frank had been a homebody.

Why, even now, he was right there with her. And he had always been right there with her. And she knew without a bit of doubt that he had not gone to hang out at bars of an evening and take up with the likes of Dede.

Maggie had gone some distance by now, well out of sight of the campground as was her intention, she was pretty sure. Far from Dede. Far from Dede's innuendos. It didn't matter how she had gotten out of Dede's range, just that she was.

She had stepped into some brambles and gotten scratched, she had walked into a cedar and had scratched her nose, she had gotten beeped at out on the main road when she didn't look when crossing. She had in fact just walked away, not toward anything. She'd had no plan. She had her reliable Ernest, and that's what she needed, all she needed.

But then all at once she returned to her right mind. She realized that Dede had made it all up. Maybe there'd been a guy named Frank, but he wasn't her Frank. And at that moment she turned around and walked back to the campground.

But now, instead of putting one foot stalwartly in front of the other, she took little skips along the way, walked around the trees, watched for traffic, and in no time she found herself in the campground, where she stuck to the roadways and took Martin and Dede by surprise by appearing from a different direction from where she'd gone.

Dede and Martin had been sitting at the picnic table again, but they weren't talking. And then Maggie had appeared -- she could see how startled they were -- and they had both jumped up. Possibly they were feeling guilt, possibly they had assumed she had walked home, possibly they assumed she had walked into the ocean and drowned. Whatever current mental image they had of Maggie, she wasn't matching it, and suddenly there she was right upon them, she and Ernest both.

And before she stopped walking, she got really close to Dede. Dede tried to step back but the picnic table bench wouldn't let her, and Maggie's face ended up very close to hers.

So Maggie didn't need to say anything very loud, and in fact she realized she didn't need to say anything at all if she didn't want to. So she just shook her head no, smiled, and mouthed, "Not my Frank!"

Then she went into the RV, and pulled Ernest in with her. Martin caught the door before it shut and looked questioningly up into her eyes. She smiled at him and waved him in. Then she waved goodbye to Dede and disappeared inside. When she got her shoes off her sore feet and looked outside again, Dede was just driving away.

Maggie didn't know what to think, except for questions surging through her mind of where she fit in. She was there in the RV at the beach, after all, and Dede wasn't. But then Dede was his 'as good as divorced' wife. Almost.... Before she knew it, she found herself asking.

"Ok. So you're married. Then why did you ask me to come with you?"

"I wanted to spend the weekend with you!"

Maggie was remembering recent kisses. Martin had been quite generous with them. So this was probably the boy-girl thing that she had thought it was. But what if Dede was his girlfriend too, even though they were 'as good as divorced'? Or thought she was? Or what if I think I am, Maggie suggested to herself, but I'm not?

'Kisses,' said Frank. 'That's how you know.'

Maggie had never thought of Frank as much of an expert on the subject of kisses, but it was good to hear right now. Although what if Frank had been much more an expert about kisses than she'd realized? And then her inner Frank said to her mind, forget Dede. She's nothing but trouble.

"You're not listening!" Martin said.

Maggie looked at him. He was being serious.

"Look," he said, "we came to spend the weekend together. I like you! I want to spend time with you!"

Here he paused. Maggie could tell he wasn't done. Would he say 'but'? Or 'and'? Such as, "I want to spend time with you, BUT -- sorry about that -- I'm married." Or would he say 'and' as in "I want to spend time with you, AND here we are! Let's go have fun!"

She waited. He was clearly thinking before he spoke. Not easy to do, she always found, but it was admirable.

And then he began again.

"Let's pack a picnic and get on with it! The day is beautiful after all!"

That sounded wonderful. But Maggie had to make sure. No matter what Frank said. No matter about all those kisses.

"Is Dede really gone...." but she couldn't get the rest out before he kissed her full on the mouth and said, "Shhh. No more of that. This is about us.

And then she started to say what was on her mind, that that was his WIFE, but certainly he knew that and she couldn't think of any reason why she would want to remind him of it, so she said nothing at all and helped pack the lunch.

And hoped she could remember not to think of Dede. And in fact starting now, she would not....

She looked at him. He turned and smiled at her, gave her another kiss, added some napkins to the basket, and said, "That's better!" just as if he was reading her mind, and then said, "Let's take the binoculars," and he started talking about the birds he'd seen from this very beach.

They walked along the beach with the picnic basket and a pail and shovel. Maggie had gone back for her jacket, but now it was tied around her waist. The day was gorgeous, the wind barely stirring the cedar branches on the trees beyond the beach. And Maggie was lost in thought.

She had been silent for quite a while. He looked at her but she didn't want to be interrupted.

They had their lunch, they tossed the Frisbee around, they made a sandcastle until the tide came in and washed it away. The tide was indeed coming up, the breeze was cooler now, and when she looked back toward the parking lot, it seemed far far away. And the campground was well beyond that.

And then Martin was brushing the sand off his hands and gathering their toys and she picked up the towels and let the breeze carry the sand away so they wouldn't dirty the RV. Martin had already paid for another night, and she for one didn't want to sleep in a sandy bed.

Frank started to murmur something but she cut him off.

And then her train of thought led her back to Dede. As they slogged along in the sand, with wind in their faces and the threat of rain hanging from the sky full of clouds, Dede seemed to fill every corner of her mind.

Why had Dede really shown up? If they were as good as divorced? Which meant, presumably, that they were done with each other...???

"She thinks you're sleeping with me, doesn't she...." The thought had just come to her, and she actually said it out loud, though she certainly hadn't meant to.

This was a huge revelation to Maggie. She was a bit proud of herself. It made her feel less out of it, less old-fashioned. Suddenly she could see it all clearly. Martin had been married to Dede before, and now he was hanging out with her, Maggie! Quite astounding when you think of it. When you think of the gorgeous well put-together Dede compared to the more mature, robust, even sturdy, Maggie.

And when it could only be concluded that Dede thought they were sleeping together. Because Dede and Martin had been sleeping together.

'And that is why nice girls don't go away for the weekend with guys in their RVs' came a voice from deep in her mind. But not Frank's. It was her mother's.

Martin seemed to be hearing the clicks in her mind as she got it, got all the its, one after the other.

"Yeah, so you see, my dear," said he, "Dede is jealous. And for good reason, don't you think?"

She wasn't ready yet to think those thoughts. She looked at him with his sweetly hopeful look. The thing is, she was thinking, that it's nighttime and here we are and this time there's no Dede.

"And I was thinking you were being such a gentleman sleeping out here on the couch!"

"Is that where you want me to sleep?" he asked. She knew the innocence she was hearing in his voice might be anything but.

And she absolutely did not want to answer that question! So she said, "umm".

"Yes, that's what I thought, that is where we started this conversation."

Maggie couldn't deny it, to herself at least. She had known they would be overnight together in the RV and that it would involve the twinkling of eyes and kisses and all that went with them.

She sat on the foot of the bed, THE bed, the only bed, with her arms folded. She knew she knew, he knew she knew, and yet she couldn't get her grown-up, mature-woman person to say no. Couldn't find that mature woman inside, the one who could give consent as an adult, because 'she wasn't the kind of girl who did that'.

And she knew she wouldn't. Knew she wouldn't get some disease, or get pregnant if she did, just that she wouldn't. Not unless they were married.

He was waiting. He had taken off her shoes and socks and had been rubbing her feet with lotion. It felt incredibly good. He sat next to her and took off his shoes. He began to unbutton his shirt. He looked at her. She was looking straight ahead but she could see him well enough. She didn't move, didn't say anything. He got up, leaned over and kissed her, then left the room and pulled the curtain over. He took Ernest out and she heard them return from where she had hidden, under the covers where she had slept last night.

She suspected he was disappointed. Probably she would not see him again, except when Ernest needed a bath if even then. But still, feeling somewhat courageous, she called out, "Good night, Martin. And Ernest!"

"Woof," said Ernest.

Chapter 23

They left the state park right after breakfast. Martin was business-like in his setting out the cold-cereal breakfast, and not his usual flirty self when they were sitting across from each other at the table. He took Ernest out one last time and before coming in had lowered the awning and done his usual routine for getting underway. He hadn't said a dozen words to Maggie.

She was confused. She didn't know whether their sleeping apart had anything to do with it. Maybe her not letting him crawl into bed with her was a bigger deal than she'd thought.

Maybe she had turned him down, not just his desire for sex but the whole of him. So it loomed up in her. When they got home, they had casually gone their separate ways, and he hadn't appeared at suppertime. And then well after the mid-summer sun had set, he had knocked on the door. She was already in her nighty, Ernest was already asleep in her bed, and she was ready to crawl in herself. And so she had sent him home.

As morning dawned and she awakened early feeling they had somehow misunderstood each other, she realized she had pushed him away, said no aloud and also deep in her soul, not wavering. And he had left. She was in turmoil. She couldn't sleep in as she'd planned. She realized she probably couldn't expect a hot breakfast, a lazy batting around of plans for the day. Despite the early hour she swung her feet out of bed and went to the front window.

Each morning she went to the front window and craned her neck to see if he was already at work with his truck. Or his other truck or his little boat. Often he was. Often he sensed her there and looked up and waved. (Or else he was always looking up, which was in a way more reassuring though less cosmic and cool.) Often Ernest stood there with her.

This morning it was earlier than usual. The sky was lightening but there was no color to it, no rosy-fingered dawn, certainly no sunlight. The clock said 5. She should go back to bed.

She heard Ernest click his way across the floor and soon he was standing with her, yawning hugely. She kissed his nose, then resumed her wool-gathering at the window. It was silent except for birds. And now the sound of a lawn mower, someone getting a start on the weekly chore.

Except it wasn't. It was Martin's truck, the one with the hitch, and it was now moving into the street, now, at 5:00am. It had the little boat trailer attached, and on it was the boat! He was heading out, it seemed.

Without her.

She stamped her feet and stamped them again. She balled up her fists and pounded the air. She screamed at Ernest, 'Where is he going? Where is he going without us?'

Ernest looked at her and yawned again. He went to her bed and climbed up and set his jowls down on the pillow (the other pillow, not her pillow, ok, his pillow, Martin's pillow as she thought of it since he had crawled in with her way back).

She stood in the door with her hands on her hips. She thought about taking a shower, getting some cornflakes. They wouldn't do. That's not how life was anymore! She rejected it all and threw herself on the bed and cried into her pillow and cried some more and fell asleep.

He was gone all day.

She sat on a hard chair she had dragged up to the window. She didn't go for a walk, didn't make a meal, ate more cornflakes for supper, sighed with reluctance when Ernest needed to go out. It was like being hypnotized by the window and what might happen out there. But it didn't happen.

Martin was still gone, and the sun was setting. The late northern summer sun, that kept the night lit until well after bedtime, was setting. Still she sat.

Ernest had wandered here and there all day long. Now he was at her side. She had finally left the slider open and he had been coming and going, in or out, without her having to leave her seat. But now he was bouncing at her side, clearly trying to get her attention.

Gradually her obsessed, disturbed mind became aware of him. She absently scratched his ears. He ran to the front door and back to her, then to the door again. She told him to lie down. But he didn't. She looked back out the window.

Then he scratched at the door.

"Ernest, no!" she whispered.

Still he scratched.

In bellowing tones she roared at him, "NO!"

He raised his head to the sky and howled. And scratched at the door.

She dragged herself out of her chair, went to the door, let him out. The sky was fully dark, so maybe it was 11pm. Still no Martin.

Ernest had run only a short distance, for all his fussing, and was now back at the door, wagging his tail at her. She stepped out. The evening was warm, a soft wind blowing a bit of cool from the sound. Ernest ran in through the door and returned with his leash. Half-heartedly she clipped it on and walked him around the cul-de-sac, then covered the same steps a second time.

A little bit of appreciation trickled from one brain cell to another: It was a beautiful summer night.

(A counterbalancing silent roar erupted from nearby cells telling her she could be lying beside him right now if only....)

It might have been Frank, she realized. He never had liked the lying-beside, not for more than a minute or two. And she hadn't liked it much with him, either. But when it came to Martin...she could only imagine!

If only. If only she had let him have at her. If only she hadn't had the standards she had, or maybe it was programming.

She thought, if he was here now, all that would change! I love him. I really do. And if I have to be one of his many women, then that's better than none at all.

(I don't know about that, whispered the dead Frank.)

Memories of opportunities lost passed through her mind. It was hard to imagine that only weeks ago they had nearly died of hypothermia when the boat had been caught in a squall, and how fortunate they were to be able to get themselves home. Ernest had gotten really chilled that night, and the thought pulled her into the abyss. It had taken both of them to get him dry and warmed up.

And what if right this minute the very overdue Martin was clinging to his life just minutes from home, as they all had been? Well, that was pretty dramatic. But as he had said, the sea was unpredictable.

The thought mobilized her. She let go of the leash and ran for home. The door was still open. She grabbed her keys and purse. She opened the car door for Ernest, and raced to the driver's side. The two miles to the boat ramp seemed to take forever.

The parking lot for the beach and park and boat ramp were almost empty, except for trucks and empty boat trailers hitched to them. Maggie let Ernest out and he ran directly for the very familiar rig Martin kept in his yard, or just as often, in the street.

"Good boy," she yelled. She couldn't get over to it fast enough. She fully expected a tired Martin had fallen asleep in it.

But then, where was his boat?

No boat. And no Martin!

She began to shake in the light warm breeze. He was out to sea, lost perhaps. All because she wouldn't sleep with him.

(You see? Said the all-knowing very dead Frank.)

The parking lot was entirely empty of people. It was, after all, around 2AM. Maggie sat on a log and shivered. Ernest sat by her side. What could she do? He was gone, either for the night or forever, either for her or for humanity. She became calm, not worrying about his being dead of hypothermia someplace out in the sound, but that was only because she herself was growing numb with cold and the need to sleep. She pulled Ernest closer and lay across his back and fell into a dreamless state.

Sometime in the night Maggie must have eased herself off the log. She awoke with first light to find herself sprawled on the ground, damp all over with dew, her head on Ernest's back.. Ernest was still snoring as she pushed herself back onto the log, but soon he woke up and trotted off to do his business. She watched him go. The light was growing stronger. She saw him sniffing around at the edge of the woods. Then she thought about her own needs and stood to look toward the picnic grounds to remind herself of where the public toilets were there. Much as she didn't like them, she couldn't put it off much longer. Unless she went home.

And should she go home? Definitely! She called to Ernest, and he turned from sniffing deep into the woods and started back toward her. But then he veered off toward the shoreline. It was fun to watch him run like a young dog. She followed him with her eyes. He ran straight down the shallow boat ramp and into the water and began to swim.

She called him back but he bulleted through the water at an amazing speed. Her eyes followed his trajectory and way out she could see a small boat heading in. Other than a pair of ferries, it was the only boat on the nearly flat waters off the north end of the island.

Could it be Martin? Anyone could be on the seas as the sun came up. But not anyone would cause a mature bloodhound to take to the waves.

Maggie could see the seal-like enormous head bobbing sloppily in the calm waters, and felt a sweet wave of love. She could almost see herself plunge faithfully into the sea too. And for very much the same reason.

But no! Good heavens, he would see she had followed him, maybe even stalked him! He mustn't see her! She must find a way to avoid that!

It might be hard to explain about Ernest, of course.

She thought about calling the dog back. The early morning was so quiet that she hesitated. And however would he hear her? Still, maybe he would turn back in time for her to keep her dignity. Which meant before Martin saw him.

By now she could barely make out the splashes Ernest made as he plowed through the ripples.

He'd never hear her. But she had to try. She yelled once, then again much louder, as loud as she could. Nothing changed.

What could she do? She was stuck. Because she could imagine what Martin would think when he pulled ashore and she was standing there with her hands on her hips waiting for him. Like his mother, maybe, after he had ducked out to go fishing instead of going to school.

No, she would not be standing there waiting! She ran for her car, veered off to the bathroom. She could sit in the car, she thought. Maybe she had a book that could absorb her attention.

But then, her business done, she turned back. The little boat was much closer. It would be on shore in a few more minutes.

But where was Ernest? The sun was glistening off the ocean. Large numbers of walkers had arrived to walk the loop road through the woods at Washington Park. The parking lot was in fact nearly full with their cars. Maggie scanned the waters. She had no idea where Ernest was!

She ran as fast as she could for the shore. Martin's boat was just grating against the boat ramp, and the old dear was stepping out onto the stony beach. Safe!

She could see him reaching for the line at the front. She was twenty or thirty feet away and he hadn't seen her.

And still she couldn't see Ernest. She turned her eyes back to scanning the waters. Nothing.

And then Martin said, "Maggie, come here and hold the painter while I get the truck."

She knew the routine. And he knew she was there.

"Good of you to come help me haul the boat out," he said. He was smiling.

"Martin, help! It's Ernest! He's out there in the water! I can't see him anymore!"

"Hold this," he said. "I'm sure Ernest will be all right."

"No, he's gone! I'm afraid he's drowned!"

"I don't think so," said Martin. "Here, hold this! I'm getting the trailer."

Maggie trudged to the little boat, glancing all the while at the gentle waves, the undisturbed waves. Surely Ernest would have turned around to follow Martin – if he could.

Tears were coming to Maggie's eyes. She was worried about Ernest, and she was sad that Martin wasn't worried. Or maybe she was mad. She'd been so worried about the man, and now she was worried about the dog.

She bent over and sobbed.

An unpleasant scratching of something on metal penetrated her misery. She opened her eyes, turned toward the boat. That massive head popped up as the scratching stopped. Ernest was in the boat.

But only for a second. His toenails found a grip on the slippery wet metal. He catapulted himself out and knocked Martin over into the grass at the edge of the narrow beach, and sprayed Maggie with cold sea water as he shook himself.

Martin held out his hand, and Maggie took it and helped him stand. She was shaking, maybe because she was wet. Or maybe because she mad. Or maybe because she was relieved. She couldn't tell.

Martin had begun backing the truck down the boat ramp, and by now the trailer had reached the boat. Maggie automatically took a hand at hoisting the boat onto the trailer. When it was secured, Martin helped Ernest into the truck and drove off. No words had passed between them, though both of them told Ernest a great deal of what was on their minds in low mumbling tones of the sort that only dogs understand. Grumbling thus about the teasing she had taken, on top of the worry that had made her sick inside for more than a day, helped only a little.

And now that she was on her own – it appeared – she felt free to raise the volume. She did wait till her car door was shut. And then the grumbles became roars and the roars became tears and she couldn't see to drive.

Well, let him wait! Maybe she wouldn't go home at all! That would serve him right.

Unless he didn't notice. Unless he made soup and decided to take it to some one of his other girlfriends! Maybe even Dede (though Dede didn't seem much like a soup sort of person, more of a steak and lobster sort). And Ernest? He clearly had chosen Martin.

But Martin couldn't have him! The nerve! He had driven off with her dog, her old rescue senior decrepit adorable huge Ernest! HER dog!

And he couldn't have him!

She wiped her smeary eyes and aimed her car toward home to rescue Ernest. All the way she shook her fist at Martin. Wait till she gave him a piece of her mind.

It was two miles to her house. By the time she got there she was smiling. But only to herself. She would smite Martin with neglect!

She pulled into the driveway. Ernest was standing in the yard looking at her. And Martin was standing at the front door with a big pot of soup.

Maggie's insides sagged. She was hungry, two days' worth of hunger had built up in her. She eyed the soup pot. She bowed her head, then opened the car door. Her anger had disappeared.

And now she bustled to the door to unlock it, and even – this she thought was really absurd – felt guilty for not being home so he had to stand and wait.

And that absurdity, the realization that she felt she owed him something when he clearly owed her peace of mind at very least (at VERY least, she reassured herself), made her mad all over again.

She realized she needed a good talk with herself.

She went to the stove and turned on the flame as he set the pot down. Obviously it would be cold after sitting at his house for two days! And neither of them could afford cold soup right now, Martin because he was still in his Ernest-drenched clothing and Maggie because of her cold cold heart.

Because mentally she was taking a step back. What WAS this!?!! She had spent 24 hours pining for this relative stranger! And now she wanted to pound him with her fists and send him home for warm clothes and tell him to hurry back.

And she also wanted to ask him where he'd been.

Because it was now only the beginning of the day, and he had been gone overnight. Where had he been gone overnight? With whom had he been gone overnight?

And why did she care?

Well, she did.

And then he did go home to get into warm dry clothes and then he did hurry back and then he handed her a bunch of carrots with limp green tops, and roots that still had dirt clinging to them.

"These are from Sylvia," he said.

"Sylvia?"

Suddenly the pieces started to fit together. Sylvia, her forlorn gardening friend from Guemes Island! Martin had gone to Guemes and somehow had met up with Sylvia!

It made sense. Sylvia lived a rather isolated existence on the island just north of their own, one that could be accessed only by boat, or by an hourly ferry during the day. She loved company.

Hmm, thought Maggie. How much did she love this company?

Because it was dawning on her that Martin must have spent the night with Sylvia.

And as that thought landed with all its weight in her lap, she lost it.

Martin was still handing her – or trying to hand her – the carrots. She ripped them from his hand and threw them to the floor. She stepped closer to him and pummeled him with her fists. She was screaming words at him, which words she didn't know but it didn't matter.

He grabbed her wrists. She could see Ernest standing nearby shifting his weight from one foot to another, and she could hear a rumbling in his throat. Still she screamed at Martin, throwing out the story of the past day and more in jagged fragments of words, like boat and gone and waiting and corn flakes and worried and find you and drowned and Sylvia. Sylvia! Really?

"Really, Martin?" she screamed.

He kept holding her wrists so she flailed her head around and when she could she pounded it into his chest. But somehow he had managed to walk her toward a chair and he forced her to sit and stepped away.

Finding herself detached from him, she opened her eyes. He had a quirky smile on his face. It enraged her yet again. But as the rage built up to the point where it would become audible again, that smile created a detour in her soul. She lunged out of the chair, the better to hug him. He took a step back but she was too fast for him. She grabbed him around the chest and held on.

He was stumbling backward, and she was propelling them. He grabbed for the doorway as they fell through it into the hall. She didn't want to break him! So she sat down and he caught her shoulders and balanced himself and did not break his hip as he might have, and she was glad.

She started to cry, then to laugh. She couldn't get up. He gave her a hand, and helped her to her feet. While he was at it he gave her a kiss. A nice one, soft and smoochy and lingering.

"I didn't sleep with her, you ninny!" he said.

Maggie was worn out. A day and more of worry, and then more worry, and then? Well, then a tantrum. And then pounding, and jealousy, burning jealousy. All of it was exhausting.

She staggered a few steps to the couch and lay on it. Ernest came over and lay on the floor at her side. Martin busied himself in the kitchen. She could hear him scraping the carrots.

Chapter 24

They ate a hot lunch. Martin told her Sylvia had called and asked him if he was ever coming over to Guemes she'd make him lunch, and could he please bring a big bag of wheat from the health store? Because when she took the ferry, it was always as a walk-on and she couldn't carry that much all that way.

Frank, thinking he should straighten things out in this conversation, offered that Sylvia probably mentioned Martin's strong muscles, or maybe that was Maggie herself having that thought.

So, Martin continued, he had gotten the wheat and instead of driving over, had decided to go by boat and fish along the way. So he'd left early, had forgotten to tell Maggie the night before, had realized it was too early to let her know, had expected to be home an hour after lunch.

While he was telling this tale, Maggie was looking at her hands in her lap. She was reserving judgment. Now that she knew how much she cared, she was growing cautious, or careful of herself or for herself. She was listening hard. She was rooting for him. But she wanted the truth more.

This was perhaps a watershed moment in their relationship, she thought. (What relationship, inserted Frank but she chose not to hear him.) Watershed because now she knew she truly wanted a life with this man, and that to have that, there would be barriers. And one of those would be other women like her who could see the quality of this man. Anyway, that's what it looked like.

Just like high school.

And now he was saying that Sylvia had asked him to do some chores around the place and then to stay for supper and then it was late....

And here he stopped. And here her curiosity peaked. Because she herself had once gone to Sylvia's, had done similar errands for Sylvia, who was a vendor at the farmer's market and who seemed to have these needs for help quite often. And Sylvia lived, at least back then, had lived in a travel trailer with just one bed and a table and no couch for a guest to sleep on.

So Maggie was listening at the peak of alertness, fully conscious of the deep meaning of the moment, and it was at this instant when Martin had stopped talking. She thought he had in fact been in mid-sentence.

He sat there and she sat there and they stared at each other.

And then she knew he had lied to her earlier, and he knew that she knew. He stood up. He flapped his hands against his sides a few times, then turned, picked up the soup pot, and stepped toward the door.

Ernest followed, but Maggie called him back.

Chapter 25

The afternoon wore on and she was very much alone. And she was hating it. Who was this guy and what motivated him? He liked women, that was for sure. And there she was, one of many women, and she could either get used to it, or end it.

Or maybe he'd drift away naturally, since she wouldn't sleep with him, not now, not unmarried, not when he was such a... such a....

(Vagabond, said Frank.)

And Maggie liked the word, the traveler, adventurer. But she also liked companion.

Because – well, she liked him, so she was inclined to find something to hold onto that was good about him. Maybe that was all. But what did she know? How long had he been on his own? (Well, not counting Dede.) (But maybe there had been other wives.) (And, Frank added, don't forget your own list of guys!) (What, retorted Maggie, you mean you? And Simon of course? And nothing since? Not one little fling? That's a list?)

Well, the fact is, people lived their lives the best way they knew how. She for one had barely been alive these past three years, had let herself be buried with Frank, was still succumbing to his commentary on who she was, on who SHE was! And maybe it was the same for Martin.

It was no doubt the same for him, and that meant that whatever had gone before, it had landed him here now, a loving, affectionate, perhaps overly generous man. Her pot of soup was someone else's overnight visitor. He was just that way: you had a need, he came to the rescue.

Like Ernest. She had rescued him from the pound, but Martin had put life back into him, made it fun for him. And fun for her.

When had she even used the word 'fun' in recent years? (In how many years, she wondered. And Frank took that as a question and said FUN? What do you mean, fun? And when she heard him, she said EXACTLY.)

Fun! Martin was fun. Martin liked fun. Fun to Martin meant feeding, finding, feeling! (Fleeing, said Frank.) (SHUT UP Frank! Implored Maggie. Or I will rout you out and leave you ... somewhere.)

Chapter 26

Anyway, about Martin. Maggie was swelling with love for him. She called to Ernest and opened the front door. She scurried through the maze of vehicles in his yard, counting them as she went. They were all there! He would be home.

She knocked on the front door, knocked again. He appeared wrapped in a towel. In dismay she turned her back to him, then turned back and looked at him squarely. She understood that all this was disturbing to Frank, but she was Maggie and she was in love with this man who stood all but naked before her.

He had smiled when he had seen her at the open door, in a bland sort of way. But now his expression changed. It seemed that he changed at that very moment when she had spun back to look at him with an appreciative eye. Could he tell that's what she was feeling, appreciation for all he was?

Just an hour ago she had caught him in a lie and he had known it. And now they had both moved beyond it.

She felt a deep love for him grow and tears form in her eyes.

"What is it?" he asked, so gently that she took a step forward, still looking at him, all the while finding the love she felt deepening moment by moment.

What to say in response! What indeed!

"I was worried," she said. "I thought you had drowned at sea. I couldn't breathe, all day yesterday. I don't care about Sylvia. I'm glad you're safe."

"Hold on a minute," he said. Ernest followed him into the house, but Maggie stood safely at the door.

And then she thought, yes, I stand here safe on the threshold but why? Whose rule is that, to pretend like this, to pretend I'm not welcome in there, to pretend I don't want to see what's under that towel, to do as I'm told?

A roar grew in her insides, not one that would make noise but one that would send up waves anyway. She felt her clay mold crack. It was as if she were taking a deep and deeper breath, so big a breath that her little short tubby mortal body couldn't contain it. The roar filled her head with sound or song or swishing or the sound of waves, and the deeper breaths sustained the sound until suddenly it stopped and she could hear the world around her with new ears. She was Maggie, and she was on her own and would make her own choices.

And now Martin was at the door in his jeans and blue pullover, looking like some old politician with outrageous white eyebrows and head full of white hair. And how she loved him! She had never felt love like this!

She walked quietly to where he stood, and took him by the hand. She reached up and kissed his mouth, with a little help from him. She ran her palm over his just-shaved cheek, sniffed his hands, one and then the other. His feet were still bare, and she reached down and ran her hands along the tops of them and between his toes. He sucked in his breath. She lifted his arms and ran her hands down each side of his torso from armpits to feet and up inside his legs to his thighs and then around back to his buttocks and up his back and over his shoulders and down his front to his belt. He stood still while she explored.

And then he started to shake. If he was going to laugh, it would be ok because she was on her own and she was giving him all of her in the best way she could. But it wasn't a laugh, it was something else.

He stood there with his arms out to the sides as she had set them. She was now feeling every bit of his face, using her fingers symmetrically and slowly and gently like delicate brushes. She finally felt his ears, then his eyes, then his mouth. He shuddered again.

She reached up and pulled his head down and kissed him while once again tracing the shapes of his ears. His mouth was passive at first, then engaged.

He wrapped his arms around her but she pressed them to his sides. She took his hand and led him to the couch and bade him lie down. She sat at the far end, away from his head, and took his bare feet in her hands and caressed them in intimate detail. A knit blanket lay over the back of the couch and she covered him with it, except for his feet. Those she massaged deeply at first, then ended many minutes later with light strokes. In her heart she had an abundance of love-stuff to share and she was pouring it into him in every way she could think of, in every way that it came into her mind to do. This was love. Not passion. He knew passion. She wanted to be sure he knew love, Maggie love.

He had fallen asleep, and gradually she tapered off her caresses and lay her head back and slept too. When she woke Ernest was curled at her feet. The open door let in gentle breezes of warmth and summer smells. Martin was still deeply asleep. She closed her eyes and slept again.

When they roused each other and stood and stretched and marveled that it was already past suppertime and decided to eat the rest of the soup and set about heating it – this time at Martin's, where Maggie had never been before – the love filled the room. Martin wanted to hug her, but it wasn't that kind of love, or really it wasn't necessarily that kind of love and they could feel it even without hugging.

And it made Maggie wonder if Martin had really been loved at all, these years when he had had so many girlfriends. And so she, now that she had found herself, was dedicated to loving him until he was full. She hoped they had life enough left so that she could give him all that he needed. All the love he needed.

But first she had to tell him the way it was with her. Because he was Martin the generous-hearted, and she had been a willing recipient of what he had had to give. But now she was Maggie, and she loved him, and she would not tolerate that love being abused, being set aside, being dallied with, being made less than what it was. She would not receive the Martin who made soup and washed dogs and mowed lawns. Or the one who did errands delivering wheat and staying behind to be companion and consort to a needy neighbor. She would love him, but if he would be hers, she insisted that she be his, one and only.

No more Sylvia. No more whoever else was on his roster. And certainly no more Dede.

So she told him. And she watched him as he listened and absorbed her words. They were standing across his kitchen from each other. Ernest was asleep on the rug in front of the sink. Martin had been clearing the table, and

Maggie had stood up and folded her arms and sized him up. Her inner Maggie was strong as steel and she knew what she was about, nothing wavering.

So she said, "Martin. I love you. And I always will. But it is because I choose to love you. I will love you through and through. And there will be no room in it for any other woman. No room for any other woman! Do you hear me?"

Martin stood looking at her. She wasn't even a little concerned that he might object. If he did, she would walk away. Because she meant it. She loved him. But if he was going to persist in needing his other women, they were done.

He didn't object. He stood still. He seemed to be holding his breath. He nodded a tiny nod. Still he didn't move.

She walked over to him, took the bowls from him and put them in the sink. She stood a foot from him with her hands on her hips. She would not let his eyes drift away from hers. She felt like a giant standing there, though she was more than a foot shorter.

She was not trying to diminish him, or shame him, or bully him, or domineer him. She was waiting for him to find the true Martin, to find his own truth about his women, and about her. She knew it might not happen today.

Still he seemed to hold his breath. Then he whirled around where he stood, one full turn. He held his face with his hands. He looked at her as if he hadn't really seen her before.

"What have I done, Maggie?"

"Nothing that can't change when you want it to. Because of me."

"Oh yes, Maggie. I want it to. Because of you. You change everything. You have changed everything, only I didn't know it. Tell me it's not too late!"

"I already told you I love you. Now you know. From now on it's all about you and me, if you want it to be. I do."

It was hard to part that night. Maggie was tired but wanted to see him comfortable and settled, and he wanted to do the same for her. And there was the undercurrent of passion. He exuded it, and Maggie felt it growing deeply within her too.

And since she was now Maggie on her own terms, she would – if she wanted to. But as urgently as she was beginning to feel the desire to couple with him, her terms were that she would not. Not yet, not now, not sloppily and just for its own sake. She wanted it to be a spilling over of all that was in her, not just a temporary fix for a mortal need.

In the end, because they were so reluctant to part, he walked her home and they crawled into her bed with Ernest between them, as they had that night months before when they had barely survived the storm at sea. They held hands until they were asleep.

And when Maggie was sunk into oblivion, Martin said, in a loud voice, loud enough to wake her a bit but not all the way so she thought she was dreaming, “OK. OK! I agree. And it makes me happy, too. Good night.”

And then Martin was snoring, Ernest was snoring, and Maggie was wide awake. She was smiling, and she couldn’t get back to sleep.

Chapter 27

Each day they ate their oatmeal and their soup -- a different soup each day depending on the what the garden or the farmers market was providing. They'd go fishing or do errands or mow the lawn or in Maggie's case, walk around the block with Ernest while Martin fixed something. The summer drifted along, the berries ripened. They played cards in the evening, or Scrabble. They were in love and in friendship and in joy and in happiness and in sunshine or sunsets or sunrises, and they were happy.

Chapter 28

Maggie lay in bed a long time. Ernest got down. She thought he seemed a little stiffer than usual. Maybe it was some weather system off the coast. She didn't want to get up at all, but she knew he needed her to let him out.

Martin had left again.

She wandered around in the kitchen in her nighty. She couldn't tell if Martin was back, not without going outside to see if the RV was in the driveway, but why would he be so early in the morning? She had breakfast, cereal and toast. She missed Martin's cooking. Ernest had gone back to bed under the table and was looking at her with sad eyes. She felt tears forming, dribbling down her face.

It would not do! She would have to figure out something she and Ernest could do, just the two of them.

And she needed to do it fast! It occurred to her that if Martin did come home, she might even look as though she was waiting for him, and that would be the end of her dignity, just as her nightgown was, just as the toast crumbs on the counter would be if she didn't take steps to remind him of how independent she could be.

Frank's voice rumbled like distant thunder: "See how you really are?"

"I am not!" said Maggie fiercely. Ernest yelped with the sudden noise. He raised his head to look at her.

"Never mind," she told him. "I'm going to get dressed, and then we'll go on our own walk. You just rest up." Ernest put his head back down. As she turned away, she whispered, "We don't need Martin," but not so Ernest could hear her.

Half an hour later she was clean and tidy. She quickly cleared the table and wiped the counters. When Ernest looked up, Maggie said, "I don't care if he's back or not, Ernest, I truly don't. We're going for a walk anyway. A nice long walk. OK?"

Ernest continued to lie on his bed under the table. She got the leash and even then he followed her only with his eyes. Even when she put on her walking shoes he continued to lie there.

She eased herself down to the floor beside the table so she could reach him on his bed below. She rubbed his ears, ran her hands down his side, felt his legs, looked at his paws. She was awkward and uncomfortable down on the floor. "Come on," she said with energy, the better to get him up. "Let's take a walk!"

She pushed herself to her knees, to her feet. With a great heave he stood up and ducked under the edge of the table, then followed her to the door. She ruffled his ears, the scruff of his neck. He looked at her with his usual bloodshot eyes. She kissed him on the nose and opened the door.

She could see from her driveway that Martin's RV was not next door. He'd been gone twenty-four hours, or more if he'd left the night before after she'd said good-night to him. Ernest headed toward Martin's house, but Maggie called him back and secured the leash on his collar. "Let's go, Old Sweetheart," she said to him. "We can go around the cul-de-sac and then head up the hill." It was up or down once she got to the main street, and either way she ended up on a long stretch of uphill, where she would slow down. Better to get it out of the way.

They took the cul-de-sac slowly. Ernest was still stiff, and now, after all their walking, she was faster than he was. Especially today when he was at his all-time draggiest. "But don't worry, Old Man," she said, "we can just go slow if that's what you want."

So they circled the cul-de-sac and when they got to the main street, she chose to go uphill. Not that long ago, Maggie reminisced, she would have circled the flat cul-de-sac two or three times and called it a day. But now she was eager to extend the walk. The sun was over the ridge now, causing the cedars to cast deep shadows. It was just a bit cool, perfect walking weather. A gentle breeze seemed to stimulate her ambition.

"Let's do that forestlands hike!" She hadn't thought of it for today, but why not now? The trailhead was only a quarter mile or so up the road, and though the trail was steep, they'd be up at the level of the ridge for the whole rest of the hike, and the way home would be all downhill!

Ernest continued to put one foot in front of the other, and his pace was picking up somewhat. He'd like to see something new, no doubt about it. There was wildlife up there, birds and bunnies and deer, no doubt. Maybe raccoons. Coyotes certainly -- she could hear them at night.

Soon they were at the trailhead. Someone was coming down the steep decline to the road. Maggie looked up. And up and up. It was steeper than she'd thought.

"Well, you know what they say!" she chirped at Ernest. He looked at her with his ears perked in interest. "They say, one foot in front of the other! So let's go!"

She did put one foot in front of the other, and so did Ernest. They were both shuffling upward at a pace that would not cause any of the wildlife out there to take notice of them at all. The slope upward went on and on.

Twenty minutes of ascent went by. She looked back at the trail. She could still see the road below them, way below. And still the trail ascended. But she had come so far... "Ernest, we've come so far now. It would be a pity to go back now, don't you think?" But it was tempting. "You'll never make it," Frank whispered.

She and Ernest were the only ones on this spur of the trail. She hoped she'd reach the top and be able to walk on the ridge soon, where she expected the trail to be flat. But Ernest was dragging and she needed to use a bit of her energy to help him. A flat part of the trail would be very welcome. Someplace to sit and look down on their house would be wonderful and despite her flagging energy, the thought was enticing. "Come on, Old Thing," she said. "We're almost there!"

Indeed the trail was leveling off, though it still ran uphill. In another few feet it turned to the right -- the right direction for the ridge to run, if she was visualizing it right -- and she could no longer see the part of the trail they had climbed. The trees, cedars and other evergreens, were dense all around them.

A shape partly obscured by vegetation loomed just beyond them, and the trail split in two. As they got closer, she could see the shape was a gigantic water tank. One section of the trail was wide enough for vehicles, service vehicles she figured. For people who took care of the water tank, who climbed the ladder that went up step after step until the whole stairwell wound out of sight. She opted for the other trail, which she felt must be the one for hikers, for people without vehicles. For her and Ernest.

The trail she chose was indeed quite flat, with tree roots to step over and a few tiny streams to avoid, but otherwise harmless, much easier to walk. Ernest stopped at the first stream to drink water, then lay down in the shade. "Good idea!" said Maggie. She sat next to him on a broad and gnarly root. She looked up at the tree attached to it and could not see the top, just the broad trunk with the intensely blue sky as a backdrop for its high-up branches. It was beautiful and she felt content.

And Ernest looked content as well. He had picked a shady spot just off the trail, up against a bush of some sort, on a grassy patch. The ground was dry there. She took off her jacket and bunched it up against the tree trunk and leaned back against it. It wasn't all that comfortable but the peace of her surroundings helped her feel content. Even with a few wispy thoughts that gave her belly a twist of pain at the thought that Martin had abandoned her, even if for the moment. After all, he did live next door, alone. "For the moment," inserted Frank smugly.

Maggie squirmed around to find a better position. Ernest looked sound asleep. She closed her eyes and wasn't sure if she nodded off or just daydreamed for a bit. She peeked at Ernest and he was still snoozing. She found a way to lie down and put her head on his chest and fell soundly and peacefully asleep.

Chapter 29

Maggie didn't know how long she had slept, but the sun was overhead, so it was midday. Ernest was still asleep. She was thirsty, found her water bottle in her jacket pocket, thought Ernest must be thirsty, called his name. He didn't stir. She called out again, tickled him. A moment later his tail raised itself once, twice. Then he raised his enormous head and hoisted himself to his feet. The leash was still attached. She also got on her feet ("that wasn't very graceful," opined the dead Frank) and took up the leash. "Let's go see if we can find our house!" said Maggie to Ernest.

"And let's see if Martin's back," thought Maggie to herself.

They continued along the ridge path. It certainly was not one that showed a lot of use. It was narrow with shrubs close on both sides, rugged with roots and mossy rocks. Mushrooms -- or were they toadstools? -- grew right in the footpath. A small bridge that had been built apparently to cross a damp spot was collapsed and Maggie tripped on a spike that had become exposed. She caught herself against a sapling and regained her balance.

They went on. She had wrenched something in her back, it was becoming obvious with each new step. But she was determined to finish the hike, find a place where she could look down on her house, her car, her cedar tree in the front yard -- would it reach up to where they were now? And where she could look down and see whether Martin's RV was there. Not that it mattered.

In a way it was true that it didn't matter. He hadn't been there and she had been fine. And then she had gotten Ernest and then he had been there and then they'd had a good time, spending day after day having mild adventures, and then he had disappeared from time to time. And she knew he’d be back. At least after all their walks she was now enjoying walking every day. And she still had Ernest to keep her company.

A twig broke under her foot and split the air with sound. The trusty Ernest continued along. The ridge headed south toward the bay, and would end soon, when it reached the edge of the island. She decided to leave the path so she could get closer to the edge of the ridge. She didn't know if the ridge was just a steep hill or the edge of cliff that could prove treacherous with a false step. She was scared enough for herself, but what about

Ernest? She tied his leash to a sapling before leaving the path herself.

Trees were everywhere. At first she couldn't make any headway, then she found an opening with clear daylight showing through. She took a step toward it, but all there was beneath her foot was a pile of leaves caught against the edge of a sapling. She sat down hard. She was partway down a leaf-covered slope. She was surprised, jolted, but unhurt. And then she began to slide. Seated as she was, she stopped her descent by catching a narrow trunk with her heel. She struggled to roll over, also to grab anything within reach that would slow her descent. Flattened as she was on her belly, she reached her arms as wide as she could and tried to dig in her toes. A tree was within reach and she held on tight with both arms. It took several minutes before she was willing to try to scramble up the hill, and then it was slow-going.

As she inched upward, she could see the scar made by her slide. A slick muddy trail showed the way back up to the path and Ernest. She still had maybe ten feet to climb.

A few feet more and she rested, face down. While she lay there, her arms wrapped around another small tree along her path, she became aware of a stinging on the back of her head. She felt it with her hand and came away with a smear of blood on her fingers. Both hands likewise seemed abraded. Not too bad. Not too bad if she could hold on and climb up and get back to flat ground. Could then hobble back down the trail to the water tank, could make it down the steep trail to the street below, could walk herself and Ernest home.

It seemed overwhelming.

"Obviously this isn't going to work -- you'll never be able to do it!" rejoiced Frank from inside her head.

"SHUT UP!" she yelled. Ernest let out a deep woof from where she had tied him.

She was still prone. The ground was mostly dry, though she felt dampness through her jeans where one knee was pressed into the ground. The forest was still. If she didn't try to hold her head up, her nose pressed itself into the soft bed of old cedar needles or whatever they were. Some sort of plant material that smelled old, pleasant. She needed to find a way to ascend the hill or she'd just melt into it, disappear, turn into compost on the spot.

"Now that's funny!" whispered Frank.

It dawned on her that she really was on her own, and she'd better do something about it right away. She had no idea what time it was. She was thirsty. Ernest was stranded, tied up, without her. No one knew where she was. She was sliding slowly down the hill, too, a little bit more each moment that she lay there, lubricated as she was by leaves on mud.

But she didn't know if she had the strength to climb up. She was afraid to try to stand. The trees would give her handholds, and maybe something to push her feet against. But what about in between the trees? She'd have to scramble up fast to keep from sliding down, but the slope was so steep she was not sure that would be enough, the scrambling and grabbing for trees and finding possible toeholds against the roots.

Well, she had to try. She raised her head, looked around but saw only tree trunks and forest debris. She looked above her for something to aim for, something she could hold onto if she were successful in lunging upward a few feet.

She could hear the occasional car below, the sound of children playing. It all sounded so normal. And here she was dangling somewhere above them, or almost dangling. Lying on steep ground, trying to make a plan, out of earshot of anyone except Ernest. And Frank, of course.

"Ok, Frank, if you are so smart, what would you do? How about a good idea for once?" She knew she had said it out loud when Ernest woofed again.

"Sing," said Frank.

She was losing her mind. Frank had never liked her singing. And why now?

In desperation she tried to scramble to her feet, rose up on her knees, flopped forward and reached for the nearest tree. She missed, slid back down, kept sliding, spread her legs out, and was saved by a tree below her, now caught between her legs. She was not going to make it out by climbing. The more she tried, the more it seemed she would end up on the roof of someone's house, or wherever the ridge ended up.

She had no idea how far she had to go. The muddy track she had left on the way down disappeared above her into the trees, into the evergreen boughs she had slid through. She was tired and done with this adventure. And nothing was working.

"I said sing," insisted the voice of her tormentor and long-dead husband Frank.

Sing? In her awful voice? Sing what? Something loud? No one would hear her.

But it would not be for the random person to hear! Ah yes, she thought to herself: It would be for Ernest.

She let herself slide down so her legs straddled the tree and she could raise herself up to sing without inhaling forest mulch. She sang the first thing that came to mind: Oh say can you see, by the dawn's early light. It was a good loud song, and she loved to sing it. At first she was a bit timid, but the discomfort and fear that had turned to hope finally gave her the courage to belt it out. She sang as loud as she could, as loud as her dry throat would let her. What so proudly we hailed...

And with all his faithfulness and his love of Maggie, Ernest sang too. His mournful and deep sonorities filled the little valley, wafted over the houses and cars and children below. So she imagined. She continued and he continued and it was Martin himself who finally came, not before her stiffness and dryness and unpleasant itching where she sat against the tree had penetrated her almost to the limits of her spirit, but he did come.

As they had sung their duet, she and Ernest, she had become aware of another voice, then a movement. She looked up along the track of her descent and saw something wiggling. It was familiar. It was within reach! It was Ernest's leash....

She lunged for it and grabbed it and dug her toes in and gained traction and made headway as the leash helped her move upward.

And there at the end of it was Martin, who grabbed her under her arms. He was lying across the path. Ernest was standing next to him, above her, sniffing, yodeling, frisking from one foot to the other. Martin was supporting her while she grabbed at saplings and rapidly sought for higher and higher toeholds. In a few moments she was flopped across the path with her guys beside her. Ernest licked her face. Martin helped her up and as she wobbled, held her tight so she wouldn't fall.

Slowly they walked, the three of them, down the path to the water tank road and then down the steep trail to the road below. Martin packed her and the faithful Ernest into his car and took her home and made supper while she cleaned up.

She was plenty sore as she crawled into bed. Her thought as she drifted into sleep was, thanks, Frank.

Chapter 30

She woke up with the sun streaming in. Ernest was no longer in bed with her. She turned over and found she was stiff with tender spots all over. The adventure on the ridge unfolded in her waking mind. She lay back with a smile.

Ernest's nose appeared at the door, which was open a crack. He nudged it fully open. Her sleepy mind was trying to figure out how he had gotten out there in the first place if the door were closed. And then Martin came in. He was carrying a tray of food. He set it down and helped her with the pillows and she sat and ate, thankful for the eggs and bacon. He sat on the end of the bed and watched her. Ernest lay at his feet.

"Why?" he asked.

"Why what?"

"Why did you go hiking alone?"

"It looked like fun. And you weren't ... And you were...."

She knew he had a right to be gone. She also had a right to go hiking on her own. So why was he quizzing her? Was she quizzing him? No. She was keeping all of it to herself, all the enraging, lonely, worried, ugly, independent, troublesome thoughts.

"Dede," she said. She was looking at her plate, nearly empty now. The plate Martin had brought to her, that was filling up her empty places.

"Dede?" he asked.

She looked up, then quickly down again. She wanted him to explain, to make it all seem ok. And she wanted him to get her more eggs and bacon. And crawl into bed with her. And go away so she could get up and pee and take a shower. She set the plate on the bed and pulled the covers up over her head like a tent.

"Maggie, listen," said Martin. "Dede left a message for me night before last. I got it after I left here. She was stranded on Guemes Island. She wanted me to come get her. I told her to get a hotel room for the night but she said the only hotel was full. I had to take the boat down and launch it and by the time I got back it was after midnight. She wanted to stay over. Well, that was a definite no!"

"Why?" asked Maggie. She was peeping over the covers. She didn't know if she might cry. And if she did cry, would it be for joy or fear or sadness? Or at her own stupidity? Or just from being tired and wanting to go back to sleep? Or from gratitude for Martin's kind ways? Kindness always got to her.

"Why? Dede always wants to stay over. When she called it could have been a set-up. I knew that."

"A set-up?"

"Yes, staying too long on Guemes, missing the last ferry, all on purpose. So I would have to go get her."

"Was it? On purpose?"

"I don't know. Anyway, we got back here and I was all set to take her home in the car, but she said she was exhausted and could she stay over. So I put her in the RV."

"Why? Oh! You didn't want her in the house?"

"Right. So I put her in the RV and then I got up early to wash the salt off the boat and she came out and wanted to take me to breakfast. So I decided to drive her home in the RV and get some gas on the same trip."

"But that was two days ago!"

"I know."

Maggie looked at him. He was holding her hand, massaging her arms. The massage made it hard to be suspicious about what would come next, but he seemed to be avoiding looking at her. A long silence followed. He picked up the plate and left the room. Ernest followed him. Maggie got up and went into the bathroom. When she was done getting ready for the day, she hobbled out, her feet still sore from the hike. Martin was gone. So was Ernest.

Ernest could be in the back yard and Martin could be anywhere. He could be gone again in his RV. Or on his boat. Or in his pickup. She stepped out the front door against her better judgment to see which of his many vehicles might be missing. A tightness was growing deep within her and tears were forming, all against her will.

Once she was in her driveway, the truth was right before her eyes. The RV was there, as was the boat. As was his pickup. As was the little old red pickup he cherished. Unless he had another vehicle she didn't know about, he was nearby.

The usual background noises of a Saturday morning didn't disturb her joy of realizing that they might still spend the day together. Because spending the day with Martin was her joy, had become her joy, even though it had taken his absence of two days to be sure of it. The squirrels were scolding, the various birds were declaring their territory or looking for mates, the lawnmowers were grinding away.

Her reverie was burst when a lawnmower sound penetrated her awareness. It was Martin on a riding lawn mower, mowing her yard.

"Ha, so there was another vehicle you didn't know about!" chortled Frank. "You don't know as much as you think you know!"

Maggie turned toward the approaching tractor. Martin turned it off and slid from the seat. "Side yard's done, front too. Let's go to the farmer's market."

Maggie's thoughts were zigzagging all over the place. Partly she wanted to know all about his absence, about Dede. She also wondered where Ernest was. And how Martin had found her yesterday. And whether they would have lunch once they got to the market. And if they would go to the dog park again and whether Ernest would like it and what if Dede was there?

"Ok," she said.

Ernest had been in the backyard sunning himself. They got him and the cloth recyclable bags they took (when they remembered them) and her mailbox key and her tokens that were used for the market. Martin put Ernest on the leash. The RV was still in the street and Martin needed to move it to the yard before they left. He held the door for Maggie, and scooped her up the steps, then did the same for Ernest.

Ernest growled. Martin felt his legs. But it wasn't pain: his hackles were up as if he was afraid of something. He slunk into the RV and sniffed the carpet and benches.

Martin slid into the driver's seat and gave her the choice of the co-pilot's chair or a seat at the table. He told her to buckle up. Ernest crept under the table. She couldn't tell if he was tired or scared or just playing it safe. His hackles were still raised. She sat there with him, rubbed his back with her stocking feet. Martin was maneuvering the big rig back and forth and with amazement she saw he had managed to squeeze it into a space that had looked too narrow for it.

He was done, turned off the engine. Ernest wouldn't come out from under the table. Maggie slid off the bench. Martin came around in front of her and took her by the cheeks and kissed her with great intensity.

Confusion filled her. She loved it when he did that. But why did he do it? Was the man blind? He could plainly see her dumpy body, her lack of make-up, her naturally curly uncolored hair, and now her limp from an embarrassing cascade off the ridge. Her clothes were, well, the only word for them was comfy. Her shoes were beat up and grass-stained and now muddy. She was old. Even her dog was old. And neither of them could sing.

But her arms understood. They encircled him and held on with an unexpected and unrelenting strength. She raised her face to his when he was clearly not done. She met his lips halfway. Then she opened her eyes and saw the bed at the far end of the rig and had visions of Dede lying there in all her gorgeous skinniness, skin being most of what she saw in her mind's eye, and she pulled away.

"What?" he said. "What what what?"

"Dede," she said.

He sat on the couch and pulled her down next to him. He put his arm around her and kissed her. She didn't resist and she didn't encourage, she didn't participate at all.

"OK, here it is, straight out," he said.

"You don't have to tell me," said Maggie.

"Ok," said Martin. He resumed kissing her. He kissed her chin, worked his way down her neck, and by the time he was at the V of her shirt he was laughing so hard that he had to stop.

"Why are you laughing?" asked Maggie. She was on the verge of laughing, too, but maybe it was more like crying.

"Does this come off?" he asked. He was plucking at her shirt, holding it out from her chest so he could look into it. She was about to say no when he resumed kissing her mouth and his kisses were turning into little nibbles of pure passion, or so they were by the time they got to her.

By now she was lying on the couch and he was kissing her from above and she was trying to catch her breath and Frank kept saying, Hmm, in an analytical sort of way. The last thing Maggie wanted was for Martin to come to his senses and gather her and Ernest up and drive off to the farmer's market and the crowds and sunshine and music. She wanted him right here, in the somewhat cool dark interior of this hidden away space of an RV. But then she remembered again, and explained during a moment's lull, "Dede."

It came out sounding like a squawk, but he got the idea.

"Really?" he asked. "Really? You want to talk about Dede? OK, then."

He sat up and pulled her to a sitting position too. Then he lifted her up and settled her on his knee and wrapped his arm around her and with the other one pointed at the bed. "See that bed? Dede wanted me to sleep in that bed with her night before last. Now are you happy?" He sounded angry, or maybe sad.

She didn't know what to say. Her worst fear was that he had slept with her. It had seemed almost inevitable, and now he said he hadn't and she believed him.

"Now ask me why I didn't," he said.

"Why didn't you?" she ventured. She wasn't sure she wanted to know, now that her fears were quieted. Now that she wasn't just another woman. But she had been a woman who had refused to sleep with him. Someone who had said no. For a good reason. Clearly Dede had wanted Martin to say yes.

And what if Martin had said yes?

"So that was the night before last..." said Maggie.

"Yes," said Martin.

She didn't want to keep questioning him. But what about last night?

"I drove down to Seattle yesterday for a couple of parts for the truck. I should have let you know."

She hadn't asked, but he had guessed what was on her mind. She would have enjoyed going.

They looked at each other. She was still feeling a bit uneasy.

"Well, Ok," he said. "Dede wanted to go shopping at that mall down there, and I needed the parts, so we just made a day of it. And we had an errand to do. I would rather have been with you."

Maggie had looked away and she now turned back to him, who seemed a bit lost in thought himself.

She wanted to ask him what errand, but it wasn't really any of her business. Was it? She had to think about that. Because....well, it could be.

And then he asked, "Don't you want to know what the errand was?"

She looked down, then said yes. It was a very quiet yes, but inside she was on high alert. When he didn't say anything, she peeked at him. He was looking at her with a peculiar expression, one that seemed full of love and what? Sadness? No, more like meaning. Like the moment meant something.

He took her in his arms and held her tight, like he was never going to let go of her. She was catching his mood, his state of being, and found herself close to tears. She took a deep breath.

And he took a deep breath and said, “We went to the county offices and signed our divorce papers.”

Her mind was in turmoil. He and Dede had together gone and signed the papers? Dede was cooperating? It was done?

“It’s done,” he said in answer to her question. We filed sometime last year. We signed off on the whole divorce today.

She held him tight. She wondered what it would mean going forward.

But then Dede had wanted to sleep with him, right here in the RV, just the other night.

"Why did you say no to Dede about spending the night?"

Martin looked at her. He kissed her. He hugged her head, pressed her ear to his chest.

"I learned it from you, Maggie. I’m saying no from now on."

She leapt on him, tipped him over onto the couch, reached up and kissed him full on the mouth with fervent passion. He gasped. She lay on him. He started to laugh. She started to laugh. Ernest got up and stood by the couch with a worried look between his eyes, a grin about his mouth, his long pink tongue looking dangerously moist. He joined the laughter by guffawing in a hound-like way.

Martin rolled her onto the floor. She bounced against Ernest, who let her drop. Martin was on top of her in a moment. They were giggling so hard she couldn't catch her breath. Finally she said, "You old silly! I know you're not in love with her! But I'm really glad you said no!"

Martin kissed her tenderly. "Let's get married," he said. "Yes," she said.

Chapter 31

They went to town for errands, and Martin said he'd take Ernest to the dog park so she could go to the knit shop and library. And to herself, Maggie said, to Duncan's office. She was on foot and was lucky these public places were all so near each other. The day was beautiful and the boys would have a great time at the dog park, and she didn't mind if Martin found Dede there, even.

She decided to go to Duncan's first. He was probably there, but if not she could come back after the other errands. She had only to climb the tall staircase once again.

She knocked and he himself opened the door to his suite. He looked older than she'd remembered. His equally old secretary did not appear to be in.

"Well, come in, Maggie! What a surprise!"

He expressed his delight, they exchanged their reflections that it had been a long time, and now they were seated in the lovely leather seats with deep and polished wood arms he'd always had. His office was vast, with tall windows that overlooked a couple of roofs. Her view of the sea to the north was obscured by a three-story equally old-looking building just down the street. She was wondering vaguely exactly why she was here, and hoped her pensive appreciation of the view gave her sufficient gravitas that Duncan wouldn't think she was wasting his time.

But as time stretched on, she didn't have any clever ideas, and heard herself blurt out, "I'm getting married."

Duncan looked at her with astonishment. "At your age?" he asked.

"Well, yes."

"Well," he said.

"Well," she said. "Yes, to Martin... Well, you might know him, tall fellow."

"Martin, yes. I know him."

"Ah, so you do know him!"

"I know of him." Duncan wasn't looking happy, but since she'd come in he had had a stressed look about him, or maybe it was sadness. So chances were it wasn't about Martin. Thank heavens!

"So, well, I wanted to tell you -- I haven't really told anyone, so you're the first -- that Martin and I will be getting married!" Maggie tucked her head down and smiled into her lap in embarrassment.

"Really!" exclaimed Duncan in a loud voice. It didn't sound like a question, but more like a bit of a challenge. He was quiet. He was tapping his left forefinger on the arm of his chair. He was looking down, then out the window, and still he tapped. Maggie could see his fingernail was overgrown, his fingers were stained yellow. She knew sometimes he smoked cigars.

The silence was getting to her and she was feeling the need of some easy conversation. So she said, "How's Doris?"

Duncan turned his head slowly and raised his eyes to her. They were filled with tears. "I guess you didn't hear," he said. "She passed away. Last winter. Pneumonia."

Maggie gasped. She and Doris had bumped into each other around town often, and she was a regular at the knit shop. How had she not noticed her absence?

She stared at Duncan. Then she got up and gave him a hug. She walked around the spacious office trying to give him time to compose himself. And she mumbled, "Sorry, Duncan. I'm so sorry." She meant sorry that she hadn't known, sorry Doris was dead, sorry he was so sad, even sorry he was crying. Crying where he had no privacy, where she could see him.

She herself was used to Frank being dead. Pretty much. Well, not entirely. She shed a few tears, too, feeling sad for the ways of mortality. At least she had Martin and Ernest.

Even if they were old. Even if she was old. But not as old as either of them, if you translated dog years into people years

Duncan had gotten out a notepad now, and Maggie collected herself and went back to her chair. "What can I do for you, Maggie," asked Duncan.

"Well, I don't know. I thought that since I was getting married, I should see if ... I don't know, if I should do something with my will or whatever. Or my other papers? Or money? Anything?"

"Do you have a will? I don't remember one, but maybe you had someone else draw it up?"

"Well, Frank did. Right? That's why I got all his property?"

"He did but you would have gotten it anyway. He just made sure we knew that's what he wanted. For example, we knew he didn't want to leave it to his brother."

"Well, his brother is dead. Has been for years!"

"Oh, sorry, I guess I'm getting old and confused. I thought you and he were divorced. But I didn't know he was dead! I thought Frank considered putting him in his will!"

Now Maggie was feeling confused. Certainly Duncan was remembering that part wrong. In her mind Simon was dead. He had died in Israel where he'd had a colleague and his mother on hearing the news had decided to have him cremated there and his ashes sprinkled in the Dead Sea. Fitting, she'd said.

But she couldn't think about that now. She was getting married, and she wanted to do it right. "So, Duncan, about my will..."

"Let me get back to you. I need to look it up. Or if you think you might have it at your house...?"

"I don't know. Frank took care of everything. And you."

"Well, one thing you can do, if you're looking for advice, is to let me set things up for you so Martin can't get a hold of your house if you die. Or that piece of land of yours. Nice property!"

"He can have them. I won't want them."

"True, but you don't know him."

Maggie pondered that. What was there to know?

But Duncan was talking. “You know, you could donate that land. To the community forestlands trust so it can be enjoyed by everyone. That’s a nice piece of land you have!”

“Interesting! I’ve been hiking up near there myself.” She was remembering her long slide off the ridge and how her lovely boys had rescued her, both Ernest and

Martin. She wasn't quite sure where her land was, but not far from there.

And while she thought about how nice that land would be for everyone to enjoy, Duncan surprised her by saying, "And then you can see whether Martin still wants to get married if you do that!"

"What?" said Maggie. Duncan didn't say anything and she was trying to navigate his meaning without further clues.

She got up to leave. "Be careful, Maggie," the old lawyer was saying. He gave her a quick hug and opened the door. She hastened away, feeling uneasy though she was not sure why. She was no longer in the mood to go to the knit shop or library, and hastened to the dog park to find her boys. She decided to keep their conversation to herself.

Chapter 32

The next day, as usual, Martin had made a fine breakfast. Maggie was glowing with eggs and bacon and love. She rubbed her feet over Ernest, who had moved from the cozy bed he shared with Maggie to his own cozy bed under the table. The sun wouldn't be around to this side of the house for a while yet, and she thought he might be shivering a little in the morning air. She got his blanket and wrapped it around him. He slept on.

Martin had just gotten up from the table and was clearing the dishes. Since Maggie had been walking every day, she was losing interest in her second piece of toast, and Martin flicked it into Ernest's dish over by the sink. Normally when he heard something land in the metal bowl, he jumped up to make sure he got it before anyone else did. Maybe there'd been other dogs in his previous home, Maggie thought.

But today the toast landed with a plink and he didn't get up. Martin added a few scraps of egg. "He's not eating," said Maggie.

"He can eat later. They'll keep," said Martin. He put his hands on his hips and looked under the table at

Ernest. "He's just sleeping. He's probably tired out from climbing that trail."

It was true. Maggie herself still had aches in her legs and would have been happy to crawl back into bed.

But it was another beautiful day outside. The sun had climbed over the ridge now and the backyard was filled with patches of light as well as the deep shadows of the cedar that grew in Martin's yard and blocked the sun in her own. Martin wanted to go out and pick raspberries. Maggie felt like a dunce in the garden -- Frank had always done it all, his way -- but she wanted to be with Martin, so she put on her shoes.

"Come on, Old Dog," she said to Ernest. "Let's get out in the sun!"

Still he didn't stir.

She knelt down beside him. He was breathing quietly, deeply. His nose was cool. He seemed in a very deep sleep. She decided to let him sleep some more.

Martin was waiting at the slider for her. "Want a basket?" he asked.

She liked that about Martin. Despite her clear incompetence at picking raspberries -- she mushed some, had to taste others, and generally ended up with few in the basket -- he seemed happy to have her help, to have her next to him. She took the basket and they went out.

They had picked maybe ten of the forty feet of berries planted along the fence when they heard a sad yowl. Ernest was awake. Maggie went to let him out. But he wasn't standing at the door. He was still lying on his bed, with his eyes looking her way. "Come on, Ernest," she said. But he didn't get up.

"Something's wrong with Ernest," she called to Martin. She went in and looked at him there under the table but she was afraid to get closer, afraid she would find something wrong, afraid there was something wrong with her old sweetheart.

(You've only had him a couple of months, whispered Frank. And don't forget dogs are nothing but trouble.)

"Shh," said Maggie. Ernest looked at her.

Martin arrived and knelt down by Ernest. Ernest wagged his tail, but only once. Martin handed Maggie the baskets of berries and scratched Ernest's ears. "What's the matter, Old Guy?" asked Martin. He rubbed his ears again, then let his hand drift over Ernest's neck, his throat, his front legs. Ernest was patient, still. Martin continued down his chest, his back, his belly. Ernest winced and trembled.

"Something's wrong inside," said Martin to Maggie.

Maggie looked at Martin. She didn't know what he would do, didn't know what she wanted him to do, wanted the problem with Ernest, whatever it was, to go away. if there was a problem inside, it was probably not from hiking up the trail. Her own legs were sore, she expected his to be, but his belly? What could that be?

"Do we need to take him to the vet?" Maggie asked.

"Could," said Martin. "Or wait and see."

"Wait and see what?" asked Maggie. She was afraid she wouldn't like the answer. No matter what he said.

"Just give it time, see what his body wants to do, see if we find out more. Right now a vet would just be guessing, I suppose."

"But what could it be? We don't know, right? Wouldn't it help if we did know?"

"Help us, or help Ernest?" Martin wrapped his arms around Maggie, who was feeling tears fill her eyes. "Let's not assume it's something horrible unless we have to," he said.

She knew he was being reasonable. But she was scared. Her own belly tightened into a miserable, almost unbearable pain of sadness for Ernest. She got down on the floor and stroked the massive red body. Ernest lay quietly, not objecting but not obviously enjoying it either. She worked along the fringes of the silky ears, down the wrinkly face, under the massive jaw to the loose skin beneath it. She tenderly smoothed the skin on his chest and between his front legs. Then she ran her hands down his legs slowly, hoping to find a tender spot that could account for his malaise. But he didn't wince, didn't complain. She picked up each of his front feet and carefully checked between each toe. She cleaned out some debris. There were no thorns, no briars wedged there. She stopped.

"He doesn't feel good," she said. "What are we going to do?"

"Would you like to take him to the vet?" asked Martin.

"I don't know. I don't think he would like it. I think he just wants to be quiet."

"Would you want to go to the hospital if it were you?"

"I don't know. I wouldn't want to be sick, but I wouldn't want to go through all those exams and tests either. What about you?"

"I don't know."

They sat together on the floor with Ernest. Maggie covered him up better. She was getting uncomfortable but she didn't want to leave him.

"He's old, isn't he..." said Maggie.

"Yes," said Martin.

"I wonder how old. No one knew. They thought maybe ten, more or less. But he climbed all the way up that hill."

"And then he waited patiently where you tied him."

"Yes, that must have been an hour. Or more."

"He loves you."

"And I love him."

"He saved your life. Well, he helped you save your own life."

Maggie smiled. Yes, he had understood her. He had helped her.

And now he was worn out. And maybe something was wrong inside of him. She hadn't thought....

"What if he ate something up there? Maybe that's why he has a bellyache."

"Maybe," said Martin.

Time went by. Martin stood by the table, Maggie sat on the floor. She wouldn't last there much longer. And Ernest lay on his big red dog bed under the table and slept.

Maggie realized sometime later that Martin had left. He came back with a couple of pillows from her bed. He laid them beside Ernest's bed. Maggie lay on them and Martin covered her with part of Ernest's blanket. The day wasn't cold but the blanket was a comfort to her. Martin pulled a chair from the family room close to Maggie and sat in it. Maggie laid her arm across Ernest.

Maggie had fallen asleep when Ernest tried to get up. He was unsteady on his feet. Martin had gotten up and opened the slider and Ernest went out. He had trouble walking. Maggie watched from the floor. Martin helped Ernest walk across the deck, then helped him ease his way down the stairs, and back up after Ernest had relieved himself in a nearby spot of lawn. He had always used a spot at the back of the yard before. Martin brought him back in and offered him some water. He took a lap, then lay down again.

"I think he's pretty bad, Mags," he said.

Maggie nodded. She stood up and went to Martin. "But he's happy, isn't he? Happier than when we found him. But I wore him out!"

"You made him happy. He loves you."

"He's a very good dog, Martin. He does everything he's supposed to do. He's no trouble at all! He makes me take him on walks! He loves to go to your house! He likes the water! Don't let him die!"

"Ok," said Martin. "Maybe a vet can help him. If you think that's what he wants. But he looks content here. He's not suffering."

"Oh, Martin!"

"It's ok, Maggie. It's the cost of love."

"I know. Oh, I know." She leaned against him sobbing. She looked at the still form of Ernest and watched till she knew he was still breathing. How she loved him!

"I love you, Martin," she said.

He held her close for several minutes. "Do you want something to eat?" he asked.

"No. I couldn't," she said.

But Martin went and made sandwiches, tuna salad. He brought them over and sat her in the comfy chair from the family room and sat on its arm and handed her a plate. She looked at it. She was hungry after all. She leaned her head against Martin's arm while she ate. The knot in her belly eased. Maybe it wouldn't last forever, but for now she was with her guys.

I'm here too! insisted Frank.

"I know," said Maggie out loud.

"What did you say?" asked Martin.

"I was talking to Frank."

Martin gave her a squeeze.

Without thinking, Maggie reached over and offered her crust to Ernest, as usual.

He lifted his head and looked at her. Then he turned and flopped on his other side. He waved his front paws in the air in rapid circles. He pulled his rear legs up. He arched his back and flopped back to the side he had been lying on. Then he stood up and shook himself and took the bite of sandwich.

Maggie pinched off another piece for him. He gobbled it down.

"Better not give him any more right now," said Martin. "Let's find out if that agrees with him."

When no more sandwich was coming his way, Ernest went to the slider. Martin let him out. He walked slowly across the deck, then down the steps and all the way to the back of the yard. He was there a long time. But when he got back he was good old Ernest.

"Let's go for a walk," said Martin.

Chapter 33

Martin was tender with her for the rest of the day. They walked hand in hand through the market, stood in rapture at the bluegrass band, swooned in unison as they ate fish tacos, and avoided the dog park. Instead they walked around town looking in shop windows. They kissed openly. They bought chocolates and fed them to each other. They shared an ice cream cone.

Afterward, they went to the park where the boat launch was and sat at a picnic table and watched the sun sink down, the ferries coming and going with their dazzle of lights, the birds heading for the trees. They watched frisbee players, they followed the return of small boats. They were a-tingle with awareness of each other. They were gentle in their speech, tender in their touch, prone to smile, to laugh, to cry, to turn to each other.

They were in love, and a powerful passion was also growing strong and urgent between them. The RV was in the parking lot beckoning. As the air grew cooler and a breeze picked up, they walked toward it aware that the two-mile drive home could be perilous for their resolve, for their yeses and no's. She was 65, he was 76, and all they could think of was love. And touching and being touched. And falling into the bed instead of the driver's and co-pilot's seats.

Ernest was shivering. Martin unlocked the door and once again scooped Maggie, then Ernest, up the steps. She paused, waiting for him. He closed and locked the door. This was the moment. Would they go home now? Before he reached the top step, she reached up and whispered in his ear, "I love you."

"I'll make soup," said Martin. He slid into his seat and started the engine. She sat and buckled and smiled at him. Because she loved him they would wait. Only a little while. They had talked about marriage all day. They would wake up some morning and go off to the marriage license place in town and then go find someone to marry them. The end.

Maybe tomorrow.

A good part of the conversation had been about Ernest, to take him on their honeymoon or not. They would decide later. Another part had been about Dede. But Maggie was over Dede. She didn't think about her as a threat, or someone who should be taken along with them on their honeymoon. Martin had tried to apologize. Maggie had sat looking at him, shaking her head.

The sun had set as they pulled into the RV spot at Martin's. They quickly disembarked. The moment of unbearable passion had passed and now they bustled about getting supper picked, chopped, cooked, eaten, cleaned up. They kissed chastely at the door and Martin went home. Maggie put on her old cozy nightie and took care of hers and Ernest's bedtime needs and was asleep in moments.

Chapter 34

They did have an awkward moment first thing the next morning. It had rained in the night and continued now. The house was chilly, and Martin had gotten soaked on his way over with scrambled eggs and sausage. Ernest had opted to stay in bed, and so had Maggie. Martin stripped off his wet coat and trousers and sneakers and socks and crawled into bed with them. It made for a tight squeeze. Maggie, partially awakened, found Martin's warm presence appealing and drew closer to him. He struck sparks in her. But she was so sleepy she turned her back on him, and when she was awake again, he was making kitchen noises and all was safe, she thought, until their wedding night.

Their wedding night! She was aghast! It sounded so ... intense? Contrived? And yet hadn't she asked for it? Hadn't she set it up so their first night together would be formal and scheduled? Ew, she thought. How is that going to be? It sounded steeped in embarrassment!

Not that she hadn't had a wedding night or two, of course, she reminded herself.

Well, sort of. By the time she and Simon were married, they had been sleeping together for months! It had just happened. They were not happy in theory that it had just happened, but then they didn't stop either. So that on their wedding night, they had felt smug, experienced, though now she thought that was laughable. But she did remember feeling that way.

And then there had been Frank. Oh dear. Frank was never her lover. In so many ways he had just taken over from the missing Simon. Except there was still the need to sleep together in some sense of the word. And even as they had undressed the night of the wedding without any sign that it was anything special, they had ignored each other. They had changed in the bathroom, one after the other. There had been one bed and as Maggie had put on her pretty satin nightgown given to her by Frank's -- and Simon's -- mother as a wedding present, she had wondered how they were going to negotiate that one bed.

Her heart had still been in serious pain that night, both for the inexplicably missing Simon (the Simon she had divorced in absentia Oregon-style at the insistence of her mother-in-law, or she would not have been free to marry Frank) and for her dead baby, the sweet little boy who would have been six, almost seven, months old right now. The thought that she might love Frank was so inconceivable that it didn't enter her mind, had not once entered her mind all day. Frank's mother had engineered it all, of course. The whole plan had served her needs, namely to provide a wife for her socially backward son, and to play martyr to some degree by reminding everyone at the very large wedding that her other son, her beloved and lovable Simon, was gone. Probably dead, but that part was never spoken of. It was too soon. And Maggie had never believed it.

So Maggie hadn't given the wedding night any thought. She had kissed Frank at the wedding as people did and then had danced with him once, and had shaken hands with guests and had given and taken hugs while he stood off to the side. She didn't know if he thought she was attractive or not. She didn't know if he'd slept with anyone else, ever. She didn't know much about him and she didn't care. She only felt sad about Simon and their baby and didn't think of much else at all. She had learned to smile just to keep the peace, just to make people around her comfortable.

And now here it was, her wedding night. Frank had changed. He had emerged from the bathroom with his robe on, over what she had no idea. No frolicking exhibitionism for Frank! But that was ok.

She followed suit. The nighty from her mother-in-law -- her former and now once again mother-in-law -

- was sleek and slinky and revealed just enough of all she had to offer to appeal to just about any man, she thought. And a hand could caress a body through that fabric and find it supple -- the fabric, she meant -- and slippery enough to be pleasant and suggestive. But would Frank notice? She didn't know. She wrapped the terry robe from the hotel around her and tied the tie in not one knot but two.

She readied herself at the door. She would turn off the bathroom light before making her entrance, all the better to be subtle, she thought. Or invisible. Now that it was upon her, she was embarrassed, anticipated more embarrassment before the night was out.

She turned off the light, opened the door. The room was entirely dark. She shuffled along hoping not to bump into anything. She ran her hand along the foot of the bed. She didn't know what side Frank was on. About halfway across she felt toes, feet. They disappeared from her touch.

This would not do. He had said nothing. And neither had she. She was a married woman! A twice-married woman. She could do what was needed. Because truly it was needed. Wasn't it? She knew her level of romanticism was a bit sub-par, but she was willing to get the deed done. If Frank was. Obviously she would need at least some of Frank's attention.

But wait. As she thought back on this second wedding night, she knew she was doing Frank a disservice. He had not known what to think of this, his brother's wife. Had he? Yes, he had descended on them in their home! He had made himself part of a three-some that included Simon and her almost from the beginning. And she had thought it was because she was attractive to him, at least in part attractive. Why else? He hadn't seemed to have much in common with Simon, not the science that connected her in a profound partnership. But often she had caught Frank looking at her like a coiled snake.

So she picked at the knotted tie until it came loose, all the while determined to do her part. She had slid under the covers and faced him.

Her third wedding night, the one with Martin, promised to be fun. Once she got over the first part of actually acknowledging it was the Capital-W Capital-N Wedding Night that was often accompanied by tittering or fireworks or ceremony formal or informal, they could have a jolly time. Not necessarily much sleep, but a lot of fun.

Frank had never actually been fun, exactly. But he had loved her in a Frank sort of way, which meant a running commentary on how she was doing with life in general. That night he had started out by telling her her hands were cold. That she was on his side of the bed. That he hoped she had flossed. That night she had not decided not to care. Later she learned that that was just how he was, and she had learned to love him. A bit.

That night she had intentionally moved to his side of the bed, as he so correctly had pointed out. She had wrapped her arms around his neck so she could get yet closer to him. It helped that the light was out. She had kissed him and he had turned away so her lips met his cheek. Even so, by now she had thrown her cares to the wind and that turning away of his had made her giggle a little. It also made her try again. She was feeling sassy.

He had struggled to rearrange himself in some sort of comfortable position, or possibly to move away from her a bit. He tried his back. She slid yet closer to him and because she was dressed in slithery material she was able to slide with ease up onto him. His arms were over his head, and she could kiss his lips with ease. Then she gathered up his arms and pulled them down over her back. She slid a little this way and that. She had never enjoyed satin before but it was just the thing for this sort of wedding night.

Frank had his pajamas on. She wanted to see if he liked satin against his skin as much as she did, so in her giddy state of mind, she pushed up his shirt and gave him a feel of it. He made some sort of sound then and she thought it might be approval.

The slitheriness proved useful all in all, she recalled. Whatever impression she had had to begin with of reluctance was soon replaced by a sense of enthusiasm, hers and also his. The unlikely had become the accomplished in a matter of minutes. Breakfast the next morning had been sweet and chummy.

So wedding night number two had turned out ok, more than ok really. She wondered what kind of nighty she would wear for -- with -- Martin.

Chapter 35

Maggie decided to use the time to get some laundry done and finish off some odd chores. The afternoon was bright and lovely, and she also indulged in some time on the deck with Ernest, who was still acting a bit tired. She missed Martin but was feeling virtuous for letting him attend to his own things.

But he was knocking at the door after all. Surprised, she got herself up off the deck and stiffly walked to the door. By the time she got there he had knocked again. Had she locked it? Why didn't he just come in?

Why indeed! It wasn't Martin!

It was Duncan. He had on his jacket and bow tie, so he'd probably come right from the office, and in fact it seemed a bit early still for him to be leaving work. Or maybe he had shorter hours these days.

"Hi, Duncan," she said. "Come on in! I'm surprised to see you. I suppose you brought that paperwork about the land? You didn't need to bother...."

He came in and she motioned him to the living room and a comfortable chair there. It's possible, she thought, that he had never been in their home before, even when he and Frank had had estate things to talk about. In any case, he seemed ill at ease. Why, she wondered.

Duncan had worn a hat, which he was now holding and rotating in his uneasy hands. He wasn't looking at Maggie.

"Nice of you to come," she said. She was at a loss to guess why he was there.

"Oh, I'm so glad!" he said. He had tripped on his way down the two little stairs to the living room. And was she smelling alcohol?

That was a bit over-enthusiastic, but if he would just continue, maybe she'd learn something about why he was so over-wrought. Or why he was there at all.

All she could think of was his possible dislike or mistrust of Martin, but that might have been just her imagination. Or maybe he knows things, opined her inner Frank. She mentally said 'shhh'.

"How times change!" he said. "Frank gone, Doris gone. May they rest in peace."

"Indeed," said Maggie. She was wondering why he was here by mentally running through the possible places where important papers might be filed. Stashed. Stacked. Or maybe he was here about the land donation, something she hadn't gotten back to him about. But a house call?

“I suppose you miss him terribly,” said Duncan, and Maggie took the liberty of supposing he was still talking about Frank.

“Don’t you?” he asked.

She reviewed quickly and was able to pick up the train of thought. Miss Frank. Well, in some ways it was very much like he was still there. But that would be hard to explain.

“Well, I miss Doris,” said Duncan. “I don’t like going home to an empty house. I’ve thought of downsizing.”

Maggie wondered if he was hinting that she should downsize? That could have something to do with marrying Martin, maybe? To keep her house from him? But she liked her house, and she hoped she had years to live in it. And now instead of one person, she would have three. Not a good time to down-size. Of course Duncan didn’t know about Ernest.

But Duncan was saying, “So much space for a single person. I never thought I’d be all alone!”

Maggie did her best to look sympathetic. She couldn’t remember where Duncan and Doris had lived. But none of it explained what he was doing there.

“Frank left an office full of papers. I can’t imagine what to do with them!”

"That's ok," offered Duncan helpfully. "And I suppose you have all sorts of fabric and yarn and so on? It really doesn't matter!"

Maggie understood perfectly well that it wouldn't matter to Duncan. Though probably it had for Doris, whom she could so easily picture being one of the regulars at the knit shop. As for her, she was more concerned about the stacks of magazines she had lying about, but once she made up her mind to it, she could certainly throw them all in the trash in a matter of an hour.

But what did that have to do with why he was here, or his need to down-size?

"To tell you the truth," he was continuing, "I had a hard time throwing out Doris's sewing, her clothes too! But after our little visit the other day, I got right down to it and cleaned out everything and feel ever so much better about moving on!"

Maggie was sure now that she was smelling alcohol on his breath. Had he been so upset by cleaning out Doris's belongings that he had taken to drink?

"Well, good for you, Duncan!" said Maggie. She was thinking they might move beyond this subject, and if it was upsetting to him, maybe she could help get the conversation back on track. Whatever track that was. She was getting hungry, she was afraid that Ernest might come in, or worst of all, that Martin might come back, since Duncan had seemed a bit disapproving of him.

But she was missing something again. He was definitely sounding more enthusiastic. "Oh, Maggie, I'm so glad you see it that way! I know you were fond of Doris and would always try to keep her best interests in mind!"

Maggie was glad it seemed that way, but what had she said? She had been fond of Doris. (No you weren't, exhorted Frank. You thought she was a gossip!) And if he was more at peace about moving on, well good!

He seemed to have come to some sort of understanding. Maybe he had just needed a friend to confess to about Doris's belongings. Because he had stopped twirling his hat, and he was beaming at her.

"I'm so glad we've had this little talk, Maggie, and that we see eye to eye, and that I've gotten here in time. Let's set the date right now!" And having said this, he leapt up and gave her a kiss on the cheek and said, "Let's go celebrate over a nice supper downtown!"

Maggie was starving and this last sounded like progress, so she grabbed her summer jacket against the evening chill and was ready to go out the door before he had climbed the steps from the living room. He reached for her, so she gave him her hand, assuming that he needed to be steadied. But he surprised her by raising her hand to his lips and kissing it moistly several times.

She pulled it back and wanted to wipe it on the seat of her jeans, but restrained herself. Still it left a chill spot on the back of her hand.

"Let's not wait," he said, so she opened the door.

He chuckled. "That's what I love about you, Maggie! Always having fun. I meant -- you knew this of course -- let's not wait to set the date. I'm not getting any younger and neither are you!"

She looked at him silently. "What?"

"The wedding! Let's not wait any longer! You can bring your fabric, I made room for it! Let's eat!"

Click click click went Maggie's brain. All the pieces fit. But this time she didn't believe the story that was emerging. So she decided to be nice to poor Duncan, have a pleasant dinner, and not commit or even come close to committing to anything. Because, she realized, she could find herself with Doris's ring on her finger.

And that would be hard to explain to Martin.

So they ate fish tacos at the seafood place. Duncan was chatty and sweet. He ordered a couple of beers. And he talked about Doris a lot. He rubbed Maggie's arm or squeezed her hand. And he never stopped smiling.

And she ate and smiled and listened very carefully and vowed never to say yes to anything. And then she told him she was really tired. She was concerned about Ernest out on the deck, though the summer sun had not actually set and there was nothing he could do except sound like a hound in distress and have the neighbors report her to the HOA. And maybe that one neighbor would rescue him and all would be well.

Meanwhile Duncan was looking a little droopy. Maggie hurried to finish her second taco, stood up, put on her jacket, and when he offered it, took his hand. But only until he was standing. Then she hurried -- she hadn't intended to hurry exactly, but she wanted this very peculiar evening to be over -- to the car. She had to wait till Duncan unlocked it.

When they got to her place, she hopped out of the car, ran around to the driver's side, and offered Duncan her hand to shake. She had thought about how to avoid a kiss on the lips all the way home, thinking on the one hand how absurd it was to worry about such a thing, and on the other how he was rubbing her hand with his when he should have been keeping it on the steering wheel, and how much more he might have in mind once the car had stopped.

So she offered her hand and when he moved it to his lips, she shook it up and down and let go and fairly skipped to the front door, waving good night. He flashed the headlights at her.

She let Ernest in and started to bed. As an afterthought, she went back to the family room, gathered up all her magazines, and dumped them in the recycling. Might as well make room for Martin!

Chapter 36

The phone rang rather early the next morning. She was just coming out of the shower. It was Duncan.

"I'm sorry, Maggie," he said. "I had one too many last night before I came over. I'm afraid I made a fool of myself. Forget everything I said, whatever it was. Whatever I did. Have a good day. And oh yes, don't under any circumstances marry Martin."

He hung up, and Martin, who was dishing up oatmeal, said, "Who was that?"

"Boyfriend," said Maggie.

Chapter 37

They were headed out in the boat again. The weather was perfect and the forecast said the seas would remain calm for the next several days. They had breakfast, gathered their things, and were out the door by 8 AM.

They'd had no time for conversation, but as soon as they were underway in the truck, the boat on the trailer behind them, Martin said, "Which boyfriend?"

"Haha!" said Maggie with a big grin.

"What?" he asked.

"You live next door! How many boyfriends have you seen coming and going?"

"I can't see your house from mine. For all I know, you have a dozen, or at least two or three. I know I'm not the only one. You have Frank, Simon, and whoever this one was...."

Maggie was astounded that he seemed sincere, genuinely questioning her.

"Well, you forgot Ernest!" she said.

"If you don't want to tell me, it's ok," he said.

"That? On the phone? That was Duncan. The lawyer."

"What did he want?"

"I stopped by Duncan's office a few days ago, then he came by the house yesterday afternoon." She stopped right before she added, 'and proposed marriage to me.'

What did he want? Good question.

Frank had his opinion: he wants that land for himself.

So without thinking much of it, Maggie said, "I think he wants to get his hands on some land I own, now that Frank's gone."

She realized as she said it that she never would have mentioned the land in the normal course of conversation, especially after the warnings Duncan had issued, that perhaps Martin wanted to marry her for her land, maybe for her house. Ridiculous!

But now that she'd said it, she looked at him frankly to see what his reaction was.

And Martin was staring at her.

And she didn't know what that meant. She was trying to think it through when he said, "How would he do that? Unless he married you."

And then Maggie blurted out, "Well, he did ask."

And then she realized that what Martin had said could mean he had already figured out that the best way to get her land was to marry her.

But then he said, "But it would make more sense for you to just sell it. Or donate it, for that matter, if it's close to the Forestlands property."

And then it seemed as though he heard her words for the first time, Duncan's words: "Well, he did ask."

Because Martin said, "Well, he can't have you. Give him your land if you choose, but marry me, please, Maggie!"

They had a nice day on the beach of their little island. All was calm, little wind, few waves, also maybe not as much fun as the first time: no storm to hide from, for one thing, and then there was the strange silence between them. Maggie was thinking about what Duncan had said, and then what Martin had said, and now what Frank was saying: I wonder what else you don't know, Maggie, my love.

As for Martin, he was also very quiet. But Maggie had so much on her mind that she didn't pay much attention.

The sun was setting as they arrived back at the boat ramp, and soon they had had their soup for supper and had gone their separate ways, Martin to his house and Maggie, Ernest, and of course Frank to their house and a restless, sleepless night.

Chapter 38

Maggie left Ernest home, outside on the porch in the corner under the eaves and out of the wind. Mostly. And if it didn't rain hard, and the wind didn't blow much -- if this October storm was the last one of summer instead of the first one of winter -- he would be all right. And if it poured, surely Martin, wherever he was, would check on Ernest just due to an abundance of caution.

All this Maggie thought to herself as she visualized a lovely lavender skein down at the knit shop, and the cozy group of ladies she knew from there and what fun it would be to stop in and sit and knit for a while.

And maybe she should also go to the bank and see to things, given that she was about to go on a long trip.

As Maggie drove along on her own, though, especially as she drove into town and could see Duncan's office towering above the other downtown buildings, she thought of the old lawyer's admonition to her that no matter what, she mustn't marry Martin!

It was confusing, because the very thought that she would soon be married to him made her deeply happy, and she was counting the days, the few days, until all the little practical details were taken care of and they would load up the RV for the long wedding trip, make a brief stop at the Justice of the Peace, and head down the highway as husband and wife.

But she could still stop it!

And why would she want to do that? She didn't.

But Duncan had issued a dire warning, had been firm in his admonition, and then had closed his lips and had given her not a single clue more.

All this weighed heavily on her, and somewhere between the post office and knit shop it dawned on her that she would have to ask Martin if there was anything more he wanted to tell her.

And that was something she couldn't picture doing. How do you say to someone you love, darling, my lawyer says I shouldn't marry you under any circumstances. What more can you tell me?

No, that would not do.

Nor could she picture asking him if there was anything he would like to tell her before they tied the knot. For heaven's sake, he was seventy-six years old! Surely there were many things a person might say in response to a question like that without ever even understanding what she was asking about.

She bought a lovely lavender skein of bamboo yarn. The idea of yarn made from bamboo was enticing. She didn't know what she wanted to make, but she could take it home till she figured it out. She idly thumbed through a few pattern books just because she loved them. Not that she knit very often. And not that she was very good at finishing things and using them.

The books were spread out on a large table and some of her knit-shop friends were knitting together, while a small class was receiving instruction in the room to the back. Maggie settled in as she had done so many times before. It was a cozy place to her, a place where she could believe she would do all she dreamed of doing, in knitting and life.

The bell dinged as more women – and the occasional husband – came in or went out. It had always been thus. Once she had brought Frank, once she had offered to bring Martin but he'd said he'd watch Ernest outside. That time she hadn't sat and settled in but had hurried back without doing her intended errand.

Today she had no intended errand but that little purchase, she just wanted to be on her own, to think and cogitate. So she thumbed through the pattern book idly without seeing anything. She caught bits of conversation going on around her, smiled vaguely when someone brushed past her, looked without seeing at her purchase.

A gust of wind pulled at the door as other customers came in, and the women shook raindrops off their umbrellas before entering. How long had it been raining? It sounded heavy. Maggie got up to walk around some shelves so she could see out the window. The rain had already caused little rivers to form in the gutters. She should go home.

Or maybe it would be better to wait it out. It was October. Was this a late summer shower, or an early winter storm, one that could last for days?

Ernest! He was on the porch. A real storm would whip rain in stinging sheets into every corner, even under the overhang that protected him. Would Martin be home to check on him?

She looked at her own skimpy jacket. She would be soaked before she could get to her car! She'd borrow the shop's phone and call Martin.

She tried his line, then hers, but there was no answer.

A rosy lady, the shop owner, came over to her. Helen was a warm sort of person, the kind who always wore an apron and who knew how to make things right. She was the center of knit-shop life. She was easy to talk to.

And Maggie found herself blurting out: My dog! My dog may be getting soaked out on the porch! I should go rescue him!

Both women turned to the window. The rain seemed to be coming down even harder.

"Isn't there someone who can take him in for you, Maggie?" asked Helen. "You'll drown if you go out in this! You'll be soaked!"

"I can't reach him!" said Maggie. "I tried calling!"

Helen looked confused. "You tried calling someone?"

"Yes, Martin," said Maggie, talking over the rain. We're getting married next week," Maggie blurted out.

A hush came over the knitters. Not a click or clack or quiet voice could be heard. And when Maggie turned back from the window, every eye in the knit shop was on her.

Maggie's first instinct was to hide. She had not intended to tell anyone that she was getting married, and right there before her eyes was verification that it would just put the world on high alert and everyone would eye her with suspicion and new interest, and all that made her blush and turn back to look out the window.

She stood looking at the grayness of the day and the sheets of unabated rain and held her breath, listening for the clicking of the knitting needles to begin again. But they didn't. But as she stood there looking out at the bleak rain, she did hear the knitters start to talk, pretty much all at once. One word stuck out: Martin.

Maggie was about to turn back to them out of curiosity, but Helen put her arm on Maggie's shoulder companionably and together they watched the rain. Maggie wasn't sure that the shop-owner's intention had been to keep her from the conversation, but Maggie was grateful enough for the guidance and the extra few seconds to listen and not say something she regretted to the half dozen women now speaking amongst themselves in low tones.

Oh, if only Martin would arrive and rescue her!

But then what? She would die of curiosity forever after. What were these women saying about Martin? And why? And weren't there many Martins in the world? Why were they certain that she had meant that one Martin, the one she was marrying, instead of some other? And what was so very interesting about hers? And how did they all happen to know him?

A dreadful thought came to her. These women must all be former girlfriends of his, of Martin the friendly man, the rescuer. (Or, said the long-silent but currently quite interested though dead former husband Frank, Martin the manly friend.) (SHUT UP, FRANK and go back to where you belong, hissed Maggie, just a bit audibly.)

"What did you say?" encouraged Helen.

Maggie was going to say, "nothing", but she had a better idea. "I said, how is it that they all know Martin?"

And with this question, which suddenly seemed perfectly normal and polite to ask, given that they were all talking about him anyway, she whirled toward the table and asked just that: "How do you all know Martin?"

The ladies were all silent, all the mouths shutting at once. Maggie turned back to see Helen, still at the window, shaking her head at them, just slightly. When Maggie looked at her, Helen dropped her eyes.

It dawned on Maggie all at once that this was a real thing that was happening. This was not some little whispering of Martin's name, but some actual sharing of information, or at least gossip, something that was truly of interest to them.

She put her hands on her hips. "Ok, out with it," she said.

She wondered at herself for that. It wasn't all that Maggie-like for her to talk to other grown-ups in such a forthright way. It must be all the practice she had been having with Frank.

The group sat awkward and silent.

At last one of the knitters, one she had seen only once or twice before, said, "Did you say you were marrying

Martin, that tall white-haired guy with the baseball cap?"

"Yes, I am, and yes, that's the Martin I am talking about. He and I are getting married in a few days."

The speaker looked around for support. Everyone remained silent due to the way they were holding their lips tightly shut. Even Helen remained silent.

"Well, why are you all talking about him?" Maggie asked. "What is he to you?"

Helen stepped in. "The rain has slowed down. Why don't we all go out and take a walk or go get some ice cream!"

Maggie thought Helen sounded as though she were chirping. Maggie was still curious, but also worried that something horrible was in everyone's mind, something they knew about Martin that she didn't, something the whole world knew and she was the only one who didn't.

(Deep inside she sought out Frank to see if he knew, but he was strangely silent.)

The women were pushing out their chairs, bundling up their knitting, throwing away their coffee cups. Maggie grabbed that moment to take her tiny purchase and run out the door.

She would ask Martin. Somehow. And she would ask him ... soon. She'd better ask him soon or forever hold her peace.

Maggie was dampish but not soaked by the time she got to the car. Failing to outpace the other women from the class who were going in the same direction she was, she had dropped back and then crossed the street, and then she had had to cross it again to reach her car. Her hair was soaked and dripping, her jacket had not protected her shoulders, and she was cold.

And now she had to go home and either get warmed up by that guy everyone seemed to know better than she did, or not get warmed up and spend a dreary night of dashed plans and unbearable curiosity.

And then there was Ernest. How was he?

Chapter 39

The western sky looked as though another storm cell was fast approaching, and the afternoon sun was weak. She desperately wanted to get home. A traffic light stopped her, then another. While she waited, a devilish plan formed in her brain, fulminating from somewhere subterranean, dark, and – at the moment, anyway – delightful!

She had her plan in place just as the light turned green and would have let her go straight ahead toward home. But she turned right, barely yielding to turning traffic. She was headed downtown.

She had no trouble finding a parking place at Duncan's office, and the adrenalin that had fired through her system when she came up with this outrageous idea – this clever, necessary, perfectly reasonable, and yes, outrageous – idea, this adrenalin helped her bounce up the steps, the two extra-long stories of steps, with ease.

She banged on Duncan's door with insistent aggression. She thought she heard him say come in, so she went in. Duncan's elderly part-time secretary

Mildred took a step back as Maggie approached the front counter.

"I need to see Duncan now, " said Maggie, with all the patience she had.

"Hi, Maggie," said Mildred weakly. "He's about to leave for an appointment."

"When does he get back?" Maggie asked. She had been on the verge of barging into his office and hijacking his keys so he couldn't leave, but then a new idea overtook her. It would work if he'd be back by suppertime....

The pixie devil in Maggie was giving way to a much more fearsome creature, Maggie in full frontal attack, Maggie as a force of nature.

Maggie grabbed a nearby pad of paper, and with barely a moment's thought, scribbled an ill-tempered, ill-bred note to Duncan. Then she tore it up and pinched it into tiny bits and put it in her purse. Her next attempt was more like buttercream frosting, so smooth and sweet was it.

With the deep satisfaction of a job well done, and with a grin on her face – maybe a bit of a scary grin – Maggie handed the note to Mildred.

"See that he gets this on his way out," instructed Maggie.

Then she twirled about, swirling her cape, as it were, across her shoulder, and plunged into the night. It was still afternoon but the feeble sunlight did not add to the drama of the situation, nor did her genteel jacket substitute for a cape. But no matter – her imagination was on after-burner and she fairly flew down the stairs and put the pedal to the metal and careened homeward.

Chapter 40

Maggie had chilled down quite a bit by the time she pulled into her driveway, and in fact she was shivering. Her thoughts were on Ernest, on the routine and lovely hug from Martin, a few kisses...and then she remembered the note she had written to Duncan.

And the whole afternoon came thundering back. What had been going on about Martin? Something real, apparently, far more than he had told her. She could ask him, or she could entice Duncan to tell her. Just in case it really mattered. Since so many people felt it did.

Her stomach spasmed as she thought about how she had intended to weasel it from him. Here, in her own yard, the idea she'd thought so brilliant seemed suddenly quite sick.

As she closed the car door, her front door opened and Ernest came wagging toward her. He seemed dry and happy, perhaps a bit eager to get back inside, as she was herself. Her wet jacket had to give way to a hot shower and bathrobe or she would have pneumonia by dawn.

Martin was standing in the doorway. He reached out for his hug. She didn't know what to do. She could smell a hot meal. Her dog was happy and dry and well. Martin was helping her out of her jacket, sending her off to her room for her hot shower. He was so good to her.

But everyone who heard she was marrying him seemed shocked. WHY!???! She had to find out.

As she stood in the steamy shower, the conversation with Duncan that she had set in motion became a dreaded weight. She gasped, hunkered down so she was grasping her knees, screaming silently to herself. How could she?

She thought over and over about the note she'd left him. Was there any room for ambiguity in it? Dearest Duncan? I want to spend time with you? She fell onto hands and knees and was almost literally sick to her stomach.

Duncan was a nice man, a lonely man! (SO vulnerable, thought Maggie.) A man who had asked her to marry him (granted in a moment of alcohol-laced ill-advised concern for her). And now she was...what? Abusing him, yes, and betraying him, and deceiving him, and using him. ALL these ugly things!

All in desperation to find out about Martin!

NO, that wasn't it. All in love for Martin, in hope that she wasn't making a mistake, in desperation to end up married to him because he was as good as she'd thought.

She dried herself, dried her hair, put on her clothes, her special dress, her special shoes, her lipstick even. She would have to see it through.

Not the IT she had first had in mind though, definitely not that IT. She would simply need to go and apologize and do what she could to mend his feelings.

When she emerged dressed in her finest from her bedroom, Martin did a literal double-take. Ernest sniffed her all over, having never experienced this combination of clothing and Maggie before. Maggie said, "I have to go out."

She knew it wouldn't do but at least it was the truth.

The amazing Martin said OK, see you later, love you...

Chapter 41

The wind was whipping leaves from trees. The rain, torrential now, was beating the leaves into the pavement. The car was pulverizing them, or slipping and sliding on them, by turns. The windshield was foggy on the inside with her intense and rapid breathing and bleary with a heavy downpour on the outside. She couldn't see the road, only the smeared-out lights from oncoming rush-hour traffic, namely a car or two every minute. Her tear-filled eyes made it all worse.

Maggie inched along, fearful of not seeing something and killing herself or someone else. And, truth be known, she never wanted to arrive and that may have had an impact on her rate of progress.

She had invited him to dinner at an old, funky seafood restaurant that was both expensive and deserted. She was gratified to see there were only two other cars in the vast parking lot. She had no idea if either was his, but in the past few minutes she had been entertaining the idea that maybe he'd have decided to stay home on the wet evening. Or maybe he'd already had a date? Or maybe his appointment had run late, or he'd had an evening appointment already on his calendar. Or maybe he hadn't been able to read her handwriting. Or maybe – now here was a real hope -- Mildred had forgotten to give him the note!

She sat in the car for a bit. What would she do? What would the real Maggie do? What would the old Maggie have done?

Frank spoke up. The old Maggie would be home alone watching TV!

And Maggie realized then that she was on new turf because she had asked for it, had opened the door – literally – to it, and it had all started with rescuing an old, dying dog.

"And," Maggie said in a loud voice to herself, "that old dying dog was YOU, Maggie! YOU!

"And," she added, "you aren't like that anymore. You're in love, you're the opposite of lonely (whatever that is, said Frank), you've created a mess. And that's because, Maggie-girl, you're not very practiced at life, are you....?"

"NO I'M NOT!" she hollered back. "Time to go learn by doing, I guess."

Chapter 42

She opened the car door. The rain was taking a break. She had only twenty feet or so to the door with the big OPEN sign on it. It was so black out that it seemed like midnight. She looked at her watch. 6:30, right on time. Her stomach lurched.

She pulled the big heavy wood door open against the wind, and slid into the warm lobby. She barely glanced at the old sailing-ship décor. She wiped her wet feet on the doormat, hesitated, girded up her loins (so to speak), and stepped forward. Duncan rose from a bench against the far wall, and came to greet her.

Both his hands were outstretched to her, and he pulled her in so he could kiss her, first on the cheek, chastely, and then on the lips. More than once on the lips. Then he tucked her arm in his, pulled her close, and walked her to a table he had already arranged for. He never took his eyes off of her.

Maggie kept her eyes on the carpet. She didn't dare meet his. When he pulled out her chair – such a gentleman – she busied herself with her napkin. They had the end table in the quietest corner of the restaurant, where they could look out at the waves and Guemes Island on the other side of the channel and at the occasional passing boat, if it had its running lights on.

Not that there was a noisy corner to this restaurant. The other guests – guest? – was perhaps in the bar. They had the whole of it to themselves.

It was now or never. Maggie looked up at Duncan, who had sat across from her. She was framing her words so she might do the least amount of damage. Duncan was a sweetheart, and a friend, as well as her lawyer. She realized all this as she formulated that first sentence. (Frank said, my lawyer too.) That Frank was there looking out for her, or at least keeping her company, made her smile a little.

And that gave Duncan his opening. "You look lovely tonight, Maggie! So good of you to arrange this little time together."

Maggie's agitation grew. She dabbed at the roll with her buttered knife but there was no way she was going to be able to eat anything with her stomach in turmoil like this.

And what was she going to say now?

And what was it that Duncan had just said?

"So good of you to arrange this little time together (yes, she had heard all that) before you get married."

What?

"...before you get married" he'd said.

She mulled that over. It actually took no time at all: he wasn't here on a date, he was here as an old friend saying goodbye to the old Maggie who was now going to start a new life.

"What?" she asked with as much intelligence as she could gather together from her woolly agitated brain. It sounded more like WUT?

He took her hand and put the butter knife on the plate. He said, "Maggie, look."

Maggie was looking at her dress, at the hem of the tablecloth, at the napkin in her lap.

"No, Maggie, look up here!"

Duncan sounded as though he were smiling, and then she did look up and saw that delightful twinkle in his eyes and she smiled.

"It's nice of you, as I said. And I also think you'd like to have a bit of time together with just me:" (here her stomach lurched again) "so I can explain what I meant by not marrying Martin."

Maggie was beside herself. She covered her face with her hands. She sighed. She began to sob.

"Shh, shh," he said. "We don't want a scene, we want a story! It's a long story and we'll need the whole of dinner AND dessert to get it told." He was twinkling again.

Maggie dried her eyes. She looked straight at him, and he met her stare.

Chapter 43

They ate their shrimp alfredo, gummy as it was, and then Duncan laid down his fork and patted his mouth with his napkin. Maggie knew the time had come and that her future, all of it, might depend on what he would say in these next minutes or hours. She settled down to listen.

But he said, "Come back to my office. The chairs are comfortable and I have some things you'll want to see. And you may want some privacy."

She mulled that over. She was game to go to his office in any case.

He had walked to the restaurant, so she drove them, stopping at his suggestion at the Lopez Island ice cream place to get everyone's favorite treat. Hers was peppermint ice cream with hot fudge sauce and whipped cream. His was a deep red raspberry sorbet. They carried it take-out style around the corner to his office entrance and up the long stairwell.

He hung their coats and installed her in a huge real-leather chair of ancient vintage. He sat behind his desk, as he always did.

And so began the long tale of Martin, her beloved, the well-known, the kind, the loving, the seemingly predictable, the soon-to-be husband.

Chapter 44

"Martin," said Duncan, "used to live in the middle of the state. He had an antique business year-round, and a boat rental in the summer in addition. He had a wife, name of Winona, and two children, lovely kids, Alice and Andrew. Winona was a bit of a handful, came and went, left the kids with anyone who would watch them, or left them alone. When Martin was not at work, of course he had them with him."

Maggie had wondered whether he'd had kids. She turned it over in her mind. Why would he not have kids? But certainly he had never mentioned it.

Duncan was going on. "Sometime when the kids were about 10 and 12, they disappeared. Winona pointed her finger at Martin, claiming he had abducted them. It seemed so unlikely that everyone thought it was a joke. But Winona kept insisting, and an investigation was begun. Nothing came of the investigation, though, and Martin appeared to be doing business as usual – being as normal as a person can be when his kids have gone missing.

"Winona then claimed he had taken them to his mother and that she didn't know where that was. No one could remember Martin being gone – it was a small town and people know these things about each other – and Martin invited anyone who believed Winona to go visit his mother and see for themselves.

"Martin had plenty of reasons to believe Winona had taken them herself, though why she'd do such a thing was something no one could guess. And when it was suggested to her, she became hysterical.

"Meanwhile the clock was ticking and worry about the kids' survival grew throughout the community and then the state, all dissected in newspapers and TV news. Then Winona disappeared."

At this Maggie started shaking her head. It was all like some tale of a remote time and place that had nothing to do with anyone she knew.

"At this point, the community turned against Martin. He was arrested. Murder and kidnapping were just some of the accusations. He pointed out that the most likely scenario was that Winona had taken them to begin with and was now joining them wherever she had hidden them, but the townsfolk had made up their minds and he was just about lynched for stealing his own kids.

"It got worse. There was no sign of any of his family. As time went by, he was convicted of custodial interference and put in jail. He lost his businesses of course. The years went by and pretty much all of it was forgotten. He got out of prison, he moved here, he had barely escaped a murder charge, he had served his time, but his name was recognized wherever he went from months if not years of newspaper articles. He could barely hold down a job before someone would point the finger at him and say, 'hey, it's that guy who murdered his wife and kids' or some such.

Then several years ago, he said he got a phone call from his daughter. I think she was maybe 30 or 35 by then. He thought it was a prank at first but she remembered him well and could tell him not only factual things like his birthday and his name, but also little pet games they had together, stories she loved – and she could tell him where she had been and how she had gotten there and how she had found him."

Maggie was still in a state of disbelief. He had a grown daughter! Then why hadn't he mentioned her? And why was everyone still on edge about him if the daughter had shown up?

Duncan was looking at her. She had the impression that he was trying to decide whether to tell her more of the story.

"There's more?" she asked. She didn't know if she wanted to know the rest, but she'd never be at peace if she didn't.

"There's more."

"It's bad, I guess," said Maggie.

"It depends on your point of view, and how much you love Martin, and how much faith you have in him," he said cryptically.

Maggie contemplated that. What more could there be?

But she knew she was all-in. She couldn't imagine Martin doing anything bad, and so far he sounded as though he'd been an unwitting victim of a mad woman.

"Yes, Duncan, tell me all of it. Whatever it is."

"Hmmm," he said. "Well, Maggie, I'll treat you like the mature woman you are. You deserve to hear it if you want to. And mind you, I probably don't know all of it myself. But from what I do know you'll see why he has a certain notoriety, why his name is known far and wide and causes a stir. Especially among women."

Maggie had her own theory about why he caused a stir among women. She'd been thinking along those lines herself, that he may have dated many of these women, including the ones at the knit-shop, had perhaps taken them to the beach, out to the islands, to the state park. But that might cause discretion on their part, not a universal abhorrence or curiosity.

"Go on, Duncan," Maggie said. "And don't stop until you are through." She knew she was sounding a bit testy, but her anxiety was building up and it was also getting late. The ice cream had long since melted, forgotten. Martin would be worried about her.

At least she thought he would.

And then something happened. Doubt started to creep in. What if he... What if his stories about those women were cover-ups? What if things had happened? She didn't know what things, but something ugly.

She caught herself. No, she couldn't believe it any more than she could believe Ernest would turn into a wolf and eat her in her sleep one night.

"Duncan, NOW! Please!"

"OK," said Duncan. "But first, Maggie, I want to say that I do believe he's a good man, and most of what people say about him is circumstantial."

"Duncan!"

"Ok, well, Alice and her dad got together. She had a kid of her own, a boy aged about 8, I think. She was single. She didn't know where her mother was, or her brother. It was the story she told that caused all the trouble.

"She was leery of him when she saw him for the first time after all those years. She had sought the meeting, but it was clear she was scared. The first thing she said was, 'Why did you take us away from Mommy?'"

Maggie gasped.

"I'm sure Martin had thought he would at last be exonerated. His daughter had not been a small child, deceived into believing some story. So her words carried a great deal of weight. And in the end, even though it was not her wish, Martin was accused again of harming his kids.

"What Alice remembered is really important. I feel it holds the keys to the case, and to Martin's innocence, if he is indeed innocent. So I'm going to give you her statement, the one she gave to the police after she met with Martin."

"Why did she go see Martin when she was so sure he had kidnapped her?" asked Maggie.

"That is a good question, and I hope you ask yourself exactly that again after you read her statement."

"Ok," said Maggie. "Let me read it and maybe it will help me understand. Because right now, it's all very confusing. And it doesn't sound like the Martin I know."

Duncan got up and carried a paper across the room to her. It was a copy of a typed list, one from an old typewriter. The first item was smudged but she could figure it out. It said, "My dad kidnapped me and my brother when I was 12 years old."

Maggie gasped. The phone rang.

Duncan picked it up. Maggie had called Martin to let him know where she was, so this would of course be Martin. Maggie held her breath while Duncan fielded the call. Maggie was thinking that she couldn't go home now, not with this piece of paper at least. She figured Duncan would make an excuse for her, whatever it might be, to explain her lengthy absence.

So she was surprised when he said, "Martin, why don't you come down to my office. Maggie has some questions for you. Let's do it now instead of waiting till morning, and let the poor dear get some sleep."

Maggie was suddenly extraordinarily tired, now that Duncan had mentioned getting sleep. But Martin? Here? Presumably to talk about these awkward things that were causing her such pain, that had obviously caused him not only pain but his entire family life?

And that is exactly what they arranged. He would be on his way in a few minutes.

Maggie was experiencing waves and waves of mixed feelings. Martin here, at her side. Martin her beloved. Martin the Murderer. And Duncan, helping her and demanding explanations of Martin for her sake.

And Maggie just wanted to go home. Not be part of this. Not hold Martin accountable for this insanity.

And that is exactly what she said when he walked in the door ten minutes later: "Martin, I want to go home!"

Martin hesitated. Then he nodded grimly to her, thanked Duncan with another nod, and took her elbow. They were down the stairs and into the truck in no time. She didn't care if she left her car – she could always get it tomorrow.

Chapter 45

And now what?

They rode along in silence. At the house, Martin opened the truck door for her and helped her slide to the ground. Ernest was in the picture window jumping up and down. All was as usual.

But it wasn't. The paper from Duncan was already crushed from her having checked it so many times, so fearful she was that it would fall out of her pocket and Martin would know she had it.

And so what if he knew she had it? Had he ever seen it? Did he know Duncan had a copy – or maybe this was the original?

So many questions! Not the least of which was what was going to happen now. What must Martin be thinking, to be called to Duncan's office like that without explanation. And yet he seemed extraordinarily accepting. Maybe Duncan had played some role back in the days of these accusations Martin had endured. (Or deserved, suggested Frank. And when Maggie silently told him to shut up, added, "I'm just trying to keep you safe. And Maggie stopped dead in her tracks on the way to the door in silent amazement.). But then her train of thought resumed: Maybe this, maybe that. Nothing made sense to Maggie and so she put one foot in front of the other and hoped she hadn't brushed away his arm when he put it around her so they could walk to the door together, as he always did.

And now what would she do? She was tired. She was shivering again, maybe from the dark cold of the autumn evening. Or maybe from that deep hopelessness that was rising up in her, a hopelessness she had never felt as a widow, not the first time and not the second time, and not the hopelessness of losing her baby. This was clearly the hopelessness of losing the truest love of her life and it was happening while she watched right there in her front hall.

Ernest had run up to them. He had nuzzled Martin's hand. He had stepped toward Maggie, but then he had turned with a whimper and gone into the bedroom and climbed stiffly and slowly up on the bed.

A moment of deep despair had descended on all three – on all four if you counted Frank – and she was convinced, for that moment, that she would not survive it. She felt her knees buckle. Nothing seemed good to her but the approaching floor, so she lay down on it and rolled herself into a ball.

And Martin stood over her with his hands on his hips, saying nothing. Waiting, maybe.

She waited too. Her supper was rebelling and she wondered if she needed to crawl to the bathroom so as not to make a mess if it abandoned her. Or maybe she could wait it out. Because Martin was still standing there, and he was staring at her, and if he was a murderer he could stamp out her life in a moment and she would not object.

And then a trickle of hope came back to her. It was a beckoning from the bedroom. Ernest sang a high note of hound-shaped tones, then dropped his voice and whimpered.

Maggie rose to her feet and threw off her coat, Martin forgotten. She launched herself indelicately onto the bed and grabbed Ernest by the neck and held him tight. He licked her face and neck and arms. She smoothed the wrinkles from his face, the hopeless and permanent and darling wrinkles. He closed his eyes and relaxed and seemed to go to sleep.

Maggie may have dozed, too.

But disturbing thoughts roused her. It all came flooding back. She rolled off the bed, leaving the sleeping red giant behind. He didn't stir. She brushed herself off, tidied her hair, tried to remember if she'd heard the front door close, because the entire house was dark.

Stealthily she slid off her shoes and walked into the living room. The street light up the street was yellow and feeble but strong enough to show her that the room was empty. Or, no, wait, it wasn't. A shaft of silver hair divulged Martin sitting in the corner chair. He was still, as still as death. She thought he must be asleep. But she caught a glint of one eye and knew he was watching her.

Which was either good or bad. He was still here. He might murder her or hug her, be understanding or angry. She stood transfixed trying to figure out all the options he had at that moment. Because of course he knew that she knew ... something.

And what did she know? Nothing, nothing at all.

She patted her pocket for the partly read paper, but it had been in her coat pocket, not in her dress. And where had she put her coat?

She turned a full circle, there in the front hall, and the coat was not where she had shucked it off.

Martin was still watching her. Slowly he held up her coat in one hand, and the paper in the other.

Maggie couldn't see his face, his expression, whether his vast eyebrows were lifted in merriment or knit in a troubled frown.

So Maggie stared at him. Her legs grew tired, so she sat on the little steps that led down to the living room. She held her face in her hands and waited.

She was waiting for herself to have thoughts, for advice from Frank, for any clue as to what to do or what to expect from either herself or from Martin, who continued to sit there with her coat and Duncan's single sheet of paper with the testimony on it.

And while she waited, a bubble of thought poked at her deep inside. It was just a simple poke at first, but it grew until she could make out the message it carried. Which was, remember! You love him!

And Maggie was stirred into action, a slow sort of movement at first, but then it accelerated until much to her own surprise and certainly to Martin's, she flew across the room, grabbed the paper, tore it into shreds as fast as she could while running and flushed it down the toilet.

And then she vomited as the water ran down the drain and finally rose to face him with a smile on her face. "I love you," she said.

They were up nearly till dawn. She had spent most of the night sitting on the couch while he paced and talked. And sometimes she had paced and he had sat or they both had paced. Once Ernest had come out. He walked past them and drank water and went back to Maggie's bed. And still Maggie listened, and Martin talked.

At times he was agitated, at times weepy, at times calm, at times loud, and a few times he had laughed. Maggie didn't join him, though, but just listened, listened with a deep intensity that gave weight to every word.

And then they slept, fully clothed, in each other's arms next to Ernest, woke too early, ate, slept again. At some point Martin had let Ernest out, and at another time Martin must have let himself out. Because when Maggie finally dragged herself from sleep, not a bit sure she was ready but the sun was shining and she didn't feel she should sleep anymore, he was gone.

Chapter 46

She made herself lunch, all the while thinking, remembering, sorting and sifting. It was such a bizarre story. But it all hung together. She believed him. And before they had finally slept, he knew she believed him, she was pretty sure.

Maggie ate her grilled cheese and apple slowly. She was musing over his tale. She was uncertain of a few parts, of a few names that had sprung up without explanation, of places she hadn't heard of that had glibly rolled off his tongue. Well, she'd ask later. The basic story exonerated him, and the details were fundamentally uninteresting to her.

"But what about your daughter?" Maggie had said. "How was it that she showed up?"

"Well, first I have to tell you that I was not at all certain it was Alice. It had been a long time, twenty years or so. Even when she told me things I thought only she would know, I was suspicious. After all, she had arrived out of the blue. Where had she been? And where was Andy? And Winona? She had no answers. I made up stories in my mind to see if I could figure out why she would show up if she wasn't Alice, and some were a bit plausible, such as maybe she was going to sue me or shake me down for hush money or something. I never really did figure it out. Because all she seemed to want was to find out why I had kidnapped her. And I hadn't. But I couldn't figure out why she said I did."

"Wasn't she twelve when it happened? Wouldn't a girl that age know?" asked Maggie.

This was the part of the story that was hard for Maggie. She had thrown away the paper that contained the testimony of the daughter, of Alice, and knew only the first point on the paper, that she had accused her father of kidnapping her. How could she not know that he hadn't done it?

Martin was silent. He had readjusted himself in his seat, then got up and started pacing again. "Yes, she was twelve," he said. "A sweetie, maybe young for her age." He said this with the deepest affection.

Martin stopped in front of Maggie. "You didn't read that paper all the way, did you." It was a statement.

"No, just the first line," said Maggie. "I knew it couldn't be true and I didn't want to confuse myself with a bunch of garbage from a deranged child – pardon me for insulting your daughter. Or maybe it was from when she was older."

"I think it was from when she was older, after she found me. I think she had some extortion in mind, though it never came to that in the end."

Maggie raised her eyebrows. Something had stopped Alice's accusations, and she had no idea what and she hadn't even thought of that.

"Well," said Martin, "you deserve to know the ugly things she said.

"No. NO! No I don't deserve that. Why would I want to hear a bunch of lies?"

"Well," he said, "most people think those things are true. They have heard the gossip, added their own uninformed versions, and passed it on. And now, another twenty years later, my name is greeted with all that knowledge, all that gossip."

Maggie was wondering where she had been. She listened closely to Martin but she also had her inner ear open for what Frank might impart. But so far he was silent, utterly silent. And then she thought about Duncan. He had known it all, had provided details Martin hadn't mentioned. She wondered how. It could have been from gossip. Or from some official information. From court, maybe. She had no idea.

And again she wondered where she had been that she hadn't ever heard of this highly visible story.

Martin had settled into the corner chair and closed his eyes. Maybe he was falling asleep. But Maggie's mind was doing a calculation. His kids had disappeared when? Twenty years ago Alice had showed up. And twenty years before that she had disappeared. Forty years! Her baby boy would be in his late 30s. While he was enduring the disappearance of his kids, she was mourning the loss of her baby boy and then her husband Simon. Maybe that's why she had missed all this.

She looked at him, slumped down as he was, either being sad or tired, but dear to her no matter what.

And that was it: No matter what.

She noticed a grayness in the sky. Dawn was approaching. She took him by the hand and led him to the bed. She covered both of them and lay there still and alert until Martin joined Ernest in the steady breathing of sleep. Then she joined them.

Chapter 47

And now she was eating her lunch, alone, nibbling at the apple. Ernest was at her feet on his bed. He'd been out a few times and was now settled for an afternoon nap. In the silence she was poking at the story Martin had told her, looking for clues. Or, she had to confess to herself, looking for discrepancies. Not that she wanted to find any.

In reality she wanted to roll time back until the day she had decided to go to Duncan's office for the first time, when she told him she was going to get married. Then he never would have said that she shouldn't marry Martin.

And then Duncan had disclosed this miserable story from the past . Of course she had begged him to. But how could she not? And why if he believed in Martin's innocence had he told her not to marry him?

That was troubling. He could have said nothing.

And then she remembered that he had lost his wife, and been a bit drunk on top of his loneliness, and embarrassed that he had asked her to marry him, and maybe he had just blurted it out about Martin. Or maybe it had been a last-ditch way to get her to say yes to his proposal, though that seemed remote now.

And then there had been their dinner together. He had seemed so sympathetic, so eager to ease her worries. And so willing to share information.

Just as Martin had said, everyone liked to talk about his misadventure.

"Even Duncan," Maggie said to herself. "Even Duncan."

She sat back in her chair, her eyes unfocused. It was hard to see how Duncan wasn't one of THEM, one of those who detested Martin for his past, for what the newspapers had reported, for the miserable story his daughter had told on him.

Should she ask Martin? Where was he, anyway? He had left at least a couple of hours ago. She needed to see him, even if she didn't get into details about all this.

"Let's go, Ernest,"

The old dog pulled himself up with a stretch and a yawn. She attached his leash, slid on her shoes, and out they went.

"Let's go see Martin," said Maggie.

Ernest set out a bit slowly but sped up. He turned toward Martin's house, then sniffed around the yard. Maggie had intended to go to his front door but Ernest was keen on going around the house toward the back, or so she thought. Then he veered to the little door that led from his side yard into the garage. The door was slightly open.

Maggie was debating whether to knock, but Ernest stuck his huge nose in, and the door swung open. Ernest tugged at the leash and ran over to Martin. Martin was sanding something at his workbench.

"Hi," Maggie said.

"Hi," said Martin, not looking at her. He kept sanding.

She came up to him and gave him a hug. He didn't respond. She waited while he sanded something small in his hand. Ernest poked him with his nose, but Martin ignored him.

Maggie could see he was suffering. Just why or just what was going on in his mind she had no idea. She wanted to comfort him, but he didn't seem to want to let her in.

So she wandered randomly around the inside of the garage. It was filled with tools, equipment, automotive things, gloves, boots, fishing equipment, a backpack, scraps of wood, thick branches, paint cans and brushes. On the wall was a locked gun rack with three rifle-like guns inside, not that she would know what kind. There were shovels, rakes, bottles of screws, all sorts of things, all tidy. Some of the tools were old and worn, some were new.

She peered closer at the hundred tiny bottles, baby food jars she thought, with tiny nails and screws and loops and who knew what. It reminded her of the quilt shop wall with all its needles and knives and sewing-machine feet for quilting.

"I do like the quilting ones better, though," she told Ernest.

But Ernest was not at her side. She twirled around to see where he was, and he and Martin were no longer in the garage. She looked around again to make sure, then went out the side door to look for them. Was he avoiding her? And if he was, why would he?

Suddenly she was tired of the whole thing. She didn't care about it at all, that was her deep-down reality. At first she was going to look into the backyard or go around to the front door, but instead she decided to go home. Let her boys find her when they were ready – she was done.

And she hoped she'd remember that later, when being alone wore thin, now that she was used to having Ernest around. And having Martin around, to be honest, and also when some new part of this story came to her ears and rekindled her curiosity. Would she remember then that she didn't care about it at all?

Chapter 48

For now she was done. Maybe the late late night was catching up with her. Maybe she really just simply loved Martin. Whatever it was, she wanted nothing more of his past, his story, his heartbreak, his ex, his other ex Dede, his other women, any of it. She just wanted his future, as long as it might be, forget the rest.

If she could remember these things.

So she went into the house and took off her clothes and crawled into bed and cried for a few minutes and fell asleep.

Maggie dreamt. Frank flittered in and out of her dream, and so did Simon. Happy children played in her dream, and a frisky red bloodhound puppy, all ears, jumped annoyingly on tolerant adults of some vintage. Duncan walked through from time to time. And Martin was there. He was kissing her and she was so thankful that he had returned to her side, even though she was suspecting it was all a dream.

And then she opened her eyes. And she was alone.

She grasped the quilt as if the bed were tipping on its side and held on. She gasped for breath, couldn't catch it, gasped again.

A warm tongue licked her face. She reached for her beloved Ernest, and fully expected Martin to be right behind him. Ernest had heard her, no doubt, and they knew she was awake.

But there was no Martin.

What time was it, anyway? She opened her eyes. Dawn was arriving. Or maybe it was sunset. The clock said 6:00 and that didn't help.

She was completely disoriented.

She staggered out of bed. She felt like her brain wasn't working. She was afraid she would fall. She lurched toward the bathroom door and held on. But it didn't work. She slid to the floor. When she didn't get up, Ernest lay down with her.

Chapter 49

At some point she went back to sleep and the dreams came back. But they were more grotesque than before. As she peeked into the dream scene before her, Martin was arguing with two men. She thought they might be Duncan, and maybe Frank.

It was too much. She woke herself up. She struggled for consciousness. She grabbed for Ernest, wrapped her arms around him, held on.

Maybe she was sick. Maybe she was feverish. She couldn't get herself collected. At one moment she was drifting back into sleep, at the next she was pulling herself awake. Finally she slept soundly.

Chapter 50

At 9:00 a.m. her alarm went off.

She hadn't set her alarm.

Martin!

Whether he was there now or not, he had been. She had slept for hours and hours and sometime in those hours he had come in and seen her there with Ernest. On the floor.

She got up to turn off the alarm. Ernest stirred. She slipped into her bathrobe, looked out the window. Maybe he was in the kitchen making her breakfast.

But it wasn't Martin. It was Duncan. He was sitting in Martin's seat in the living room.

She stood in the hallway looking at him. What was going on? Her stomach lurched. She was filled with fear.

"Did you set my alarm?"

"Yes. I needed to talk to you."

"Where's Martin?"

"Gone on errands, maybe. I saw him pull out in his RV."

"Does he know you're here?"

"Yes, he saw me come."

"Why are you here?"

"To tell you the rest of the story."

"I don't want to hear it."

"Yes, you do."

"Then Martin can tell me."

"Not really. He will just protect you and you will never hear the truth."

"I don't want the truth, I just want to marry Martin and spend the rest of my life with him."

"He's a murderer, Maggie."

Chapter 51

Maggie covered her ears but it was too late for that. She opened her mouth to say something, anything, to get him to stop, but all that happened was that her mouth stayed open. And while her mouth stayed mute, her mind was going click click click. The pieces, the fragments of Martin's story, were aligning themselves.

But she was missing a few pieces, and she got it that Duncan wanted to supply her with them, however it might be that he knew them.

So Maggie sat. Whether her knees buckled or she just decided she was better off on the floor, that's where she ended up. Ernest came over to her and she idly rubbed the silk of his ears between her thumb and fingers. She was waiting. Because she knew it was coming, and she knew...what? That she would maybe be asked to make a big decision or something. Something serious.

Duncan was merciful. He stayed in his seat. He recited the facts. He supplied the pieces. He filled in the missing elements. It was over in ten minutes.

He said, Winona had left her kids at her brother's cabin up in the mountains and had gone off on an overnight date with some guy passing through town.

Her brother had come home to find the kids sleeping.

He had disposed of Andy – had probably killed him – to get him out of the way.

(Maggie's mind was keen and alert and here she knew what was coming next, and she was right.)

And he wrapped the still sleeping Alice in a blanket and carried her into the woods and raped her.

Alice knew she was in the vicinity of her uncle's cabin, and at dawn she staggered back to it. She wanted to tell her uncle that she had been abducted and raped and get his help. He pretended to know nothing about it, and comforted her and cleaned her up and gave her several reasons why she shouldn't go to the police. He made up a story that he had seen her father's truck nearby the night she was raped. He was the one who originated the story of the kidnapping.

Then her mother arrived. This was days after she had left the kids at the cabin. She sized up the situation, and ordered Alice into her car. But her brother was afraid he would be found out, and killed Winona. Alice saw him do it, so he continued to make up stories to tie together the lies he was telling, centered on Martin and Winona wanting to get rid of the kids and setting himself up as her savior.

Maggie was feeling her stomach rebel, but she needed to hear it out.

Somehow Winona's brother wasn't investigated. Presumably Alice stayed with him for the rest of her childhood. That's what she told us. She said she had a baby when she was about 15. That would make him in his late 30s now.

When she came to see Martin, she still believed the story the brother had told her, that her father – Martin -- had kidnapped her, and that he had killed her mother. She didn't have any idea about her brother. No matter what anyone said or did, she stuck to her story.

"What happened to her?" asked Maggie. "That was a long time ago now."

"I don't know," said Duncan.

"Is there any hope Andy survived?"

"His body has never been found. That is the only hope I have."

"What happened to the brother? Has he ever been found?"

"Martin found him."

"And?"

"He killed him. That's why he went to prison."

Maggie was done. She stood up. "HOW DO YOU KNOW THIS, DUNCAN?" she screamed.

"Well, that's gratitude for you," he said. He got up, put on his hat, adjusted his jacket. "I'm just trying to be helpful, Maggie, to save you from a terrible mistake, marrying that despicable murderer. When I could give you a fine home, a lovely rose garden, companionship!"

"So you know NOTHING! Am I right? It's all rumor, ancient hearsay."

"Everyone knows this story! Where have you been? Didn't you read those accusations that his daughter made?"

"No. I didn't. I flushed them down the toilet where they belong. Now get out."

Chapter 52

Maggie had wanted to ask Duncan calmly how he had gotten involved. How accurate was his knowledge. How much could she trust him. But she couldn't, not now.

She looked after him as he drove off. She could have been nicer. She thought of all he had told her and it became a buzzing in her ears. She noticed she was still in her bathrobe. Ernest needed to go out. She needed breakfast.

She was silent. She couldn't speak, even to Ernest. She needed time to herself. She was glad that Martin was gone, though she was also worried that he was permanently gone. So be it. She needed time to think. She needed to take a walk. A long walk.

Her mind began to work like clockwork. She ate a sensible breakfast. She packed a sensible lunch and water bottles. She went next door and borrowed Martin's backpack from his garage. She clipped on Ernest's leash. She changed into a white shirt so if she was out after dark, she would be visible to drivers. She took a jacket and tied it around her waist.

She headed out the door. Then she went back and got a notepad and wrote a note to Martin. She noticed he had his RV with him and his truck was sitting in his driveway. She wouldn't think about that right now, she would just write him a cheerful note of love and let him know she was looking forward to a future with him. And that she was going for a walk.

So she started to walk. She walked and walked. She went out by the airport. She walked down the main road. She walked into Old Town. Never had she walked so far and her legs were tired. She found a bench down by the ferry to Guemes Island and ate her lunch and gave a chunk of it to Ernest. She drank some of her water. She watched the ferry come and go and decided to go the next time it headed out, as a walk-on. She enjoyed the cool breezes and being out on the water. She walked off on the other end and resisted letting other passengers pet Ernest, but she did smile.

She walked up the hill from the dock and kept walking. It took her a couple of hours to reach the other shore of the small island and sat on a good-sized rock to rest her legs.

And meanwhile Frank kept trying to explain it all to her, to apologize, or maybe even to get her to be mad. But she just trudged along, not letting herself be drawn in. Repeatedly she turned her back on him -- no mean trick, she realized -- and he became more insistent. "Come on, Mags!" (Mags? He had gotten that from Martin! How dare he! Had he been listening to their conversations? Had he turned into a Peeping Tom? And just what had he seen?).

And suddenly Maggie was mad mad mad. She slid off the rock. She looked around, peering into the growing darkness of the wet late afternoon, the cloudy, drizzly afternoon. No one was nearby, so she let out a scream. "Frank, listen to me! You are DEAD! Now get lost! Go! Now! You and I are done. I will always love you, I suppose, and I'm not glad you died. I'm really not. But I'm getting married, and we don't need you! Martin and I don't need you! BE GONE!"

And as far as she could tell, he went. And aside from Ernest, she was alone, completely alone.

It was refreshing, enlightening.

She was exhausted and had no idea where to go next. And then she thought of Sylvia's. Sylvia was over on the west side of the island, so Maggie walked that way. It took her another hour before she noticed that the sun was setting. She had no idea how much farther it was to Sylvia's or where it was exactly, and the road was narrow and the sky was getting dark very rapidly.

And she was running out of steam. And Ernest was running out of steam. And now what.

And then she realized she was probably just setting herself up for a rescue. For Martin to rescue her. As he always had. Wherever he was. And maybe not in time.

Ahead she saw a good-sized boulder beside the road. She thought she might sit on it and have a snack. It wasn't comfortable like a chair, but it would do. She slipped off her backpack and rummaged until she found a granola bar. She shared it with Ernest, and gave him some water in her hand from her water bottle. And then she waited to start feeling refreshed.

Instead she felt more tired. She thought she might lie down for a moment on the rock, but it was not shaped like a bed and she gave up trying to get comfortable.

And now what?

Chapter 53

"Now what, Ernest?"

He looked at her. He looked worried. But then of course he always looked worried. How she loved him and his wrinkled face and droopy jowls and long wagging tail.

How could she find Sylvia? For one thing it was nearly perfectly dark. The moon kept going behind clouds. No car had driven by since she had chosen this narrow country road.

She had been to Sylvia's little farm once, just once. You drove down this street – or some street – and then turned down a driveway to the right.

"Ernest! Do you remember the name of Sylvia's farm? Something – a little old-fashioned, I think. Like Lavender Farm. But not that, not quite that. I think I'd know it if I heard it. Do you remember?"

Ernest did not remember.

Maggie took up the leash and put one foot in front of the other. She resolved to look at every sign along the road until she found one that sounded like Sylvia's.

Or, she thought, maybe I'll just stop at any house I find.

That seemed like a very smart idea. If there were any houses. Right now there was only woods and more woods. Except for the occasional bramble, no longer covered with delicious blackberries but bare, preparing for winter.

She put on her jacket.

Ernest seemed to be feeling more refreshed from his snack. He had picked up his pace. He was in fact being a bit hasty for her, but she did her best to keep up. Truth be known, he was actually helping her move along.

The night was growing cold. She was feeling weary enough to give up and find a soft spot in the grass beside the road and sleep until morning. But Ernest was being enthusiastic about the path they were on. Let him! She could manage another few minutes, and maybe by then she would come to a driveway.

Her feet hurt. But the rhythm of her steps was comforting. She was drowsy and that's why when he stopped she ran into him and almost fell.

But he didn't really stop, he had turned and what lay ahead appeared to be a break in the woods and that might mean a driveway.

She felt her blood quicken. A driveway! Usually that meant a house! (She listened for Frank's agreement, but he was indeed gone. Quiet beyond silent.)

As she put one foot in front of the next, appreciating the moonlight that illuminated the street or driveway or whatever it was, Maggie was vaguely wondering why it was that Duncan was telling all.

"And why why why was Duncan telling all?" she said out loud.

So you will marry him, you ninny, said Frank. And then he added, well you asked!

Chapter 54

The moon was now hidden by clouds and a gentle rain had come up, not enough to soak through her jacket. Not yet, anyway, thought Maggie. The driveway glistened when the moonlight hit it but otherwise it was hard to see. But Ernest was steadfast in pulling her along.

Then the rain hit with full force. She pulled her collar up and held her free hand over her eyes. Her glasses were blurry with raindrops. She held on extra-tight to Ernest's leash. If he ever got away, she would be lost.

She looked off into the distance. Where was he going? Was there actually a house down here? They were headed in the general direction of the cliffs at the north-west end of the island, though they should be some distance away. And those cliffs were covered with lovely homes. But where might Sylvia, on her little acreage, in her small mobile home, live? She'd had a view of the sea through trees, that's all Maggie could remember.

Well, it didn't matter. Maggie knew she needed to get out of the storm, and surely any one of those residents would take her in and let her make a phone call. All she needed was a house, any house, a single resident, to help her out of her rather threatening situation. She was tired and wet and couldn't see herself lying down on the edge of this road or driveway, whatever it was, and sleeping. Not in the rain. Not under any circumstances, really. And she couldn't do that to Ernest, either.

Ernest did seem a bit anxious. His speed had picked up. He seemed good at tracking the roadway they were on. They had not once gotten off onto the verge regardless of how dark it had gotten.

But now the roadway had turned to gravel, and the footing was uneven. She slid, and she stepped into puddles. Her sneakers were full of water. Had they gotten off the main roadway? Ernest was pulling as strongly on the leash as before.

And then she saw what might be a sign.

"It's a sign!" she exclaimed to Ernest. "I mean, there's a sign right over there! Do you see it?"

Ernest had slowed for a moment then, but when he started up again he was pulling yet harder. And he threatened to go right past the sign.

"Stop, Ernest!" she yelled. And he did stop.

It was so dark that she couldn't be sure there were words on the board she was now leaning against. She knelt down directly in front of it and traced what letters she could see with her finger. The sign was old and rough. The first word was indistinct, but she thought it said Farm at the end. She hoped. Or maybe she had made out the word ‘farm’ because she had wanted to so badly.

If only she could remember the name of Sylvia’s tiny enterprise, the acre or so where she grew veggies and kept her tiny travel trailer that served as her home. (You mean the one where Martin spent the night that time, asked Frank? So he wasn’t gone. Well, she was almost glad.)

“YES, that one, Frank! Shut up!” said Maggie loud enough that Ernest turned around. He was tugging on the leash but Maggie was still trying to decipher the sign.

“I’m sure it says ‘farm’, Ernest,” she said.

And then it came to her what Sylvia called her farm. Not lavender! Alyssum! Another very common flower. Some people planted it, and others tried to dig it out because small as it was, it became a weed. “Odd name for a farm, Ernest,” said Maggie. “Maybe because it’s such a little place.”

And once she knew what the name was, she could see it. She traced out Alyssum with a finger. This was it: Sylvia’s place, or the driveway to it. She would be warm and cozy in just a few minutes.

She got up off her knees. As soon as she was upright, Ernest pulled vigorously on the leash and they were off down the gravel lane.

It was narrow, barely a car's width across. It was uneven and filled with puddles, which she couldn't see until she stepped in them. It couldn't be far to Sylvia's trailer.

Chapter 55

Headlights!

Her retinas were fried. She held her arm up over her eyes. Ernest bounded forward and she lost her grip on the leash. She was afraid she'd be run over, that he would be run over. All this in an instant, followed by the thought that Sylvia didn't have a vehicle.

She stepped to the side of the driveway and ran into brambles that poked her all over. Ernest came running back, then bolted off again. A voice was calling her name. Martin's voice was calling her name.

"Here!" she called out, but her voice was feeble.

"Where are you, you crazy woman?" asked Martin.

"Here," she croaked again.

Ernest came up to her and woofed and she grabbed him around the neck. Then Martin came up and she grabbed him around the neck.

"You're wet," he said. "Come get dried off."

Chapter 56

After she had been boosted into his RV, after he had backed up into Sylvia's yard and she had come out of her trailer, after Maggie had changed into some clothes she'd left in the RV for 'next time', after Ernest had been thoroughly dried and watered and fed some of the scrambled eggs ('VERY fresh, said Sylvia) that Martin prepared for her, after she had been sat, wrapped in a blanket but still shivering, in his favorite chair in the RV, and after Sylvia had said, "I'll leave you two" but Martin had detained her with a hand on her arm, a familiar hand on her arm and she had looked hard at him and said "Are you sure?" and Maggie had had a sudden horrible feeling in her gut, Martin sat down across from her and took her hands in his.

"Maggie, you know Sylvia."

Maggie nodded.

"I have a confession to make."

And here it comes, thought Maggie. The end of life as I had hoped it would be. And the word 'murderer' flitted through her mind. Murderer of hopes and the delicious romance of kisses and hugs and more kisses and so on and so on and so on.

She would be brave. It was all a matter of a few minutes and then she would be on the other side of this intolerable moment and she would be back to being just Maggie.

She looked over at Ernest. He was lying, snoring, disloyally at Martin's feet.

Sylvia was still standing. Martin pulled her down to sit next to him on the couch. Martin put his arm around her thin, terribly thin shoulders. He was smiling broadly.

Maggie wanted to slap him. She started to cry. She covered her face with her hands. Anything but to look at the two of them, sitting there together, the end of all the sweetness, all the adventure of her recent times with Martin. She couldn't think of anything to say. Even Frank had nothing to say.

But Martin did, apparently. He leaned forward, still with his arm around Sylvia. Maggie peeked at them through her fingers.

"Maggie, look at me!"

Maggie shook her head and stifled a sob.

Martin reached across and pulled her hands from her face and wiped them on the blanket. Maggie continued to look down.

He stood up, stepped over Ernest, bent down and kissed her on the lips. She pulled her head away, while thinking, wow, that was quite a kiss, and then she remembered it could be her last kiss ever. And she started to cry all over again.

"Maggie, you idiot! Will you look at me? I want you to meet my daughter Sylvia. Who used to be known as Alice."

Chapter 57

Maggie found herself on two different trajectories, on two paths. One was dark with hopelessness, the other was catching glimpses of good things, of respite, of relief, of hope, of what? Laughter!

Her sobs turned to a snort of laughter, then giggles. She started to giggle and she couldn't stop. "Teh heh heh heh heh", she said. She covered her face again and giggled and sobbed and slid to the floor and held Ernest as tight as she could.

Martin leaned over her. Sylvia said, "I really am going now" and went out the door. In the end Martin lay down on the floor too and held Maggie until she fell asleep, then covered her and lay down on the couch and held her hand.

Chapter 58

The next morning Martin woke her. They were taking Sylvia to the farmers' market and were about to get underway. The dawn light was barely visible. He needed to load Sylvia's wares -- her veggies, eggs, some apples -- and then they would leave. Maggie's breakfast was in Sylvia's trailer, but please hurry....

But Maggie had awakened achy and cranky. It was all well and good for Martin to be so easy with her and also easy with Sylvia, but, Maggie thought, I just want to go home. To MY house. With MY dog. And if possible, with MY tall, blue-eyed, cozy fiance. Yeah, that was her dad, but. But but but.

It was as if the two of them -- she and Martin -- had just had a baby. Adopted a baby. In her case, without being asked.

Yes, she was grumpy, she realized that. For one thing, why had Martin let her think that he had slept with Sylvia? And then looking back on the conversation, going back to when he had brought Sylvia's carrots home and she had thought the worst, that he had slept with her, she was suddenly struck that it was just her, just Maggie, and that he had been crushed that she thought that about him. And that it was time to trust him.

And then she realized that if one of the threesome was cranky, that person might be left behind, and while she wanted to go home, she also didn't want to be left behind at home, while the two of them went off to the farmers' market and then maybe to the park and then maybe for a hike and then maybe....

It wouldn't do. Could she fake being brave and enjoying having Sylvia around? She didn't have time to figure it out. She had to have breakfast over in her trailer so they could go to the farmers' market with her veggies in time to set up.

Sylvia's trailer, Sylvia's eggs for breakfast, Sylvia's veggies and eggs, Sylvia's father!

And what about her? She was now Sylvia's stepmother! STEPMOTHER!

"What did you say?" Martin wanted to know. He had opened the RV door just as she had said that.

Maggie noticed that he had a funny smirk on his face. She knew she looked grumpy. She tried smiling but her face wouldn't do it.

Martin turned and fiddled with the lock on the RV door. She expected him to sit in the driver's seat. But he didn't. He approached her where she sat on the couch.

He took her by the shoulders. He knocked her down on the couch, and she wouldn't have been surprised if he had knocked her teeth in, given the thoughts she was having. But instead he kissed her. A lot.

She couldn't catch her breath. But he wouldn't quit, not till she stopped him from choking her, or actually, he wasn't trying to choke her, he was trying to put his hand down her shirt. And that realization, that he wasn't trying to drown her and choke her but to punish her with passion, made her start laughing, and that led to her grasping him around the neck and pulling hard and then when he landed on her, uttering an ooooof that got cut short by more kisses.

It was a tangle and who knows where it would have ended if it had not been for the knock on the door. And neither of them was in a good position to answer it.

After a minute or so of rapid clothing adjustment and so on, Martin, ever the helpful gentleman, croaked, "Just a minute, Sylvia!"

By the time they got the door open, and Maggie was sitting sedately at the table eating a granola bar and Martin had made himself very busy indeed with a stack of maps -- despite the fact that he would not be leaving his very own town -- Sylvia had transported all her wares for the market to the door of the RV. Now she loaded them up the stairs, and Martin stashed them in places where they couldn't roll around. Maggie kept sitting at the table, but put her seat belt on. (Showing, she said to herself, that I know a thing or two about this RV.)

Sylvia sat in the passenger seat and adeptly buckled her own seat belt. Ernest had slid in with Sylvia and was happily snuggled under Maggie's dangling feet. It was time to go. The sun was just peeking over the trees. The ferry was due in a few minutes.

While they waited, Martin turned around to Maggie and said, "Home or market?"

Home, hot shower, hot food, clean clothes -- or Martin, RV, Sylvia, veggies. And probably the trip back to Guemes to drop off Sylvia...and then what? Or maybe Martin being gone all day to do those things while she sat home alone. Just like the old days. With Frank!

Or wait -- what if Duncan came by?

"Market, please," said Maggie.

Martin threw her a grateful smile. "Market it is," he said.

Chapter 59

Later, after they had dropped Sylvia back on Guemes -- she had sold all her wares and had had to do some shopping before returning home to her seriously isolated existence -- Martin and Maggie and Ernest pulled into his driveway. He did his usual tidying up of the RV while Maggie let herself and Ernest into her house. She had left the front door unlocked, and that reminded her that she had departed just about 24 hours earlier for a walk around the block.

Ernest wanted to go out the back slider. It was raining and turning chill, compared to the day before. A good day for a fire, Maggie thought, if I'd only bought firewood. It was not even October and that winter damp raw air was piercing her to the bone. Of course she had been soaked last night and her clothes weren't really dry by morning, and really she needed a hot shower except she didn't have the ambition for it.

Except it might help her avoid The Conversation with Martin. She still didn't want to know what had happened, had no inclination to listen if he chose to Tell

All, didn't even care -- right now anyway -- how he happened to be in touch with Sylvia.

Except she did want to find out why Martin had left her with the impression that he had slept with Sylvia. He couldn't have. No, certainly, he wouldn't have.

So she got her shower and found her nighty and crawled into bed and got up again to let Ernest in and found him wet and had to dry him off and ended up using her dryer he was so thoroughly soaked. And then Martin came.

He had hot soup with him -- of course -- and it smelled of veggies and things and she found she was starving. Even though she knew that if they sat down to a meal together The Talk might happen. So be it -- she was hungry.

Martin seemed to be extra-charming and extra-cheerful, and very caring: did she want this, did she want that? She had expected serious and she was getting solicitous. She was becoming suspicious.

It was sweet having him there, but it seemed safer overall for him to go home and keep his need for confession or divulgence to himself. Didn't it? Why did she ever need to know? Why couldn't they just get married and forget Sylvia and the missing Andrew and the murdered Winona....

Ah, Winona. That was the issue, wasn't it. Because ... well, was he a murderer, though he had been let free when the conviction was overturned? Or, if he had not murdered her, and no one else had either, then maybe she was still alive. And in that case, he was still married.

Hmm hmmm hmmmmmm.

So that was it. She was convinced. She stopped eating. She stared at him. The soup dripped from the spoon and rolled off the table and Ernest licked it off his back. She couldn't stop staring at Martin.

Martin smiled rather weakly, then took the spoon from her hand. He stared back, then lowered his eyes.

"Yup," he said.

She nodded. "Thought so," she said.

It was sometime after midnight when she asked, "What were you going to do about it?"

"Just let it go. Who would know? Why would it ever come up? Why would it even matter?"

"Well, Duncan for one," she said. "He seems to know a great deal."

"Really? I don't see how," said Martin.

"Well, he is a little out of date on some points, such as that you killed Winona. That is what he said."

"That gossip is maybe 40 years out of date, at least!" said Martin.

"Maybe he isn't..." The thought had just come to Maggie that maybe Duncan knew the whole story, but had told her only the part that suited him. (See? Said Frank.) (Maggie had to think about that -- had Frank thought that Duncan loved her, back when he was still alive? Back when Doris was still alive? HAD Duncan loved her back then? Why would he?)

Maggie was silent for a long time.. They were sitting in the living room, a dozen feet between them, having promised each other during dinner that they would have a calm discussion of possibilities. Ernest lay at Martin's feet, having voted early and often, sending with the beat of his tail on the chair leg the code for 'let's keep him'.

Maggie wanted to keep him, too. She looked at the long lean figure slumped on his chair, at his overgrown white hair, his sweater with the holes where fishing hooks and firewood had ripped at it. Yes, let's keep him, she thought. But how?

The question Maggie hadn't asked, the key one if she wanted to get married, was where was Winona now. It hadn't really come up, though she had the impression that Winona had disappeared long ago.

She yawned. They really needed sleep. Their brains weren't working.

"Let's finish this tomorrow," she said.

She had startled him awake. He sat up suddenly and looked at her, seemingly a bit dazed. Then he grinned. "Sure!" he exclaimed. "Can I sleep over?"

Chapter 60

After she had kicked him out and given in to Ernest's decision to sleep on her bed, she lay awake for a surprisingly long time. And then maybe she had slept. And then she was definitely awake. She had had a dream, quite a vivid dream, so vivid it had startled her awake. Frank had been there, the real flesh-and-blood Frank. He was telling her he wanted to marry her. And she had said, but I'm married to Simon! And Frank had said, we don't need him. Why not, Maggie had asked, and Frank had said, You can divorce him here in Oregon without his say-so. And then we can get married.

And now as she lay awake she remembered that's how it had been.

Chapter 61

The next morning, they busied themselves with packing the RV. Neither had an inclination to invite talk of Winona into their plans. They worked it out as they passed each other going from their two houses to the RV: take the 11 AM Guemes ferry to pick up Sylvia for the wedding, have lunch as a family, take Sylvia and Ernest back to Alyssum Farm, and head out of town as a married couple. It was now 8 AM. In four or five hours they'd be underway!

They'd attend to Winona's divorce when they got to Oregon.

Martin started carrying boxes to Maggie's. When he passed her, he winked. She stopped in her tracks: He was moving in! When they got back, they would share the house.

The RV was in the street. Now Martin was moving the boats, the truck, the little red antique Ford.

Soon they were all in Maggie's yard and driveway and garage. And last of all Martin attached Maggie's car to the rear of the RV.

And then he returned to his house, came back a minute later carrying a shopping bag, and locked his front door. "We'll drop the key off with the landlord on our way out of town," said he. And then he handed Maggie the shopping bag. "Happy wedding day, my dear," he said.

She looked at him. They were standing in the front yard. "Do I open it now?" she asked.

"No, tonight," said he. "It's something to wear -- later."

He was actually blushing. Maggie didn't think she'd ever seen him even remotely uncomfortable or self-conscious but there he was, blushing! She couldn't wait to peek in the package!

And then they locked up the house, put Ernest, who had been stuck in the backyard for hours, into the RV, and said good-bye. It was pretty much on time. They would be married within the hour.

In the end they decided to leave Ernest at Sylvia's. And Sylvia said she'd gladly walk home from the ferry. So they said their vows, had lunch at the salmon place, and dropped Sylvia at the Guemes ferry before 1 PM.

And now what?

The plan called for them to go on the Port Townsend ferry to the Olympic Peninsula. They needed to allow nearly two hours of driving time to be sure to make it, but it didn't set sail until 7:30.

As they drove through town, Martin slowed down and pulled over. Maggie had wanted to do just that! But he couldn't be thinking what she was. She looked at him, only to find he was looking at her. He opened the door. "Duncan!" they said in unison.

They walked hand in hand to his office a few blocks away. Would he be in? He was always in!

The conversation took all afternoon. Martin was the very example of calmness. Maggie? Not so much. At times as he held her hand he squeezed very hard, and then she remembered to be kind, even when Duncan held on to long-cherished opinions and felt free to speak them forcefully.

But this was their wedding day, and in the end they abandoned him and his thoughts of conspiracy and intrigue and murder and whatever else he came up with as he tied a terrible story out of tiny threads of circumstance.

And they meanwhile were having thoughts of what was to come.

And Maggie wondered what was in the shopping bag Martin had given her.

So they left. Had a bite to eat. Drove down the coast, crossing Deception Pass bridge on the way, checking out the turbulence below one more time. And when they got to the ferry line, Martin stepped from behind the steering wheel to fetch the shopping bag for Maggie. He barely had time for a kiss before the line opened in front of the RV and he was guided to tuck it against the rail of the ferry for their crossing.

The evening was calm, the waves no problem. They would need to undertake the crossing in the passenger area, and had just a moment before they were expected to exit the RV for Maggie to open her gift. She felt inside the open top of the shopping bag. What was there was soft, familiar. He kissed her again as she drew it out.

It was that old tee shirt that she had worn after getting soaked the first time she'd gone out in Martin's -- in their -- boat.

She kissed him. How she loved him! And who else would give his bride an old tee shirt -- soft and cozy, with the old faded heart that said I LOVE YOU -- for her wedding night? She couldn't wait to put it on and crawl into bed with him!

Chapter 62

Maggie awoke to full sunshine. It took a moment for her to put together where she was and why. She could see the kitchen from her bed, and the little pot of geraniums next to the sink. The sun was just getting around to that little window with its rather masculine plaid curtains. She was in Martin's RV. And she had just spent her first night with him.

It had been a most wonderful night! She felt rosy top to bottom, head to toe, front to back, inside and out.

She was drifting back to sleep. Martin was snoring a bit, nothing bothersome. She looked at his ear, his messy hair, the hint of beard, the great bushy bright white eyebrows, his fine nose and full lips, his closed eyes that would show bright blue as soon as he opened them. She was trying to stay awake but sleep would have its way with her, she realized.

And then the world shifted. She was rocked from sleep back to full wakefulness. Something was odd, wrong. She felt her stomach lurch with it. She grabbed for the bed. Who was this guy she was lying next to? Who was this guy she'd ... Oh! Not in 40 years had she felt such feelings as she had last night, maybe even early this morning, and impossible to contemplate, joyfully again at dawn as the birds were just waking!

All that had left her feeling so rosy. And because of it, for a moment she was remembering Simon, whom she had loved, and had thought -- that kind of thought that comes without any real thinking about it -- that it was Simon next to her.

It had been a fine thing, she remembered with great fondness, to be a young wife, newly married, receiving compliment after compliment about how beautiful, how fit, how creamy and delicious she looked as they lay side by side. But that was then.

And actually, this guy lying next to her, who was now stirring and reaching out for her and now pulling her toward him, had told her how beautiful she was just a few hours ago. And hadn't she been every bit as naked then? And hadn't those words been sweet to her, and caused her to glow and feel love for him and want to get closer to him, closer and ever closer?

The husky voice behind her said, "Maggie, my love! Good morning!" He nuzzled against the back of her neck. His warm body aligned itself with hers. Her memories became wispy and unimportant.

Maggie turned and snuggled against him, Martin, this man she shared so much love with. She tucked her chin where it fit, under his jaw, the better to nibble on his ear. And whispered into it, "We must find Simon."

Made in the USA
Lexington, KY
04 September 2019